Inanna

and the

GIANT

Pearl —
Thanks for the
First Read & The
Encouragement

Mark West
(Rии fₐₙₗ)

Mark West

MinRef Press

ISBN 978-1-930322-25-7

Cover Design by Rick Lawler
Cover Photo by Jean Alves

MinRef Press

This book is dedicated to
my mate of 39 years
my two children
and first reader Pearl
and professional proof reader Susan

"There were giants in the earth in those days; and also after that, when the sons of God came unto the daughters of men, and they bare children to them, the same became mighty men of old, men of renown." ---Genesis 6:4

"Extinction is the rule. Survival is the exception."
—Carl Sagan

PROLOGUE
c: 1996

They had been digging into the huge mound for several months, braving dust and heat and cold. This location in Turkey did not offer a particularly hospitable climate. What it did offer, however, was something that had never been seen before. A young archaeological intern, named Josh, dumped a load of dirt and rubble into the screen box, then began shaking it back and forth. The dust and loose dirt fell through, leaving stones and rocks and, surprise, a primitive stone cutting blade.

He picked up the find and tossed it over to a colleague. "Looks pretty rough," the other said, handing it back.

"Yeah, still. Maybe it was made by a beginner. Kind of like we are." Josh had photographed the dig site before he'd shoveled dirt into the screen. He photographed the screen when the detritus was gone, then imaged each angle of the worked stone. He recorded the depth of his dig, grid coordinates, and the date and time. He tossed the primitive blade into a pile of similar artifacts and promptly forgot about it. They had bigger fish to fry.

The lead archaeologist, a German Professor, was away, hoping to get the Carbon-14 dating results from animal bones and other organic materials found at the site. More scientists were back at their base camp, pouring over the Ground Penetrating Radar survey results for the entire artificial hill.

He looked over his shoulder at the main dig site. A ring of 20-foot tall, massive stone T-shaped pillars, weighing 10 tons or more each, reminded him of both Stonehenge and Easter Island. C-14 couldn't date stones, of course. But it was those stones that grabbed everybody's attention. Most of the pillars were crude representations of humans, the top of the "T" representing the head. Arms were carved into the sides and front, and many of the pillars had animals carved into the stone as well. While the representation of humans was crude, the pillars themselves were smooth and expertly made, almost as if they had been machined.

Josh stood up as a well-used Land Rover approached from the east. It arrived at the site a few minutes later, sliding to a stop in the dirt, a cloud of dust momentarily obscuring the vehicle. The lead archaeologist emerged from his car and strode quickly to the dig site, gesturing for the workers to gather 'round.

"We got the C-14 results," he said in English, with a noticeable German accent. Most of his interns and workers were university graduate students from the United States, so English was typically spoken. "This," he held up a piece of paper, "changes everything." He looked at each of the workers, ensuring their attention. "Our work here is even more important than we thought."

"Go ahead," prompted Josh, "shoot us the results."

The leader took a deep breath and shook his head. "This site dates back to almost twelve thousand years ago."

A stunned silence followed his revelation.

"You're joking, right?" someone exclaimed. "Christ, that's back to the end of the last ice age." Excited conversations broke out among the workers. "That's before human civilization existed. Before writing, before cities and villages, before domestication of animals and agriculture. That can't be right. There's got to be a mistake."

The archaeologist held his results high and shook the pages. The workers quieted. "They tested numerous samples from various locations within the two excavated areas. All were consistent."

"This changes everything," said Josh.

"Indeed," the German agreed softly.

Before more discussion could continue, a battered Jeep drove up and stopped next to the Land Rover. A Turkish scientist from the Department of Antiquities got out. "I have," he said, striding into the group "the results of the GPR scans."

"Yeah? What now?"

The scientist swept his hand in an encompassing arc. "In addition to the two circles we've dug, this whole mountain is filled with buried circular rock pillars. The whole thing. Twenty circles, over 200 pillars, 10 tons each. This puts Stonehenge to shame. And I have more news..."

The lead archaeologist collapsed into a folding chair. "I can't take much more," he said.

"You'll like this one," the Turk replied. "This entire site, the whole mountain, was deliberately buried. We think that happened about 8,000 years ago. This temple, this whatever it is, was 4,000 years old when that happened. Somehow, somebody buried the entire site. This changes *everything*."

BEFORE

A large carnivore, probably a cave lion, loped across a distant meadow, stopping once to sniff the air.

The human hunter knelt at the edge of a drop-off, surveying the meadow and a lush green forest below. High above, ice stretched into the sky, covering the entire mountain range. Down where the hunter watched, the ice was thinner and covered in snow. The air was cold and crisp. There were trees and bushes and patches of bare ground. To the left, a small waterfall trickled. Lower down, water joined with other streams to form a small creek. Much farther down, the creeks combined to form a river which flowed into wide, rolling plains, and eventually emptied into the great sea.

Prey was plentiful down there, near the plains. But the hunter dare not venture that far. Where river met sea was the city of Giants. A city that stretched out as far one could see along the coast also stretched, it seemed, equally as high into the sky. These Giants farmed the plains and kept their domesticated animals there. They did not like hunters from the mountain tribes intruding.

The hunter gazed at a faint and far distant glow from the many tall, thin buildings of the Giant city. Darkness was not, to them, an enemy. The glow of their great city fought against darkness and, within its confines, won.

The hunter lived in a small tribal village, nestled against mountains among the snow and ice. At night, the villagers had no light, except the faint remnant embers of wood fires.

Those mysterious Giants who occupied the city actually averaged only slightly taller than the hunter. They were giants not in stature, but because of the lights in their city, the sky-reaching size of their buildings, because of the way they could climb into beasts and fly, the way their boats let them conquer the sea and its bounty of fish. If the hunter ventured too far down the slopes, into open grasslands, the Giants would know. They would confront her and send her back up to where she belonged. Or kill her, perhaps. For her people, the mountain people, the grasslands were taboo.

Her tribe scratched out a precarious existence, in biting cold, just below the massive wall of ice. Along with numerous other individual hunter-gatherer tribes that populated the mountains, they subsisted on little, unless they found an elk or a mountain goat. Many of her people died of disease or in childhood, in wars or hunting accidents. Those who survived were hardy, slender but strong. All except the chief who, in his later years, had become rather rotund.

The Giants, on the other hand, ranged from tall and thin all the way to a few who were very fat. The hunter knew this because she sometimes sneaked close to the City and observed its occupants. She'd found a way along the river, and if she kept below the bank and followed the rushing water, the Giants did not detect her. If she had eaten well and did not need to hunt, she would lie in her hiding place near that wondrous city for hours and watch the Giants go about their lives, much busier and more complicated than hers.

She learned many things that other members of her tribe did not know. Giant children were playful and loud, laughing and screaming in their play. In her tribe, children were quiet and played almost silently. Cave bears and packs of wolves, and sometimes worse, hunted the upper lands. They found children to be soft and tasty, and easy to catch. Relations among various tribes in the mountains were not always friendly, and sometimes they fought each other for food or territory, or for slaves. A tenuous existence did not deter this hunter from wondering and exploring, an attribute that set her apart from others of her village.

She learned the Giants had a range of skin color. Some of them were as dark, or even darker than she and her fellow tribe members. Others were pale and pasty, but the majority were somewhere in between. She never got close enough to determine eye color. She was curious because hers were a brilliant blue, which contrasted with her curly black hair and brown skin.

The rest of the tribe, other than her little brother, sported uniform brown eyes, with only slight variations in shade. When she was born, her father had interceded with the Shaman, who wanted her killed as a defective. Because of those cursed eyes. He had interceded once again, several years later, for her brother. He succeeded, but his efforts had set them both apart from the rest of their people. They were never fully accepted, treated with mild but underlying contempt and an ever-present suspicion. This suspicion carried over to her parents, who were normal in every way except that they had produced two blue-eyed freaks.

The hunter learned that, unlike her people, Giants enjoyed laughing, talking and communicating with each other. They spent much time in their tall buildings. From her hiding place, she could sometimes see them through the windows. They often entered small beasts, some looking like giant turtles, which then sped them off to somewhere else over smooth flat roads. There were hundreds of the beasts. With these, and the flying things and the ships at sea, the Giants' city was a nest of humming activity. Their lights held back the night. Unlike the hunter's tribe, Giants feared nothing.

The hunter, by her estimate, was 16 years of age. In her opinion she was not appreciated by her tribe. She was, in fact, a nuisance. Hunters were typically male, and only the strongest and quickest were successful. This outcast blue-eyed female dared hunt like the men. Worse, dared to call herself *She-Wolf.*

She had become a hunter after her father was killed by a mammoth, leaving her, her mother, and her small brother no way to secure food. So she became a hunter. A year ago, she had tracked and killed an injured cave wolf. She'd presented its carcass to the tribe elders as was required, but kept the pelt for herself, another dubious affront to tribal custom. Hunters were expected to present prized pelts to the chief, which he used to line and insulate his hut, or, rarely, present to loyal tribesmen as gifts. He had grudgingly accepted the body of the wolf, and waited expectantly, to be presented with a new pelt.

The hunter had spent many hours preparing and curing that pelt, and it was her prized possession. Besides, the Chief already had a half-dozen wolf pelts. She had gazed at the chief, and then, defiantly, swung the pelt over her thin shoulders, its wolf head resting atop hers. The chief had grunted and turned away, presenting her with both the tribe's displeasure and her new name: *She-Wolf.*

Since then, She-Wolf had become a mostly solitary hunter, successful enough to provide food for her immediate family. She occasionally joined male hunters, and from time-to-time assisted in the taking of an elk or deer, although she was not usually privileged to share in such bounty. But typically, she hunted alone and thus knew the terrain of her tribe's territory better than any of the male hunters. She-Wolf was curious and spent time in solitary exploration, whereas the males hunted in groups and were only interested in finding prey and protecting their territory.

She-Wolf carried a spear much longer than her stature would suggest. Made herself, its tip was razor-sharp obsidian, as one of the older teenage hunters found out when he tried to take it from her. Unlike the men, she carried a small knife. The males carried larger knives and shorter spears, some of them launched with atlatls. The more skilled hunters had fashioned bows with crude, though effective, arrows.

She-Wolf was proficient with her spear since it was used primarily to impale squirrels, rabbits, rats, an occasional fish and, rarely, larger prey. She made an imposing figure, standing on an outcropping, spear butt down on the rock, its finely-worked ash shaft in hand, its glistening point a full two feet above her head.

None of the unattached males showed interest in her, and she had begun to wonder if she would ever find a mate, become a mother, and relinquish her role as a hunter. Most of the tribe's females her age had already found mates, and a couple were pregnant. Females mated early, and as quickly as possible, added members to the tribe. Death, also, came early for most. Their lifestyle used them up quickly, and few made it to old age.

Her age was more of a guess than an absolute, as the tribe elders' ability to keep track of time was haphazard at best. She-Wolf considered herself sixteen, but could easily have been a year, or even two, older, although she considered it unlikely. She wondered what her life would be like had she followed in the path of most tribal women; pregnant or already carrying a child on her hip.

Her frequent observations of the Giants was forbidden by the tribe as they feared retribution of the almost mystical city might be called down upon them. But She-Wolf persisted, keeping her explorations secret from the tribe and her presence hidden from the Giants. She would be away from home for days, and sometimes even longer if she had provided sufficient food for her family. Her furtive trips to the city of Giants could take up to a week getting there, and at least another week on the return.

Although wiser than her years might attest, She-Wolf was, essentially, a rebellious teenager.

*

Ogenus loved his job. He rode a great cargo ship on an elevated bridge overlooking the endless rolling sea. Not that a navigator had all that much to do. A global tracking system and the onboard computer handled most of the ship's navigational tasks.

Guild rules required that a human navigator be present on all cargo ships, along with a captain and a small crew to assist stevedores with loading and unloading the giant ship, and a few to tend the engines and ancillary functions.

Ogenus shared responsibility on the bridge with the ship's captain. It was his job to guide the ship from one port to another; the vessel's captain made sure the ship moved where its navigator designated. In reality, GPS and the computers did most of that work, with the humans merely overseeing.

Staring out at the endless water, Ogenus was anxious to reach port. They had been sailing for three weeks down the western side of the Great Southern Continent. They had made several stops along the way, but Ogenus hadn't had an opportunity to leave the ship. Here, near the southern tip of the continent, they would dock for several days at a large city and shipping port, to unload most of their cargo. After, they would load more goods for transport back to the ports of Oceana. Not responsible for those jobs, Ogenus would be free to walk the dry land, meet people, and explore.

Rough water rocked the giant cargo ship gently. Ogenus enjoyed the motion. It was as relaxing to him as it was nauseous to land dwellers. He watched eagerly as details of the land became clear, and he could finally see taller structures of the distant city.

Several hours before sunset, the ship approached a designated dock. His ship carried tons of wheat and refrigerated vegetables, along with containers of handmade goods and other products, and a few tons of frozen beef and pork carcasses. The ship had loaded most of its cargo at the home port of Kursatta, and the remainder from other seaports of Oceana.

As the ship slowed to a crawl, Ogenus kept one eye on the computer readout and the other on the dock. Abruptly, the ship lurched forward. The captain reached out a hand to steady herself. "What was that?" she asked.

Ogenus tapped screens, but there were no obvious answers.

The ship shuddered again and slipped sideways toward the dock. Speed was still slowing.

"There. Did you feel that?"

"Uh-huh. I don't like this," Ogenus muttered.

"I don't, either. But it seems to me to be only minor anomalies," the captain said. "Engines at slow, speed nominal. Proceed normally."

Ogenus felt another shudder and this time the ship seemed to shift away from the dock. He glanced at the docking crew waiting to tie the ship down and saw wondering looks on their faces.

"I'm taking manual control," he said. "Something's not right."

"I don't recommend that," said the captain. She glanced over at him from her screens.

Ogenus took a deep breath, then flipped up the cover and pressed a red manual override button. He grasped his navigation joystick. "On manual," he said softly.

The captain opened her mouth, but said nothing.

As a skilled navigator with seven years of experience on top of certification training, Ogenus was competent to dock a cargo ship. He handled his controls with a soft touch that belied the huge size of the vessel.

As they nestled to the dock, the ship suddenly gave another lurch, this time toward the wood and metal structure.

Ogenus quickly reversed thrust, but the ship bumped the dock with enough force to almost knock himself and the captain off their feet.

"Cut engines," Ogenus growled. The captain jabbed her screens, and the engine rumble ceased. There was shouting from both those on the ship and crew on the dock. He heard a loud crashing as several cargo containers shifted and a couple of smaller tubs toppled from the stacks.

"What the hell happened?" the captain asked angrily.

"I don't know," Ogenus said. "At the last moment, my controls stopped responding."

The captain looked out and watched crews as they secured her ship to the dock. "Not good," she said. "If there was any damage, we'll need to justify our actions. Make sure you back up the automatic ship's log. Make a written record of what transpired and the reasons for your actions. We need to assess any damage to cargo and the ship itself. Log that as well."

"I will," Ogenus said. "Was it as bad as that?"

"You took manual control. None of my screens showed any malfunction."

"But you felt the movement just as I did."

She shrugged. "The Guild will look at our ship's log, and that shows nothing abnormal."

"But it was abnormal," Ogenus said frowning. He sat down, took a deep breath, and began typing in his log screen. After he finished, Ogenus went out on the massive deck to observe any damage to the cargo or the ship itself. What he found was relatively minor, and none of the crew was injured. The real damage had been to his credibility. He gazed at the harbor's calm water, confused and angry at his bad fortune. Something had, indeed, happened. But he didn't understand the cause, and he didn't like the effect.

*

She-Wolf had decided on her most recent solo excursion out of the mountains because she and her family had eaten well, and there was extra meat cured, salted, and stored in the ice behind their hut. She and her fellow hunters had found an injured and dying bear. It had succumbed easily to their spears and arrows. Members of the tribe had butchered the carcass, and the chief rewarded with a new warm coat. There was plenty of meat for all tribe members, even those not so well regarded by the elders.

The next day, before dawn, She-Wolf left her tribe and family, and over the next week, worked her way out of the mountains. She eventually reached and followed the river down toward the Giant city, blazing brightly in darkness. During her earlier visits, she had dared venture closer and closer, following the river bank. She eventually made it to a stone and concrete bridge spanning the river. The bridge carried Giant vehicles back-and-forth over the tributary, in an endless stream. Crouching under this, she heard the growling rumble of their passage. Beyond the bridge, river water flowed into the sea. She had never dared to venture that far, to actually stand at the edge of the Great Water. That would happen someday, when her courage matched her curiosity.

As she reached her secret hiding place, She-Wolf settled back in a depression under the bridge, head cradled in her arms. Comforted by the unceasing rumble of vehicles, she relaxed and eventually fell asleep. She dreamed what it would be like to meet and know a Giant, to have the opportunity to enter, and perhaps live, in one of the structures of light inhabited by the Giants. In her dream, she smiled—a smile of wonder.

A dislodged pebble rolling down the river bank woke She-Wolf with a start. Her hand grasped the shaft of her spear and she instinctively lie motionless, listening. Too late to run, she could only hide and hope who-or whatever it was didn't see her. It was late evening, the sun still slightly above the horizon, its orange glow illuminating her hiding place. She heard another sound, then saw movement. She sat up, held very still, and watched.

A young man, a Giant, one of the tall, thin, pasty ones, slowly made his way down the steep bank and strode to the river's edge. He was a foot taller than She-Wolf, fully-grown rather than an adolescent. He did not seem to be carrying a weapon of any kind. His clothes were garish and flowing, useless, in She-Wolf's opinion, for anything but vanity.

He made his way to the river, stooped, picked up a pebble, and plopped it into rushing water. He stood silent for a while, watching ripples flow toward the sea. Then he turned, bent down and picked up a twig. As he stood, he saw She-Wolf, hidden in lengthening shadows under the bridge. The man froze, his expression surprised but not frightened.

The two remained thus, separated by a few yards, for an intense moment. Then She-Wolf was on her feet and running past the Giant, following the river back up, her moccasins silent on rounded river rocks. She heard the man call after her, but he did not follow. She-Wolf was soon swallowed by the deepening shadows of dusk.

She had intended to make haste back up to the heights, but an old broken tree trunk lying at the river's edge provided a good hiding place. She ducked behind it and looked back toward the bridge. The Giant was slowly moving in her direction, but gave no indication he saw her among deepening shadows. His posture remained relaxed and fearless.

The Giant watched for a long moment, took a few more steps in her direction, then stopped. He gazed intently into the shadows. She-Wolf ducked back, then cautiously peeked around the stump. The man called out, a few words into the night, in the language of Giants which She-Wolf, of course, didn't understand. The tone of his voice was not angry or demanding, but seemed friendly and encouraging. She was tempted to step out and confront the man. After all, she had a spear and he had nothing. But legends of the Giants kept her hidden until the man eventually turned and made his way back up the bank, out of the growing night and back into a comfortable glowing, brightly lit city.

*

She-Wolf took her time, working her way along the river next to fields and meadows, up into rolling foothills, and finally into the forest and higher mountains toward her home. By the time well-worn paths of the village greeted her many days later mid-morning, she had carcasses of two rabbits and a squirrel hanging from her belt. She located and acknowledged the sentries. As usual, they ignored her. Upon her arrival at the village, a young boy, coincidentally named Rabbit, saw her and came running up.

"You've been gone a long time," he said, breathlessly. The boy, a year or two younger than She-Wolf, was small for his age. As the Chief's son, he was expected to lead hunting parties and do his part to help feed the tribe. However, his diminutive stature and an uncommon shyness kept him close to home. He was a disappointment to his much larger and far more successful father. Rabbit's siblings were protective of him, but otherwise less than kind.

"Where have you been?" Rabbit asked, accusingly.

She-Wolf grunted. While she liked the boy, he was much too inquisitive and curious. And as the Chief's son, he was a little too eager to impress his old man to suit her. Had circumstances been different, he might have made a welcome friend.

"Well, the Chief wants to see you right away."

"Let me get this meat to my hut, then I'll see the Chief."

Rabbit grasped her hand and pulled her toward the large hut occupied by the tribal leader. "He wants to see you *now!*"

21

"Okay, okay, just don't yank on my arm."

She followed Rabbit through snow and ice to the largest hut. Rabbit pushed an elk hide door aside. "She's here," he shouted into the opening.

Some noises and a grunt were followed by a deep voice. "You may enter She-Wolf."

The Chief, old and fat, dark as night, sat warming himself in front of a small, hot fire. As Chief, he was the only one with a hut large enough to enjoy inside flames. A vent made of bones and cured mud opened at the top of the structure, making a fire relatively safe in a shelter constructed of thin branches, mud, and grass.

She-Wolf momentarily envied the Chief, warm and sweating, while most tribe members huddled in cold grass huts, swaddled in varying amounts of furs, woven grass, and precious cloth.

"Come here," the Chief called to She-Wolf. Rabbit accompanied the girl until a look from his Elder sent him scurrying back out into the cold.

She-Wolf stood before the fat old man and waited, silently and unmoving, until his patience was almost exhausted. Then she touched her forehead with the tips of her fingers and bowed just enough to not further anger the tribal leader. Why she took such an effort just to annoy her leader, She-Wolf could not say. She smiled where it would not show on her face.

"While you were away," Chief said almost offhandedly, gazing at the low flames of his coveted fire, "your mother and brother were attacked and killed in their hut by one of the big cats."

She-Wolf gasped, her eyes widened, and she stumbled back and almost fell. She dropped her spear, and the sound of it hitting a rock cracked like thunder in her ears.

"You are no longer daughter and sister. You are not competent to be a hutkeeper and cook. None of the men wish to mate with you." He looked at her bleakly, his eyes flicked briefly to the wolf head atop hers, then returned to the embers of his fire. "Your hunting skills, while they were adequate for the three of you, are insufficient to benefit the tribe. You are therefore a liability to us all and I've made the decision to banish you. You may take whatever remains in your hut that you find valuable, but you must leave by sun rise tomorrow. Do not attempt to return to this village. Do not attempt to hunt within the territory of this tribe. If you do not heed this edict, you will be executed. Do you understand me?"

She-Wolf wiped her cheeks with the back of her fists. Through eyes clouded with tears, too shocked to respond, she simply stared at the Chief.

"Where are they?" She asked, her voice soft but halting. She longed to run to them, to their hut, to turn back time, to bring them back to life. If only she not been gone, playing explorer, daring to dream...

"You know the customs of our tribe. They have been sent up to the sky to dwell with our ancestors." She-Wolf knew what that meant. Her mother and brother had been turned to ash and the ash carried aloft on the flames. She would find them in the stars, looking down on her. She hoped it would not be a look of disapproval.

"You—you could have waited until I returned," she accused.

"We did not know when, or if, you would ever appear. While you were off," he waved a hand, "somewhere doing what it is that you do, we did our duty. We upheld the customs of our people. I asked you a question." His eyes narrowed as he gazed at the girl.

She-Wolf tried to replay the conversation, but she couldn't arrange her thoughts. She looked at the Chief and was silent, tears streaming down her cheeks.

The Chief raised a hand and pointed. "If you do not respond, I will have you killed immediately. I ask again, do you understand my words?"

She shouted out a sobbed "Yes! When the light returns, I will be gone!" She turned, grabbed her spear from the ground, and ran out into evening dusk, shivering but not merely because of the cold.

She-Wolf stood outside the Chief's hut for a moment, breathing hard and ignoring the furtive looks of her former tribe members. Rabbit was talking to her, but she did not hear his words. She turned and strode to the hut where she had lived since the last migration seven years ago. Her home was located at the far edge of the village, a reflection of her family's troubled status.

From outside, the hut looked normal, and she expected to see her little brother come running out to greet her. She imagined it, almost seeing him looking up at her with those shining blue eyes and his wide smile. She wanted to lift him up, hug him, and smell his hair. She expected to hear the singing and noises of her mother as she worked to prepare their evening meal. But all she heard was the soft rustling of a cold breeze drifting through tall trees. A silence greater than any mountain she'd ever seen now faced her. She knew she had to climb this mountain, enter the hut, and do what needed to be done. But oh, by the gods, she didn't want to. "Please let this task pass from my hands to yours," she whispered almost silently, a plea to the gods who so seldom answered. She stared at the opening for a while longer. Then, with a shuddering sigh and trembling lips, she reached out and pushed the covering pelt aside.

*

Ogenus barely saw something rush past him, and realized it was a girl. And by her dress, he guessed she was from one of the mountain tribes. He had been idly staring at the river when he turned and bent to pick up a twig he had intended to toss into the rushing water. There, under the bridge, hidden in the shadows, cast in an orange evening light, was something moving. He could not have been more surprised. At first, he thought it was an animal. But he'd never seen a wild animal this close to Kursatta. As she passed him, he recognized a human female.

"Wait!" he shouted as she disappeared into the growing darkness. "I won't hurt you." But he knew she didn't understand his words if, indeed, she had even heard them. What was she doing all the way down here, he wondered. He had never seen anyone from the tribes this close before, as he knew they very seldom ventured near the Oceanus cities.

He took a few steps upriver, then stopped. He would have followed after her, but he'd seen the long spear she carried. Ogenus assumed she knew how to use it, despite her size and gender. And even if he did follow her, and caught up with her, what then?

After another long moment searching the terrain, and a shouted greeting, he gave up and climbed back up to the road that led back to the city of Kursatta.

His vehicle was parked near the bridge. He got back in and told it to take him home. He lived in a high-rise apartment complex a few miles west of the river, overlooking the city's harbor.

Ogenus was six years past his second decade of life. He'd been born and raised on a farm near Kursatta. Until a month ago, he had been employed as a navigator on long-haul cargo ships. He loved being out on the open water, but his main job was making sure the computers that actually did the navigating did their job properly. Which they did. His onboard computer even handled the ship in all but the largest storms. Ogenus' mistake came when he disengaged the automatic controls during docking with the result of minor but serious damage to both the ship and the dock. This had resulted in his suspension and appearance before a Review Board hearing. Because everyone knew the computers operated flawlessly, the incident had to, of course, be human error.

The hearing was a recent, and painful, memory. He'd waited silently while his and the Captain's logbooks were examined, and entered into evidence. His explanation for the incident was weak, and he did not even fully convince himself.

"You detected an anomaly in the on-board tracking computer?" the review board Director had asked.

"That's correct, sir. The ship was docking in an unsafe manner."

"According to your calculations?"

"Well, I could feel it reacting...strangely." He'd tried to think of another word, a better description, but his mind remained blank.

The Director looked down at his screen, then back up at Ogenus. "However, both the onboard computer and satellite tracking logs showed the ship at correct speed and position for docking. How do you explain that?"

"I have no explanation, sir. I don't see how both the computer and the satellite could be wrong. I would like to point out, however, that the computer and the satellite each provided correct—but slightly conflicting—data."

"But both," the Director said, "well within the margin of safety."

"Because of this slight discrepancy," Ogenus said, "I felt it best to take manual control."

"With results that were less than satisfactory."

Ogenus shrugged. "I know my job. Whatever caused the discrepancy also caused the ship's electronic controls to respond...erratically." Again, he cursed his lack of a better word.

The company's technical supervisor had also testified. "Those GPS satellites will be properly in orbit for the next thousand years. They have, and continue to provide reliable data. The ship's computers functioned normally in all subsequent tests."

The Director made a note. "To what do you attribute the minor variances mentioned by the defendant?"

"Unknown, sir. It could have been due to a gravitational anomaly, a minor earthquake, or an electrical discharge of some kind."

"However, you have no evidence that any of these events occurred, is that correct?"

The technician paused, shrugged, glanced at Ogenus, then nodded.

Ogenus' arguments, while reasoned and with some evidence to back them up, had been insufficient to overturn the electronic data. He was relieved of his position with the Maritime Shipping Board. He was discharged without penalty, and given a new position with an administrative utility billing company. It was an office job, sitting for hours, shifting papers and jabbing his finger at screens. And he hated it. He had avoided a harsher sentence, but any decision that kept him off the water was the same as being isolated in a small room behind metal bars.

Throwing rocks into the river was not sailing the high seas, but it was the best he could do for the moment. He often visited the river near the bridge because he didn't think he could stand at the edge of open water without bursting into tears.

Ogenus lived alone, and his apartment was relatively small. His vehicle parked itself in the complex's underground garage. In the elevator, he mentioned his name. The machine zoomed him to floor 75 so rapidly that his knees buckled slightly. However, instead of smoothly and silently swishing to a stop as it had always done in the past, the elevator bumped once, then twice. The doors opened to a corridor lined with identical apartment entrances. Ogenus turned left, but stopped and gazed momentarily at the elevator. A simple, slight malfunction; but the technology of Oceanus did not have simple, slight malfunctions. Until recently.

His apartment was three doors down from the elevator. As he approached, the door recognized him but did not unlock until he had provided voice confirmation. He entered, kicked off his shoes and wiggled his feet in the plush dark blue carpet. He walked over to a bank of floor-to-ceiling windows and gazed out at an inky black sea that spread before him. All along the coast blazed lights of the city he called home. If he looked down, he could see the marina to his left, and a shipping port to the right. Other than pinpoint lights of a few ships and pleasure boats, the ocean itself was ink dark. And tonight, it took on a rather ominous tone as Ogenus watched. Then he turned to the kitchen and fixed himself a drink.

His parents had lived on a farm a half-hour's drive from the city, until their deaths five years ago. They died as a result of a farming accident and fire that had consumed the barn with his parents trapped inside. Ogenus kept the property in his name since it was where he grew up. But he had no interest in farming; his love was the sea. He leased his property to neighbors who took care of the animals and farmed the land. His parents had considered him a good son, a competent worker, and most seriously, criminally unattached. He had been happy with his job, navigating the known world and visiting far distant ports. Many of the nearby ports belonged to Oceanus, but others constituted foreign nations. Some of those nations spoke languages that required Ogenus to listen and learn enough so that he could get along with his explorations and adventures.

Now he worked in an office, auditing bills and angering strangers. He worked in a high-rise building with perhaps hundreds of co-workers whose names he did not know. He recognized a few dozen of those sitting nearby with whom he shared pleasantries and mindless small talk each morning. But most were nameless faces that appeared and disappeared during his boring workday. His apartment had become a refuge, as well as a prison. He was in it much more than he used to be, and sometimes the walls seemed to be closing in on him.

His communicator lit up and buzzed. "Ogenus," he said.

"Ionic here. You home?"

"Just got here. Come on in."

Ionic lived five floors above Ogenus, at the very top of the building, in a corner apartment. His abode was much larger and with better views, a testament to his age and wealth. Twenty years older, Ionic was a Renaissance man, with learned degrees in several sciences, medicine, music, history, and astronomy, and probably a few more that Ogenus didn't know about. Ionic was his closest friend, and they were both similarly unattached. However Ionic, despite his age, had a much livelier social life.

The door opened, and Ionic entered with a bottle in each hand and a package of sweets in his mouth. He set the bottles on the table, then opened his mouth to drop the package of candy between them. "So how was your day, mighty biller?"

"Stuff it. I hated every minute of it. Took off early. Went to the river. Saw a girl."

"Funny place to find a date, my friend."

"Not a date. Looked like she belonged to one of the mountain tribes. She was hiding under the bridge. When I saw her, she took off like a scared rabbit."

"I wasn't aware tribal people ever came down from the mountains. Should have chased her. Might have been playing hard-to-get."

Despite his dour mood, Ogenus smiled. "Not hardly. She was pretty, but had a spear that looked twice as tall as she."

Ionic took a drink. "My mistake. You are in serious trouble, my friend, if you not only don't have to fight them off with a stick, but they bring their own sticks to fight you off." He laughed heartily at his own joke.

Ogenus smiled at the dig but didn't laugh.

Ionic shook his head and took another long drink from his bottle. He was tall, with a receding hairline, long but sparse gray hair, a thick middle, a twinkle in his eye and a bright disposition that sometimes irritated Ogenus, who tended to be more reserved and less expressive.

"And how about your day? Any exciting new scientific discoveries?"

Ionic opened his mouth to reply, then stopped and stared out the window. "I'll be damned," he said softly. Ogenus watched as his friend stood and almost stumbled to the window. "Look at this," he said, pointing toward the darkness.

Ogenus joined him at the window. "Lights, dim," he said. As the illumination in his apartment lowered, they saw in the night sky, over the blackness of the sea, green ribbons of glow rippling silently. The two men watched the display for several minutes before either of them spoke.

"By the gods," Ogenus whispered, "what is that?"

"It's a display of charged particles emitted from the sun and interacting with elements in our atmosphere." Ionic shook his head. "The phenomenon is seen primarily at the magnetic poles. Rarely observed this close to the equator. This is important..."

"Okay. Why?"

"It might be an indication of increased solar activity. Perhaps the end of the solar minimum, which has given us this pesky ice stretching down from both poles. This phenomenon is often caused by coronal mass ejections, which may," he said, turning to look at Ogenus, "explain the glitches in various types of electronics." He pursed his lips. "Including your navigational anomalies."

Ogenus thought about this for a moment. "Probably not enough evidence to get me reinstated, you think?"

"It would be hard to prove. But..."

"But what?"

"If the sun is really emerging from its solar minimum, our climate may very well begin to warm."

"That's a good thing, right?"

Ionic looked at his friend. "If things warm up, a lot of that mountain ice will melt, which means rivers flowing a greater volume of water into the oceans, and the ocean levels rising. Most of our cities are on or near the oceans. We could be facing some serious coastal inundations."

"What do we do about it?"

Ionic shrugged. "Not much we can do. Anyhow, I believe it will be many decades before we see a measurable effect. If I'm right, the sun's output should slowly increase and as a result, our climate will also slowly warm." He paused for a moment, "and I'm afraid these annoying electronic anomalies will continue periodically. It may be necessary to go back and add shielding to our electronics at critical points."

Both men watched the aurora display for a few minutes longer, each silent with his own thoughts.

"Oh!" Ionic said, "I almost forgot the most interesting news."

Ogenus lifted an eyebrow.

"Scientists in Mokaya Land across the great western sea have found the body of a large prehistoric dinosaur that was not fossilized. You've seen those huge fossilized skeletons in museums, right? This one apparently died or was killed, then fell into a peat bog which was covered shortly thereafter with volcanic ash. A short time later the whole area was frozen, and it remained pretty much preserved and frozen for millions of years until it was found by Mokaya Land paleontologists."

"Interesting. Did they learn anything new with a complete animal in their possession?"

Ionic's eyes opened wide. "Tons of stuff. One fascinating thing of importance. The animal was carnivorous, large enough to eat either of us in a couple of bites. You've seen the artist's concepts. Teeth like daggers, two tiny little front arms. And," he paused, "now we know it was feathered, somewhat like a bird. We've suspected some of those prehistoric animals were feathered, predecessors of our modern birds, but this one was intact, with skin, bones, soft tissue, and those fascinating feathers. The Mokayas are calling it a Feathered Reptile or Feathered Serpent. It's on display at their Capitol museum, enclosed in a temperature-controlled glass case. It's a very popular attraction. Some of the common people are even worshiping it."

"Amazing. That's one animal I'd like to see."

"I'd give my hair to be able to study it for a month."

"I think you should be willing to give something of value," Ogenus said dryly, looking at the sparse growth atop his friend's head.

Ionic replied digitally, which bought a smile from his friend.

Ogenus glanced over at the window. "Looks like the light show is over for tonight. Guess I'll turn in."

Ionic took the hint, finished his drink, then departed with a few encouraging words.

Ogenus lay in his bed for some hours, staring at his ceiling, reflecting on the recent changes to his life, which had occurred faster than he could comprehend. One moment, he was plying the oceans of the world, feeling the power of a giant ship under him. He feared nothing the sea could throw at him. He knew where he was going, and made sure he and the crew, along with their massive cargo, arrived safely.

In ports all over the world, he had explored different cultures, other nations, and the lands they occupied. He had friends in far-flung places. He had even learned and spoke some of their languages.

Now he sailed a powerless desk that went nowhere, just like his future.

He missed his parents, and he found himself feeling very alone.

*

She-Wolf woke with a start. Wrapped in the familiar skins and furs of home, she could still smell her mother and little brother, as if both of them were simply asleep next to her. She remained completely still for a long time, remembering, followed by deep, unstoppable sobs. The night before she'd cleaned up the blood and other debris that littered their grass hut, and made a temporary repair to the back where the large cat had torn its way in. Afterward, an overwhelming weariness overtook her. She managed to make a small bundle of the belongings she planned to take with her, then fell into a deep, black, dreamless sleep.

A shaft of sunlight penetrated the hut. It was time for her to leave. She got up and took care of a few final things. Other than her spear, she would take only the clothes she wore and the bundle now tied to her fabric belt.

It was a small, pitiful bundle, comprised mostly of mementos of her family, including the stone amulet she'd made for her father. She removed the stone and looked it, holding back more tears. As a small child, she'd patiently shaped the stone, carved a primitive wolf on the face of the circular surface, then spent hours digging a small hole into the upper part. Once finished, she threaded a cord through it, tied it off, then presented the stone to her father. He was delighted and immediately slipped it around his neck and never removed it. Months later, when he was killed, his wolf stone was the only thing returned to the family.

Dawn illuminated the quiet village. She-Wolf left her hut for the last time. Women tended fires in preparation for cooking. No one looked at her as she strode, silently, past them. She kept her eyes forward, not looking back. Embers of perimeter fires glowed. Sentries kept watch on higher ground, wrapped in heavy furs to keep out the cold. They idly watched as she made her way to the village edge.

As she passed by, Rabbit stepped out from his small hut which was built against a tall tree. The boy was the only one who acknowledged her beyond that which was necessary. "You're leaving," he said. It wasn't a question.

She-Wolf stopped and looked down at Rabbit. "No choice. The Chief doesn't want me." She gazed around the encampment. "And neither does anyone else."

Rabbit did not dispute her words. He looked into her eyes. "This one was happy to have you here." He paused, looked down and scuffed the dirt with his moccasin. "Where will you go?"

She rested a gloved hand on Rabbit's shoulder. She pointed her spear to the west. "The lowlands, down near the Great Water."

"What about the Giants?"

"I'll stay out of their way. One small girl living off the edge of their land shouldn't cause notice. And if they do notice, what will they do? Send me away? Kill me? What does it matter?"

Rabbit was silent for a time, gazing at She-Wolf, perhaps memorizing her face. "It would matter to me. I'll miss you," he said softly.

She wanted to give him a hug, a proper goodbye. But that wouldn't be wise. He was the Chief's son, one of them. And besides, it would tie her to the tribe, regardless of distance. Instead, she nodded slightly, and without a sound, stepped into the shadows of a cold misty morning. She would miss him, too, but she couldn't bring the words to her lips. It was better this way.

She-Wolf followed a much-used path downhill and north to the first of many waterfalls. Then she turned west, following a path of her own making, and started down toward the valley of the Giants. She knew her destination, the place where she could set up housekeeping. She hoped the Giant who had ventured to the edge of the river that night, and saw her hiding under the bridge, would not return. If he did, she'd have to fight for her new home. If he challenged her, she'd have to kill the Giant, and she didn't know if Giants could be killed.

She didn't much care. She had no family, no home, no friends, and other than one foot in front of another, no future.

*

Ogenus finally got around to visiting the Maritime Authority offices. He had personal items to retrieve from his former cubicle, and a few people he wanted to see, if for no other reason than to say goodbye. The door guard greeted him as a friend and provided a visitor's pass. He rode up 80 floors and entered the navigation administrative offices. He went to the cubicle he'd used infrequently when not aboard a cargo ship.

He greeted friends and co-workers...former co-workers he reminded himself. They were happy to see him, but kept comments neutral, knowing there was nothing they could say, or he could say, that would change his situation.

A tall, light-haired, middle-aged woman stepped from a nearby office, saw Ogenus, smiled and strode over, her hand out in greeting.

"There you are, Ogenus. I wondered if you'd come back to get your things." Her voice was loud, and it carried.

"Eris," he said quietly, taking the hand and giving it a neutral squeeze. Eris was an executive administrator. She'd served on his board of inquiry and was one of those who had voted to release him. They had sometimes shared pleasantries but did not have a close relationship. His personal opinion of her was one he did not share with others. She was tall and rather attractive, but not really his type. She did her job competently, but in his opinion, tended to harbor grudges and punish what she saw as disloyalty.

"How are you coping?" she asked, still a bit loudly.

"As well as could be expected," he said softly, "although it is a bit of a change."

She stared at him for a moment. "I think you'll do all right," she said. "There are opportunities out there for a man of your abilities."

"I'd like to think so." Her steady gaze made him somewhat uncomfortable.

"Well, get your things boxed up, then stop by my office and we'll chat for a bit."

"Okay," he said slowly, glancing over Eris' shoulder. She followed his gaze and smiled. "There have been some changes since you left." Eris turned and strode, conspicuously, back to her office.

Indeed, Ogenus thought. That office belonged to the Chief of Navigations, a job he had aspired to, before things changed. He shook his head and dismissed might-have-beens. Eris entered her office and swung the door almost closed, leaving it unlatched, a minimum invitation.

It didn't take him long to retrieve and box up his belongings. He'd spent so little time in the facility that he never considered it his workplace. His place was on ships, sailing to those far distant and exotic ports. Until he didn't. He'd made the best decisions he could, but it turned out they weren't good enough. Because of that, he was now a land dweller. The walls of his former office displayed large photos of the various ships the organization was responsible for. He glanced at them, but did not dwell.

Wishing he had some excuse to just leave, Ogenus stepped in front of Eris' office and knocked softly. "Enter," Eris called.

He pushed through the door. The woman was holding a phone to her ear. She glanced at Ogenus, then turned away, waving him inside and continuing her conversation. Ogenus stepped in and stood awkwardly until Eris finished the call and placed the phone on her desk.

"Come in," she said, "have a seat and relax."

Ogenus seated himself, but didn't relax.

"I've read the final Commission report on your case. While I have some reservations, I think we made the correct decision. What do you think?"

Ogenus opened his mouth, then closed it. He thought for a moment before replying. "I think there is information the Board of Inquiry didn't have at the time of my hearing that may shed a slightly different light on the incident."

"New information? Such as?"

"A friend, who is an astronomer, noticed some unusual atmospheric phenomena these past few evenings. He thinks the sun might be shifting back to a solar maximum. He believes this will result in a slow increase in global temperatures. He also thinks the resulting atmospheric disturbances could be the cause of anomalies in some of our electronic equipment, such as that found on cargo ships."

Eris frowned. "Interesting. So you believe that the accident wasn't your fault at all, but the result of this, hypothetical, atmospheric disturbance?"

Ogenus answered carefully. "I believe that is a possibility, yes."

Eris stared at him for a long moment, then leaned back in her chair. "Perhaps we can discuss this sometime in more detail. Say, maybe, your place some evening?"

Ogenus didn't answer right away. "I don't think that's possible," he said softly. "I no longer work for the Maritime Commission. The Board has already made its decision. I have no evidence that my friend's hypothesis is correct, and no way to test it."

"Oh, come now, Ogenus. If the sun's acting up, we should be seeing more technical glitches."

"You're right, of course. Sooo..."

She looked at him again with that unnerving gaze, then shrugged. "I guess you're right. It would be a waste of our time. Pity, though. We might have had, all things considered, a productive evening."

He caught her implied meaning. The thought was distasteful to Ogenus. Not only was she mated, but she also had children, one of whom was no more than a decade younger than he. Any kind of relationship with Eris could only make a bad situation worse, and in his eyes at least, would be absurd. Her rather contentious attitude toward him was also puzzling.

Ogenus stood and turned to the door, intending to make a quick and quiet departure. Then he turned back. "I'm sorry things haven't worked out, but I think I'm better off leaving the situation as is," he said dryly. The look on Eris' face was... interesting, a mixture of anger, regret, and disappointment. While he had many friends on the 80th floor of this building, he knew instinctively that Eris was not one of them.

*

On his way back home, Ogenus changed his mind and decided to pay a visit to the observatory where Ionic earned most of his living. He badly needed a friend at the moment, and when Ionic worked at the observatory, he tended to be away from home for days at a time.

The traditional round-topped building housed a powerful telescope and a few other buildings. It rested on a large rock outcropping, called the Crecopia, which was located inland a couple of hours or so by air, northeast of the city. It was a place that had once been isolated from light pollution until a small village called Sesklo grew up and surrounded it. Use of the large telescope had thus declined, but a satellite dish nearby received data from space telescopes in various geosynchronous and geostationary orbits.

He secured a personal flier and took to the deep blue sky. He knew he should feel freedom in the air, but instead, strangely, felt tied to the earth, to the dry ground. Soaring high above was not the same as plying far-flung seas. It was a distinction that shouldn't have made a difference, but somehow it did.

As his flier passed over fields and hills, he closed his eyes and imagined the craft was a ship at sea. After a while, he relaxed and fell asleep. An hour later, he sensed a change in the air car's motion. Eyes flicked open, and he saw the flat top of the rock below.

In the distance, mountains covered in ice faded into billowy clouds. His airship slowly settled on the designated landing area. Had he been in the mood, Ogenus would have enjoyed an expansive view from the flat, elevated outcrop in the middle of low rolling fields.

A guard let Ogenus into the observatory building, after calling Ionic for clearance.

Ionic eschewed greetings as he literally pulled Ogenus into his lab, bubbling with excitement. "You're just in time.

Come here. Look at this," he pushed Ogenus into a chair in front of his workspace, which was decorated with a pile of unorganized papers, empty cups, and four large computer screens.

Ionic pointed, eagerly.

"What am I looking at?" Ogenus asked.

"Look right there. See that point of light?"

"Yes, I see it."

"That's a comet. A new one. At least since we've been keeping records. A big one, by the gods. I mean big! And it's headed right for us. In a year, it should pass very close to Earth. By the time it gets nearest to us, the tail will stretch across the sky. It'll be spectacular!"

"Hmm," Ogenus muttered. "That tiny little speck?"

Ionic stood and looked at his friend. "That little speck, as you call it, is about the size of the entire nation of Oceanus. Or maybe even bigger. We'll know more once it gets closer. It's going to be awesome! And guess what."

"What?"

"I discovered it! The Board has named it 'IonicB473a' after me!"

Ogenus looked away from the computer screen. "Congratulations. That's great. I'm happy for you!" He shook Ionic's hand. Then he looked again at the undistinguished speck.

After another moment of silently staring at the screen, Ogenus said what he'd been thinking. "What if it hits us?"

Ionic's smile disappeared. "What?"

"You know. A collision between that comet and the Earth."

Ionic looked back at the computer screen and was silent for a long moment. "Well," he said slowly. "I guess it could. If it hit us directly, it would probably kill most life on Earth, perhaps even shift our planet's orbit. But that's not likely to happen. We'll know more as it gets closer. There's an astronomer in the Kingdom of Naqada who's also a very good mathematician. I'll consult with her, maybe even visit her." He gazed off into the distance, then shook his head and glanced back at the screen. "Naqada isn't all that far away."

"I know. I've been there several times," Ogenus pointed southwest, "just across the sea, right next to Esna."

Ionic looked at Ogenus for a long moment. "You've visited a lot of places, haven't you?" He said quietly.

"Almost the whole world. At least those nations that have seaports."

Ionic nodded. "You really miss the sea life, don't you? Traveling to distant lands and enjoying mysterious cultures?"

Ogenus shrugged. "Of course I do. But that's over. It's in the past. Now I'm here. I'm not going anywhere. Kursatta is my home now, not just a place I visit occasionally." He was surprised at the anger in his voice.

He gazed at the pinpoint of light on the computer screen. He couldn't say why it frightened him, but for some reason, it did.

*

As she had done in the past, She-Wolf followed a small branch of the chuckling water through forests and meadows. The stream merged with others and would eventually wind its way out of the mountains to flow past the City of Giants.

While she had spent many days by herself in isolation before, she had always had the anchor of her family waiting for her at home. She had enjoyed being by herself, but now that isolation was no longer joyful as there seemed to be no end to it, no home to return to. She had to find someplace to live.

She'd decided to make her home under the bridge at the City of Giants. Near the ocean, temperatures were warmer. She could fish and hunt along the river where prey came to drink, all the while keeping out of sight of the Giants. She hoped just the nearness of those almost-gods would help fill the void of her loneliness.

Her goal was, of course, the same place where she had seen the man from the Giant city, but she did not believe that man, or any of the other giants, visited that particular location often.

She was shaken from her idle thoughts. At the base of a tall waterfall, She-Wolf saw cave wolf tracks in the snow. There seemed to be only one set of tracks, which was unusual and concerning. She had to be careful. While these large wolves hunted in packs, an old, sick, or injured wolf might be on its own. A lone wolf, hungry and unable to hunt, would seek easy prey. That made it dangerous.

Keeping an eye out, she drank from a pond at the base of the falls. The ice-cold water refreshed her, and she continued on downward, now fully focused not as a hunter but as possible prey. Her path down followed a set of waterfalls, toward the large river and eventually into cultivated land occupied by the Giants.

An hour later, She-Wolf suspected she was being stalked. She hid, and cut back on her trail, but saw nothing except, perhaps, a tail disappearing behind a rock. Later, she caught a glimpse of something moving through distant trees, but couldn't identify it. From her brief glance, she suspected a cave wolf. If so, it was likely a solitary hunter. Her familiarity with the terrain gave her a slight advantage as she climbed down through the forest. If she could reach cultivated fields, that would make it much harder for the wolf to stalk her. But those fields were still several days away; she had much climbing and forest to put behind her as she descended from the mountains.

At one point, she hid in thick foliage when the wind changed, and she observed the wolf for a bare moment. It was thin and limped, obviously injured. That gave her an idea.

During her downward trek, she kept her eyes open for small prey. First, she speared a rabbit. Instead of keeping it for herself, she left it behind her on the trail. Near sunset, a rat fell victim to her obsidian spear tip. She left that on the trail as well. At dusk, she managed to spear two fish from the ice-cold stream which she followed. One became her dinner, the other she left on the trail. That night, She-Wolf slept in a tree. While the big cats and some of the bears were good climbers, she didn't believe a cave wolf, injured and tired, would manage to reach her.

A thin fog greeted She-Wolf the next morning. As she dropped to the ground, she saw the wolf on rocks above, silent, unmoving, watching her. She turned away and hiked on, downward. An hour later, after a short chase and an impatient wait, she managed another rabbit. Again, she left the carcass in the dirt behind her.

The creek flung itself over a cliff, yet another roaring waterfall. She-Wolf used the same familiar path as before, but this time turned her head to look behind her. While distracted, she slipped on a wet boulder and fell, landing painfully on a flat rock five or six feet below. An anguished yelp escaped her, but she managed to hold onto her spear. She remained motionless for a long moment. She did not believe her injuries were serious, but she was dazed, and she fought to catch her breath. Her right shoulder exploded with pain as she tried to rise.

If the wolf was going to challenge her, now would be the time. She was injured and tired, and she felt very small and vulnerable. Back on her feet, She-Wolf used the butt of her spear to steady herself. An ankle was also giving her trouble, and she limped down toward a swirling pool at the bottom of the waterfall. It was slow going, painful and treacherous. She had only sight to warn her; the falling water covered any other sound.

She-Wolf descended the rocky path, moving slowly and carefully. The waterfall was a loud roar as she passed beside it, a fine mist covering everything. The trail turned a couple of times, following the stream down, and finally, with the roar of the waterfall behind her, she could once again hear the wind's whisper through trees and the song of birds.

She found a small pond at the edge of the stream. Beside it, large boulders made a half-cave where she would make her camp for the night. Patiently and one-handed, and despite the pain in her shoulder, she speared a couple of fish. She built a campfire to keep her warm, lined it with large rocks that she moved, again one-handed, into place. Warmed by her fire, the flames also provided sufficiently hot temperatures to serve as a pit for roasting the fish.

As dusk edged into full darkness, She-Wolf ate one of the fish, drank from the pond, and settled back against a space between two boulders. She left the other fish opposite her side of the campfire, well away from where she reclined.

It was difficult to find a resting position that wasn't painful, but she removed her wolf pelt, rolled it tightly, and used it and some brush for a makeshift bedroll. Exhausted and injured, she fell into a deep but troubled sleep.

Sometime during the night, after the moon had reached its zenith in the sky, she woke with a start. Her camp was bathed in a dim silvery lunar light. Her campfire emitted a minor glow and a few embers.

The first thing she noticed was that the fish she'd left out was gone. The second thing was a cave wolf lying on the other side of her camp fire. It raised its head and gazed at her with penetrating light blue eyes. Warily they stared at each other. Then the wolf rested its head on forepaws, turned slightly away, and went back to sleep.

With very little more to lose, She-Wolf sighed and dropped back into the deep sleep from which she had awoken. The wolf had blue eyes, she noted, similar to hers. She wondered if that was an omen from the gods. Maybe they had sent the animal to protect her. They owed her that, at the very least. She fell into a deeper sleep and dreamed of walking among ice-free high mountains, coming to the edge of a waterfall, and seeing endless water spread out before her. Striding out of the water, carrying his own spear, was the Giant she'd seen under the bridge. He opened his mouth and said words, but the words were silent. He turned, looked back out to sea and pointed. Then the dream changed, and she began to tremble with cold.

A fever washed over her. Delirious, She-Wolf regained enough awareness to realize that something warm nestled against her. A small part of her came to the conclusion the wolf was keeping her warm, protecting her. She relaxed and let the fever take her. She shivered and unknowingly grasped the wolf's fur, pulling at it weakly. She cried, softly, deep un-worldly sobs. She dreamed of her father, who'd held her when she was small. And of her mother and brother, taken, in her opinion, because the tribe and the gods had abandoned the family. A female hunter was an affront; a self-reliant one was intolerable.

Now the wolf had seemingly joined its fortunes to hers. Was that another affront to the gods? Only time would tell. She was sick and helpless, with hours of fevered unconscious-ness. Two days later, the fever broke. She-Wolf opened her eyes. The cave wolf still rested against her, its head looking out, scanning the terrain.

She-Wolf silently, and without moving, studied the animal. It wasn't old and sick as she had first thought. It was young, not quite fully-grown. Apparently an injury had slowed it down, and it had been abandoned by its pack. Left to die, hungry, and tracking She-Wolf, her idea of leaving food on the trail had helped animal to heal. And now it repaid her.

The wolf showed no fear as She-Wolf rose, stumbled to the pond, and drank deeply. The pain in her shoulder was mostly gone. She had most of her movement back except for some stiffness. The wolf watched as she returned, retrieved her spear and used it to impale two large fish. She rebuilt the fire, cleaned and cooked her catch. She shared one with the wolf and ate most of the other.

"So," she muttered to the animal, "are we friends, or are you fattening me up for a meal?" She raised an eyebrow. The wolf perked its ears and tilted its head.

She-Wolf stepped closer and raised a hand. The wolf leaned back and bared its fangs, a warning but not a threat, She-Wolf concluded. She turned and resumed her journey to the sea. She limped further down, still surrounded by trees, and noted the air was a bit warmer. In a day or two, she would be at the forest's edge. The cave wolf watched her for a long moment, then got to its feet and padded behind her, closely but warily. The teenager's lips carried a hint of a smile. She was not quite so lonely as she had been.

*

Ogenus visited Ionic on the top floor of their apartment complex. His purpose was to bid his friend what he hoped was a temporary farewell. Ionic voiced him in and looked up from his computer, its screen filled with calculations. He did a double-take. "What are you dressed for? You look silly in that outfit."

"Nice to see you, too," Ogenus replied.

"Well?"

"I'm going up into the mountains."

"On foot? Dressed in *that* outfit?"

Ogenus nodded and lowered his large backpack to the floor with a loud thump. Ionic looked skeptical. "You're either off on an adventure or you've gone out of your mind. Or both."

"Probably both. I'm going up to where the ice is. I had quite a lot of accumulated leave from my old job. It would transfer over to the new position, but I decided to use some of it instead."

Ionic stood, ran a hand over his long, thin, gray hair, making a mess. "But venturing up to the cold, icy wilderness is not what I'd call a vacation. That's a long walk, my friend. Whatever reason would anyone want to do that?"

Ogenus smiled. "There are tribes living up there, primitive peoples. I'd like to know a little more about them."

"What you will learn, my dear Ogenus, is that they eat people like you and me. You'll learn that they kill strangers first, and think about it later. Or they might capture you and use you for a little blood-thirsty fun, and then kill you. Of course, if you're lucky, they just might decide to make a slave out of you."

Ogenus laughed. "So you're an expert on the primitive tribes, now, are you?"

Ionic put a hand on Ogenus' shoulder. "I don't need to be an expert. I've read the news reports. I've seen the adventure programs," he waved toward his computer screen. "None of them turn out well, Ogenus. They're primitives for a reason. They aren't civilized."

"Perhaps you're right," Ogenus admitted. "But perhaps all this stuff you think you 'know' about them is mostly dramatic license."

Ionic shrugged. "But I wouldn't be foolish enough to bet my life on it. Remember history. We used to have wars with those tribes five or six hundred years ago, and their primitive weapons were almost as good as our primitive weapons. We don't deal with them now because they leave us alone. If they forced the issue today, it wouldn't be a battle, it would be a slaughter."

"Just so," Ogenus said. "I think it would be better if we made an effort to study them, tried to understand their culture, perhaps even communicate with them. We might find our word for 'civilization' is defined a little too rigidly."

Ionic threw his hands in the air. "Communicate with them? Do they even have a language?"

"Of course they have language," Ogenus replied angrily, then he noticed the gleam in Ionic's eye.

"Of course they do. They have words for 'kill' and 'cook' and 'yum' and things like that."

This time Ogenus laughed. "That's what I'm going to find out."

"Well, good luck with that. You on this adventure alone? Or are you taking a team of experts with you?"

Ogenus lifted the backpack with a grunt, and settled it across his shoulders. "There really aren't any experts. And I think this contact would be better served if I do it alone. Less threatening."

"Wouldn't have anything to do with the young lady you saw under that bridge a few weeks ago, would it?"

"I'll let you know the answer to that question when I return." Ogenus walked toward the door, then turned back. "You keep an eye on that comet while I'm gone."

"I surely will. If I can't talk you out of this, you need to be careful. There aren't very many people here I can call friend. I don't want to find out you were the star in a primitive tribal cooking ritual."

*

It was a much more difficult journey than Ogenus had imagined. As the woman had, he followed the river until it rose up beyond cultivated lands and farms. The going was fairly easy at first as the land rose gently toward the forest. Reaching undulating foothills, he began to climb. When he entered the forest, he sometimes came across animal tracks and sign. Some of the tracks where large. Either wolves or the large cats, maybe bears. He had never seen any of those in the wild. Actually, he'd never really been in the wild before.

It began to dawn on Ogenus that perhaps he hadn't thought this through. There wasn't really a path to follow, just up. He kept to one of the streams that fed the river. Eventually, that should lead him up to higher mountains and ice.

Alone, he was vulnerable. Any of the large carnivores might be stalking him right now. With a cold chill, Ogenus realized he could be eaten before dinner time. And what would happen when (or if) he managed to make it into the range of a tribe? They were hunters and gatherers. They were skilled at not being seen. And he was sure they didn't like strangers.

Tribes occasionally fought with each other, when food was scarce or territory too small for the population. In planning his epic journey, Ogenus had imagined a meeting between himself and members of this supposed tribe. In his mind, it had been a wary but dignified encounter, with mutual respect and curiosity. As he now climbed higher, his imagination redefined that meeting into something, he felt, was a little closer to reality. They would see him coming long before he saw them. As a loner, he'd be an easy capture. His imagination turned the dignified meeting into one where he was brought before the tribal chief secured in ropes and having suffered a beating.

But his imagination wouldn't quit. These people were hunters. He next imagined himself looking up at a ring of men who had brought him down with a flurry of spears and arrows. And, in his mind's eye, one leaned close to him, grinning in triumph, brandishing brown broken teeth and a long, sharp knife.

Ogenus stopped his upward trek and took a deep breath. He almost turned back at that moment. This was a foolish idea. He wasn't an outdoorsman. He couldn't even start a fire without a lighter. He couldn't catch, clean, and cook an animal. He didn't know which plants and fruits might be safely eaten, and which were dangerous. He was woefully unprepared to live off the wilderness. And he was even more unprepared to meet those who could. He looked back down the way he had come. He found himself missing the soft life of his city, especially that soft warm bed in his apartment. He missed the comfort of a carefree populace who inhabited that city, having everything they could ever imagine and wanting for nothing. Despite the fact that he'd only been hiking for a few hours, he envied Kursatta's citizens who had sense enough not to do what he was doing.

He sighed again. Then, lacking the courage to quit, he turned once more toward the towering mountains and began his slow climb up.

He settled the backpack across his shoulders. Carrying everything he believed he needed, the pack had become heavier with each step. He stopped again, abruptly. The silence of the evening had been broken by a distant growl. That was followed by a deep, resonating, echoing roar that pulsed through the trees and bounced off rock walls. A carnivore, Ogenus thought, and a large one.

He unholstered his beam weapon. It felt small, flimsy, and practically useless in his hand. Would the owner of that growl feel the beam, even if he could get it aimed properly? He doubted it. He stood silently for a long moment, straining to hear any sounds of an approaching predator. Of course, such a hunter would stalk him silently, the only sound he heard would be its attack.

Ogenus thought of the woman, a primitive tribal mistress who had taken the opposite course and chanced contact with city dwellers. Her curiosity evidently matched his. And she'd had the courage and the will to follow her dream and venture into the unknown.

He turned in a circle, eyes seeing nothing. He sighed again and continued his climb toward the cold and the ice and, most likely, oblivion.

*

Weak and still a bit lightheaded, She-Wolf didn't make much downward progress the days after regaining consciousness. She took her time, hunted only small prey when necessary, and stayed close to her companion.

Early one morning, something brought her awake, and without moving, her eyes flicked open. She had learned to trust her subconscious and its ability to sense very subtle changes in her environment. The wolf, too, felt something different. The forest was quiet, the only sound being the gurgling of a nearby stream. Then a deep reverberating roar seemed to shake the very leaves of the trees. The wolf froze, its hackles elevated, lips bared and teeth showing. She-Wolf stood up, then also froze, her spear up and ready.

The roar came again, if anything, closer and louder. Whatever it was, and it sounded like one of the long-fanged cats, it was coming their way, and it was angry and probably very hungry.

She watched as her companion slunk back into the bushes and faded away. Whatever it was had frightened the canine into abandoning its tenuous ties with the woman. She-Wolf was left to face whatever it was on her own.

Her eyes darted here and there, trying to watch in every direction at once. Retreat was not possible. Only vigilance and silence were her allies. The cat could probably smell her and would attack downwind. Except the morning was still, leaves hanging limply on motionless trees. Every living thing nearby abruptly became silent.

She turned quietly, spear up, eyes searching, ears reaching for any hint of sound.

There! The snap of a small twig to her left. As she turned toward it, a large brown and orange object leaped at her from between a huge boulder and a tree. As she feared, it was a fully-grown, long-fanged cat, claws extended, mouth open to expose its terrible, over-sized saber-like fangs.

Her only hope? Shove the spear down its throat! Fear gripped her, but the years she had hunted alone, depending on her wits and skill, seemed to be preparation for this one single moment. Time slowed down, yet her reactions did not. In one motion, she aimed the spear, wedged the butt of its pike against the base of a boulder, and held on. Another roar from the left got both her and the cat's attention. The wolf leapt from underbrush and snapped at the cat's rear leg. Distracted, the big cat turned its head toward the wolf. The girl screamed, and the cat turned back to her just in time to impale itself on the spear, the tip shoved deep down its throat thanks to She-Wolf's perfect angle.

The spear's shaft bent but held. The cat, mortally wounded but still alive, landed on the girl, and claws scraped her shoulder. She screamed again, this time in pain. Her wolf companion dragged the cat by its right leg, pulling the animal partly off her. She-Wolf had her knife out and repeatedly stabbed at the cat. Her efforts did little damage other than distracting it. The cat struggled against the dual attack, but the spear limited its movement. Its tip had punctured a lung and eventually worked its way to the animal's heart. A sudden spray of blood covered She-Wolf, and the cat dropped, lifeless and limp, over her legs and torso, its eyes staring blankly into hers.

She-Wolf, crushed beneath the body, took a deep, shuddering breath. Finally, she shoved and pushed the dead weight off her, and shakily stood. Her shoulder was bleeding, but not too badly. With some effort, she freed her spear and pulled it from the cat's mouth. She sighed and fell to her knees. Before she knew it, the wolf was next to her, bumping its head against hers. She reached out a hand and ruffled the ears, a ministration the wolf at last permitted. She realized they were bound together now, spirit to spirit.

She-Wolf rose to her feet and stumbled to the creek where she cleaned her wound and washed off the blood. She harvested certain plants and prepared a poultice which she applied to her shoulder wound. Feeling light-headed but a bit stronger, she built a fire, speared a fish and a too-curious beaver. Once her prey had been cleaned and roasted over the fire, she fed herself and the wolf.

Then she turned her attention to the lifeless cat. She had plans for that orange and black pelt. She used her knife and a large measure of patience to expertly skin the animal. She worked through the night, stopping only long enough to gather thin sticks of wood which she used to feed the fire for light. She continued her work the next morning and through most of the day. She removed the cat's lower jaw, then carefully split the skull at its center, leaving a long tooth on each side. It took skill and determination to keep that part of the skull and the two long fangs attached to the pelt, yet flexible enough for her intended purpose. She used strips of the animal's belly skin to bind the split upper skull together. Over the next several days, she cleaned, repaired, and dried the pelt, and cured it.

When it was finally done, she removed her wolf pelt and tried the new one on. It fit over her head, the two elongated teeth framing her cheeks. There was sufficient play in the reworked skull that it would fit an even larger human head.

The entire pelt was too big for her, and heavy. But she did not intend to wear it herself. Instead, she swung the wolf pelt over her shoulders and the top of her head. It had been so much a part of her for so long, She-Wolf felt naked without it.

She postponed her journey into the Giants' domain, turning back toward the elevated and colder heights that had once been her home. She carefully rolled the cat pelt and strapped it to her back.

She began her trek back up into the mountains. Progress was slow but uneventful. Her shoulder wound healed nicely. Hunting was good. Two days of light rain turned into two more days of snow as they climbed to higher elevations. Her wolf companion remained close despite the fact that it was back to full health and did much of its own hunting.

She approached the village of her former tribe warily. She and her companion waited until night, remained hidden and unmoving until she had located the night sentries. Undetected, she entered the village and walked silently among the trees and dark tents and huts, the wolf padding quietly beside her.

As she approached the chief's hut, a whispered voice broke the silence. "She-Wolf, you're back. Is it really you?"

"Rabbit," she whispered and saw her young friend emerge from his hut at the base of a tree where he had been sleeping. Despite the week she'd been gone, he seemed smaller than she remembered, thin and a bit awkward, so unlike what a chief's son should be.

He stood before the girl, gasped when the wolf approached and pushed its head up against the girl's hand. "You've made a new friend, I see," the boy murmured.

"I want you to do something for me," she replied, pulling the cat pelt from her back. "I want you to take this and place it in the Chief's hut. Don't let him see you, and in the morning when he asks, don't tell him where it came from. Just let it appear, as if by magic."

The boy examined the pelt. "I don't believe it. I've never seen any Chief wearing the coat of a big cat. Even at the great meeting two years ago. There were fifteen tribes, and no Chief wore one like this."

"Just so. Perhaps it will make up for some of the unrest I've caused him. But I don't want him to know it came from me. You need to promise."

Rabbit stared at the pelt, then glanced at the wolf, and nodded. He struggled with the pelt's weight, heaved it over a shoulder, and disappeared silently into the Chief's hut. He returned a moment later. "Done," he said, softly. "The old man barely moved."

"Thank you," she said.

Rabbit was silent for a long moment. "You can't stay here, you know."

She-Wolf smiled and ruffled the boy's hair. "I know. I'm leaving. But before I go, I have a gift for you. Three gifts, actually. To reward you for your friendship when everyone else abandoned and rejected me."

The boy's eyes lit up, then he ducked his head in embarrassment. "They didn't reject you," he said softly, looking up, "they just didn't understand you and that made them afraid of you."

She-Wolf barely smiled. "And you?"

"I'm not exactly surrounded by friends, either," he said. "Were it not that I'm the Chief's son..."

She-Wolf nodded. "Yes, we understand each other. Perhaps if things had been different...but no, the gods ordain our paths. I have these gifts for you. First, this animal who has followed me for days and has become my brother," she patted the wolf. "I transfer his loyalty from me to you. Let him sniff you."

The boy hesitantly lifted a hand. The wolf looked from the girl to the boy. The animal sniffed, then licked the proffered hand. She-Wolf watched her canine companion and nodded. She removed the wolf pelt from her head and back, and placed it on the boy. The wolf, seeming to sense the purpose of the ritual, calmly moved to stand beside Rabbit.

"It's now your responsibility to protect this wolf. The other tribe members will fear him, and they'll blame you. They'll try to kill it, and you must not let that happen. Do your best, be his friend, and he will walk beside you. He will share your spirit and you will share his. Over time your name will become legend."

Rabbit bowed, placed a hand on the wolf's head. "I will wear the spirit of this wolf proudly," he said softly.

"Secondly, 'Rabbit' is not an appropriate name for someone who hunts with the wolf. So my second gift to you is a new name. From this moment on, you will be known for your intelligence, your creativity, your skill, and your love of life. In our language there are two words that I give to you. 'Im' meaning 'creator' and 'Kotep' meaning 'healer of spirit'. Henceforth you will be known as 'Imkotep'"

The boy shrugged, as if fitting the name across his shoulders. "Thank you," he said, smiling. "I like this name. I will wear it and walk tall, no longer the shy, snuffling rabbit."

"And the third gift is a personal one. I will take my memories of you with me. They will never be apart from me. Though we may never meet again, we will always share a connection. Take this as a token of our friendship." She handed the boy the wolf neck lace she had made for her father many years ago.

The boy knelt beside She-Wolf, and she placed the wolf stone around his neck.

When he again stood, Imkotep looked down at the stone and fingered it gently. He seemed taller and more mature than Rabbit. He spoke with a deeper and more assured voice: "My sister, I thank you for these gifts. I accept them with gratitude and joy, and will work to honor their value." He looked her, his eyes shining. "I, too, will never forget you."

"Stand tall and walk with the wolf," she said. She took one last, long look at her companion wolf. His eyes met hers in unblinking acceptance and understanding. He would walk with the boy now, and train him up to someday become Chief. And the wolf, casting its lot with humans, would forge an alliance that would benefit this tribe in times of unimaginable chaos.

The girl turned, hefted her spear, and walked away, not looking back. She forever left behind the four most precious things in her life: A true friend, an animal in spirit with her soul, the pelt which had defined her existence, and her entire family, which now looked down upon her from stars in the black night.

Her heart had been broken more than once in that former life. In her new life, she would not let that happen. Her new life would be different. She walked alone, carrying only her spear, but with a renewed sense of purpose.

*

Ogenus threw another log on his campfire. It had taken him an hour to start it, which was an improvement. He had managed to catch a rabbit in his beam, but hated the look of betrayal in its eyes as it leapt and died, the stench of its burnt fur almost ruining his appetite. He made a mess of skinning the animal, ruined half of the edible part in cleaning the carcass, burnt most of the remainder by misjudging his fire's intensity. He angrily brushed off scorched flesh and consumed the remainder with a resigned grimace. It tasted burnt, gamey, and tough. But he considered it a victory since it was the first meal he'd had that wasn't fished from his backpack to be eaten, dried and cold.

As dark descended, his fire turned to orange embers, generating heat but little light. Night noises began, and Ogenus prepared to endure another endless hated dark period filled with insects, animals, and a cacophony of sounds. Everything in the forest, he was convinced, was evil and wanted him dead.

He rubbed the beard that had grown during his time in the wild. Shot with premature gray, he imagined it gave him a look of strength and dignity, but realized he probably just looked lost, homeless, and bewildered, with facial hair. He slapped at a biting insect and sighed.

He had made it deep into untamed mountains. Forest surrounded him. Were it not for the creek which he followed, he would have been long ago lost.

Cautiously, checking for snakes and small animals, Ogenus eased himself into his tent. It provided slight protection from a hunting animal. Ogenus climbed into the bag in which he would try to sleep. It was guaranteed to protect him from all natural elements, but he didn't feel protected. He could imagine a group of carnivores seated around his tent, debating among themselves which one was to drag him out of the tent for a starring role in a communal buffet.

He sighed again, silently, closed his eyes, and tried to sleep.

*

With a wolf pelt no longer protecting her, and no animal sharing her path, the girl realized she no longer had the right to be called She-Wolf. The only other name she could use was the one given her by her mother: *Inanna*. That would be her new name in her new life.

She made her way once again down toward the land of the Giants, carrying only her spear. Two days later, she stopped to listen.

A distant human cough caused Inanna to tilt her head. Hunters from a tribe would not venture this far down, and would never betray their location. Giants seldom came to this height as their fields and animals subsisted much further down in the valleys and plains that descended, eventually, to the sea.

The crack of a twig and a grunt indicated that the human, hunter or Giant, was moving her way. He didn't sound like a hunter, who would move as silently as the gentle breeze. She eased into the underbrush and proved her point by almost silently creeping toward the human. It wasn't difficult. She saw a man following the river, at this elevation a wide but fast-moving creek. He was not a member of any tribe, but he wasn't dressed exactly as a Giant either. The huge pack on his back caused her to smile. He was bearded. Younger members of the local tribes seldom grew facial hair; that was a privilege of the elderly. This man did not look old enough for the privilege of growing a beard.

Determining that he was not accustomed to the wilderness, the beard was probably the result of a lack of an opportunity to shave it off. That made it much more likely that he was a Giant rather than a tribe elder.

All through that day, Inanna stalked the man as he moved, slowly, up toward her former home. She was absolutely sure he would never make it, was surprised he'd actually made it this far. His movements were noisy and uncoordinated, and he paid no attention to the wind.

He would surely be killed by an animal or by one of the hunting parties that roamed through these forests. Or, if he were very lucky and got that far, by sentries that protected the village. And, there was something about him that tugged at her memory. Could it be? Perhaps...

As evening fell, he stopped and made a primitive camp. He slept inside a large tent, in a bag placed on a mattress of air which he pumped up. Inanna watched and listened, and wondered how the man had survived this far without running afoul of something large, hairy, and hungry.

Inanna shook her head in disbelief. That night she slept nearby on a bed of straw and branches.

She was awake and watching as the Giant woke the next morning and spent an inordinate amount of time packing up his camping gear. He was slow and clumsy and tended to talk to himself.

He took a crudely sharpened stick and used it to poke at fish swimming in a quiet pond off the river. His frustration was amusing, but he did, in the end, manage to spear a large fish. As he turned and raised it up in triumph, the fish came alive, writhing madly, managing to slap the Giant's face repeatedly and loudly with its tail until the fish had worked the stick loose and it flopped back into the water. The man stumbled and almost fell into the water himself.

Inanna couldn't stop herself. She fell out of her hiding place, laughing loudly and hysterically, pointing at the man, her high-pitched shrieks echoing through the trees. She laughed until tears stained her cheeks. She was, in fact, unable to rise to her feet, and stayed on her knees, pounding the ground with her fists, all the while wailing in laughter.

She turned away from the Giant so she could regain her composure, but it wasn't easy. She could not remember a time in her life when she had laughed out loud. Children were taught that any noise could bring death, so kept their silence except when among a group of tribal adults. As she grew older and endured the death of her father, there didn't seem to be anything to laugh about.

She heard a sound and turned her head in time to see the man toss a small pebble at her. He glared, then flung his stick into the water. He sat, crossed his legs, and watched Inanna. He remained quiet, and she finally turned to stare back.

Studying his face, she wondered if he might, indeed, be the Giant who had called after her from under the bridge. Had he really come all this way to find her? He couldn't be here in the forest, looking for her? Could he? She tilted her head and thought back to that night. She tried to mentally remove the beard, but had no success. He could be the same one, but most Giants looked alike to her. And, seriously, why come all the way up here? It didn't make any sense.

She couldn't even ask him. They had no language in common, of course. He smiled at her, patting the ground and inviting her to sit next to him. Having watched him for the better part of two days, any hesitation or fear of the man had been completely eliminated by a frisky fish.

She stood, hefted her spear as a mild warning, then walked over to the man. She gazed down at him for a moment. He was still smiling and again patted the ground next to him. He said a word she took as "sit."

So she sat, slowly and carefully, laying her spear on the far side of her, but keeping a hand on it.

*

Ogenus had never been so shocked in his life. Falling out of the bushes, laughing hysterically, was the girl he'd seen under the bridge. Amazing as it seemed, it had to be her! How she'd found him in this endless forest had to be an act of the gods.

He tossed a pebble at her, more in embarrassment than anger. He could still smell fish, as its slime dried on his face, tightening the skin. When the girl's laughter ceased, they both sat and stared at each other for quite a long time. Then Ogenus urged her to come closer, to join him sitting on the hard ground.

After an assessing look, she moved toward him, and he had the first opportunity to study her in detail. He was quite pleased with what he saw. Her hair was black, made up of a slew of soft ringlets that framed her face. Her skin was much darker than his, and her teeth brilliantly white. Most unusual of all were her eyes, blue and calm. Those eyes missed nothing.

She sat next to him. She had a natural, earthy, pleasing smell about her that Ogenus enjoyed. In is eyes, she was also quite beautiful, in a rather wild and exotic way. He patted his chest and said "Ogenus."

She looked at him for a moment. "Oannes," she said, pointing at him.

He shook his head. "Ogenus."

"Oannes," she repeated.

He shrugged. "Okay. That's close enough." She seemed to have trouble with the "g" sound. He pointed to her with a questioning look.

She looked down, then caught his meaning. "Inanna," she said softly, patting her chest. "Inanna."

Ogenus repeated it, and she smiled.

"Good. We're making progress." He then pointed to her weapon. "Spear," he said.

She glanced down. "Spear." Then she said the word in her language which Ogenus repeated.

Over the next hour or so, they exchanged words. Ogenus found Inanna to be intelligent with an excellent memory. Better than his in fact, as she often had to repeat words in her language, while he rarely had to say things twice. They spent most of the day learning words. Arm, leg, head, eye, mouth, lips, feet, foot, hand, fingers, and more. She had an exotic accent, accentuated with her stumbling over the "g" sound. He found her lilting voice and accent delightful. In fact, he found everything about her delightful.

He pointed to himself, and then down toward the city of the Giants. Inanna understood and nodded. She then pointed up toward the mountains, then used gestures to make it clear that she had come from there, but was on her way down. Ogenus was somewhat confused. Finally, he indicated both himself and her, and pointed down toward the city. Inanna took that as an invitation to accompany him to his home. Since that was her goal anyway, she nodded eagerly.

She watched as he hefted his backpack and settled it on his shoulders. Was he ending his trip because he had found what he'd been looking for? Her? It didn't seem logical. But then again, men did not always act logically.

As they talked and learned from each other, Ogenus and Inanna slowly made their way through the forest, down toward the plains. They kept a wary eye out for predators, but the way was peaceful and the weather mild and calm.

As dusk fell, they made camp. Ogenus found starting a fire was much easier when it was done with someone who knew how. They ate a meal of fish and some roots Inanna dug up, seasoned with salt provided by Ogenus. The meal tasted excellent, much better than what Ogenus had been able to concoct. He kept taking furtive glances at her, and found, more often than not, her eyes on him. He enjoyed catching her small, shy, smile when she knew he was looking at her.

The forest slowly transitioned from day to night, which meant the nocturnal hunters were becoming active. In addition to biting insects, other noises, close and distant, filled the dusk. Ogenus tried to relax, but felt an added responsibility to protect this young tribal woman. He recognized, though, that she had found him, he had not found her. She would be more likely to protect him than the other way around. They were, after all, in her domain, not his. She carried that tall spear and obviously knew how to use it.

Just before night fell, the forest around them abruptly became silent. Inanna tensed, looked up, then started to say something. A loud roar erupted from the trees, followed by a bear in full attack. Inanna turned, saw the animal, and realized her spear was on the other side of the fire, an inexcusable mistake.

Ogenus, kneeling near the fire, jumped back and fell. The bear was upon them as Ogenus pulled his beam weapon and began firing a thin, blue shaft of energy at the crashing, roaring animal. He prayed the beam would be strong enough to penetrate the bear's thick hide.

Inanna found herself closer to the bear, but off to one side. She pulled her knife and crouched at the ready. She stabbed at the bear's paw, and it angrily backhanded her. Inanna yelped as she was flung back. The animal followed and stood over her, its mouth open wide and salivating. The beam from Ogenus' weapon crackled out and danced across the bear as he tried to calm himself and aim steadily. The beam continued to waver, drawing burning fur and flesh as the bear howled in pain and surprise. The animal turned toward the man and roared. Ogenus could smell burnt fur and the reek of the animal's breath.

Ogenus went for the eyes, then down to where it would, hopefully, puncture the heart. The beam began to pulse as its power cell became exhausted. The bear had stopped. It looked puzzled, then slowly collapsed and lie, breathing raggedly, near Inanna, its scimitar claws resting against her left leg.

Then it died.

Inanna drew a shaky breath and stood. She walked to where Ogenus was also regaining his feet. They looked at the bear for a moment, making sure it was really dead. Inanna turned and stood before Ogenus, looked up at his eyes, then bowed her head and rested it against his chest. Hesitantly, Ogenus placed a hand against the back of her head and gently stroked her hair. When she looked up, there were tears in her eyes.

In all the time of her life as a hunter, she had never been taken by surprise by an animal. Now it had happened, and this stranger, a Giant, protected her. Her gesture gave thanks and acknowledged him as an equal in this wilderness. It was also something more, the desire of a homeless waif, alone and lost and lonely, hoping against all hope that she might have been given a chance to find a home. Inanna prayed silently to the gods that her impressions were accurate and real. Without a common language between them, much could be missed or easily misinterpreted.

Ogenus didn't understand the full measure of Inanna's simple gesture, but he held her against him for much longer than necessary, drinking in the experience, wishing it could last forever. Everything about her pulled him in, the feel of her soft, curly hair against his face, her smell, the heat of her body beating against him like a physical embrace. He let out a deep breath he had not been aware of holding. Then he realized that he had been holding it for many years. And only now did he feel a deep sense of relief and peace.

When they separated and looked into each other's eyes, both were surprised to see tears. Both looked away in embarrassment, but both had a hint of a smile on their lips.

They disposed of the bear carcass by dragging it, an inch at a time, back into the brush and trees from which it had emerged. To Inanna's experienced eyes, it was an old and possibly sick specimen. Otherwise, she suspected its attack would have been completely successful, and it would have been dragging *them* into the bushes.

After a brief rest, they continued their journey in the dark, needing to find another camp away from the bear. They found an adequate spot after an hour of stumbling through dark forest. Ogenus set up his tent, and they split the night, one sleeping and the other keeping watch. It was far from satisfactory, and Inanna didn't sleep well on the Giant's air-filled mattress. She kept waking up, and each time glanced out the opening to make sure he was all right. Ogenus, on the other hand, had a more restful sleep than he could remember, despite the few hours of its duration. When morning came, he emerged from the tent to find that Inanna had built a fire, and was busy cooking fish and some roots. The day began with smiles and another series of language lessons.

That evening, they set up camp by a large pond at the forest's edge. Earlier, the pool had once again provided a fish for their meal. Now, as the sun began to set, Inanna tested the pond's water and found it to be somewhat less than ice cold. She decided to take a bath. She stepped to the rocky beach, and looked back, glancing at Ogenus shyly. She calmly disrobed, leaving her furs and leathers on the rock, and plunged into the cold water, her arms sweeping around her. She used a small chunk of soap formulated by her tribe elders over the centuries to leave a neutral odor. Stinky hunters couldn't stalk prey, but did attract predators.

Inanna's decision was, in part, another gesture of her commitment to this gentle Giant, and a rather defiant one at that. Tribal members typically bathed by sex; women and girls in one pond, men and boys in another. If weather prohibited, which it often did, members heated water over their cooking fires and took care of bathing inside their hut, an inadequate necessity. In many cases, even mates did not bathe together. With her actions, Inanna confirmed her separation from tribal customs, and her determination to make her own rules from that point on.

Ogenus looked up from stoking the fire and watched. He recognized the trust she placed in him, and he made a conscious determination not to violate that trust.

He then tried to keep his eyes on the fire, but found himself glancing up from time to time. A while later, Inanna rose from the pool, dripping wet, hesitated for a moment, then walked, boldly, to the fire. She placed her clothes down first, then sat on them, drying herself from the warmth of the burning embers.

Ogenus was shocked to realize that the woman before him was barely that, just a teenager. He had assumed she was near his age, and that colored his perception until she stepped out of the water, nude. As she dried herself, he tried not to stare, but took brief glances. Each time her eyes met his, and she smiled. He began to realize Inanna's story was...different. Not a lot was known about the mountain tribes, but he knew that tribal women typically mated and bore children at a much younger age than his own people. Had she not chosen to be a hunter, Inanna probably would have found a mate and either had borne a child or be expecting one by now.

Neither said a word. Ogenus took the hint and excused himself. He dropped his clothes on the same rock and jumped into the water. His agonized shout caused Inanna to half rise, but Ogenus laughed nervously. "It's really cold!" he said, and shivered. His own soap, dug from the depths of his backpack, was commercially produced, and not nearly as effective in the wild as Inanna's home-grown variety.

Inanna turned her gaze back to the fire and listened to the man's splashing.

After a while she heard him approaching. He dropped his clothes onto a large, flat boulder opposite Inanna, the fire between them. He then sat on them following Inanna's lead. The periodic popping and crackling of flames was the only night sound. Both man and young woman gazed into those flames, with quick glances at each other. Ogenus broke the mood when he slapped at an insect with a loud smack.

Inanna stood, grabbed her clothes, and took a short walk into the night. While she was gone, Ogenus dressed then took his own brief walk in the other direction.

Thus dressed and refreshed, they met at the tent.

Using pantomime and gestures, Ogenus made it clear that he was willing to accompany Inanna up the mountains, return her back to her home. He wanted to make sure, beyond a doubt, that Inanna understood her choices. Using the same method, the girl nodded her head and pointed down, toward the plains, clearly indicating both of them. Then she pointed back the way she had come and shook her head, signifying a strong negative.

Ogenus raised his hands as a gesture of understanding. They would travel together, and they would travel away from the mountains. As he had suspected, she had for some reason been banished by her tribe. He wished he could know the details, but realized that such a level of communication would be many months down the road.

Ogenus then made another decision. Seeing as they were now at the edge of cultivated land, and danger from wild animals was significantly diminished, a night watch was no longer necessary.

Inside the tent, Ogenus spread his sleeping bag across the mattress, then secured a blanket from his backpack. He nervously indicated the right side of the mattress for Inanna, and the left side for himself. In his mind, he was busily rearranging perceptions that were a bit too optimistic. That she could kill him in an instant he acknowledged. The girl was both soft and gentle, with muscles that were rock hard. She was a hunter and he a city dweller. As such, he did not wish to anger her. Such anger could manifest itself in either of two directions, so he carefully discarded the choice he wanted to make and instead chose a middle ground, and hoped.

Inanna realized that they would sleep together, but not together as she had anticipated. The woman, as woman, felt disappointment at his implied rejection. The woman, as a teenager, welcomed his hesitation. He was, after all, much older than she. Not that it mattered in the long run. She had nowhere else to go. Under no circumstance would she venture back toward her tribal lands; that was no longer home.

And besides, he was a Giant, and Giants could do as they pleased. In her mind, Giants were virtually all-powerful, and any restraint he showed her was a kindness. That he didn't take her that very night indicated he saw her as a person and not just an object with which to satisfy himself.

Kindness implied friendship, and in Inanna's mind, friendship could lead to something more than just a physical relationship. And at this moment, she very badly needed a friend. Nevertheless, she wondered what it would be like to mate with a Giant, when she had no experience, indeed, of mating with one of her own tribe. Would he then consider her a partner? Or something less? Did he already have a woman or women in the massive City of Giants? She had so many unanswered questions, but her eyes were heavy, her thoughts cloudy.

She fell asleep, her mind whirling in a thousand different directions, considering an almost unlimited range of possibilities. She did not, at the moment, have enough information to narrow her possible futures. But one thing was certain. Whatever future she found, it could not be as lonely as the future she'd faced two days ago. In her sleep, she smiled.

Morning sunlight woke Ogenus. He had slept poorly most of the night, aware of Inanna asleep near him. He'd argued with himself most of that time, but was unable to win any of them. Ultimately, he made up his mind and moved a bit closer to her, not close enough to touch, but enough to feel the warmth from her. He finally fell into a deep sleep. Hours later he woke smelling her. As his eyes opened, he realized the back of her head rested against his chin. Sometime during the night, she had backed up against him, probably without waking. Now she slept, breathing deeply. She'd taken his hand and pulled it, protectively, across her chest. He remained as still as possible for as long as possible, not wanting to wake her, content to enjoy the moment.

Despite his effort to remain still, he eventually moved slightly. She woke, stiffened, then relaxed and turned her head toward him, smiling shyly, her unusual blue eyes flashing. She cuddled against him and boldly placed his hand where there would be no doubt as to her invitation and her expectations. Ogenus felt an overwhelming rush of excitement, like ocean waves breaking over him. He knew what he wanted to do, and he knew what she wanted him to do. He just wished he felt more in tune with his own intentions. He had never before had another person give themselves to him without reservation. He struggled with the weight of this unexpected responsibility, not only toward Inanna but also himself. How fast could they progress in a relationship when they couldn't even talk to each other? Once again, he chose the middle ground.

He gazed into her eyes for an infinite second, then kissed her firmly and held her tight. She did not pull away from his lips, and he stretched the kiss, his excitement building. He held her for a long time, luxuriating in this new sensation, but did not let the intimacy progress. She did not seem disappointed as she stared back at him and smiled. She kissed him again, then again, satisfied to hold the line. They both found it a very pleasant line to hold.

After some immeasurable amount of time, they rose, dressed, and consumed a simple breakfast. Ogenus packed his camping gear and hoisted the backpack. Inanna grasped her spear and small bundle, and the two started off, following the river down as trees thinned, then largely disappeared to be replaced by grassland and widely separated oaks.

They held hands, and as they walked, continued their language lessons. Hours later, in the far distance, the towers of Kursatta appeared, tiny in the mist. As foothills flattened into cultivated farmland, Ogenus pointed to a large, singular, flat-topped oblong rock outcropping that dominated a small village and farmland around it. "That's my friend, Ionic's astronomical observatory," he said, pointing it out to Inanna's attention, and confusion. The landmark told him they were getting close to home. His home, and, he hoped, Inanna's as well. He did not know what the future would bring, but he desperately wanted it to include this strange girl, Inanna.

Now that they were back in civilization, Ogenus secured a ride from a former school friend who now farmed land near the observatory. This was Inanna's first ride in a vehicle of the Giants. She was both terrified and excited to zip along at what was to her a death-defying speed. She held tightly to Ogenus' arm with both her hands, gasping when they leaned into corners and sped along straightaways.

*

As they approached the city, farmlands and ranches kept Inanna's eyes and mouth open in wonder. In her previous visits, she had followed the river, hiding along its banks, and had thus seen very little of the cultivated lands except from a distance.

After being dropped off, they strode the wide sidewalks of the wondrous city of Giants. Ogenus and Inanna both elicited curious and incredulous stares. Citizens did not often see a bearded man bearing a large backpack walking hand-in-hand with an obvious tribal woman carrying a long threatening spear. Inanna, as well, wore a look of amazement and wonder.

The city itself was unimaginable. Paved streets, flat and smooth, were filled with vehicles of all kinds zooming here and there. On each side of the street were walkways, flanked by lush trees and bushes, populated with brightly-dressed Giants, walking to and fro, smiling and unafraid. They talked to each other, and showed no fear for there was nothing of which to be afraid. Beyond the walkways were hundreds of stores and shops, brightly lit and garishly colorful. Overhead, flying machines split the sky from time-to-time, but she could barely see them for the massive towers that must reach all the way to the heavens. She thought, perhaps, the towers were how the Giants had originally come down to the earth. The gods surely smiled upon the inhabitants of this magical city.

Ogenus kept a cautious eye on the girl, conscious of sensory overload. They eventually reached the building in which he lived. She stumbled back as a door opened, silently, by itself. She gazed in awe at the size and opulence of the lobby. She held onto Ogenus tightly as her first ride in an elevator whisked them up 75 floors.

"This is where I live," he said, using gestures and pantomime to get his meaning across. He spoke to his door, and it disappeared as if it had never existed, sliding silently into the wall. Ogenus gently urged Inanna to enter, and the door magically reappeared behind them. His residence was, to her, incredibly large. She wondered how many families occupied this cavernous room, and which part belonged to Ogenus. The carpet felt, to her, much like standing on a cloud. Floor-to-ceiling windows looked out over an endless ocean. A sofa and two chairs offered relaxation and a stunning view. To the right, his kitchen and dining area; to the left was a refresher and shower, storage, and his bed. As a single male, he needed little more. Now he had decisions to make.

Inanna slowly explored the room, moving in a daze, seeing things she didn't understand, touching things that felt strange and unreal. She slowly walked to the windows and looked out. From this height, the boats, and even large ships appeared tiny.

Perspective abruptly snapped into place, and Inanna realized how high they were. Feeling dizzy, she stepped back and collapsed against Ogenus. He led her to the sofa, and she grasped his arm tightly as they sat. He said nothing. They didn't yet have enough language for him to comfort her with words. He sat next to her and held her, rocking her gently as one would a small child. He loved the way she looked; he loved the feel of her pressed against him. He loved her earthy fragrance. Without the will to resist, he pressed his face against her hair and breathed deeply. Inanna clung to him and shook.

It slowly dawned on Inanna that this entire apartment belonged to Ogenus, that he didn't share it with anyone. In her previous observations of the Giants, their lives had mystified her. Now, in the presence of a Giant, inside his home, Inanna was overwhelmed. She huddled on the sofa, and clung to the man, almost hyperventilating, unable to move. Ogenus' arms and patience calmed her eventually. Slowly she began to relax.

Later, Ogenus went to his kitchen and prepared a simple meal. Inanna watched from the sofa, then joined him as he cooked food over an electric stove, selected a package of frozen vegetables and boiled them to softness. The food was familiar to him, and utterly strange to Inanna. Ogenus set two plates at the table, then indicated that they sit and eat. Ogenus enjoyed the meal, of course, happy to be out of the forest and back where things were familiar and comfortable.

Inanna studied the eating implements, and watched Orenus closely. She tried to mimic his use of them, with varying degrees of success. She tasted each of the dishes carefully. While she enjoyed some of the food, the boiled veggies seemed to distress her. With great embarrassment, she spit them out. Ogenus laughed, and that made her feel even worse. She almost cried until he reached across the table and took her hand and nodded with a smile.

Ogenus began to wonder if this was more damaging to the girl than if he had left her in the wilderness to fend for herself. He gazed at her, then shook his head. He couldn't imagine doing that, but hoped he hadn't taken on more than he could handle. He wanted her to eventually adjust to his lifestyle, but wondered if that could actually happen.

That evening, Ogenus took Inanna to the top floor of the apartment tower to meet his friend, Ionic.

"Ogenus! Welcome! You're back from your mighty quest, and with brand new growth on your face. You look like an ape. And who's this?" Ionic said as he stepped back from his door and Ogenus entered, followed by a frightened Inanna. His eyes widened in surprise.

"Her name is Inanna. She's the one who..."

"Came down to the river!" Ionic exclaimed. "How on earth did you ever find her?"

"She found me. Inanna, this is my friend Ionic," he said, again using gestures.

Inanna smiled hesitantly. This old man seemed like a mixture of a chief, a medicine man, and a child. She did not know where he fit in the hierarchy of Giant civilization. She decided to treat him as an honored elder and possibly a medicine man. The intensity of his examination frightened her.

"I'm surprised, Ogenus," he said, looking away from the girl. "You came back in one piece."

Ogenus laughed. "It was close. But yes, I made it back. Never got up to the tribal area, though. She met me halfway. Saved my life."

"Hmm. I see. And you brought her back here to what?...Adopt her?"

"No!" Ogenus said forcibly. "I believe she was rejected by her tribe, banished. When we found each other, she was alone wandering in the forest with nowhere to go." He paused for a long time, studying the puzzled look on the other man's face. "Ionic," he said, finally, "I may have found a mate."

"What?" Ionic laughed, then frowned. "You can't be serious. She's only a child, Ogenus."

"She's a woman by her standards," Ogenus replied, angrily. "Had she not been a hunter, she would have already been mated, and probably a mother by now. Their customs, Ionic, are not our customs."

"And so you brought her here to live in our advanced culture but by their primitive tribal customs?"

"She's going to have a difficult enough time as it is. If she sees herself as my mate, then so be it. She has no one, no home. She doesn't speak our language, doesn't know our ways, but I think she can adapt. She's learning. I've never known anyone who can so quickly absorb and retain information. She knows a few hundred words already, but has no context, as of yet."

Ionic was silent for a long time, not looking at either of his visitors. Then he caught both with his gaze. He saw Ogenus, rigid, stubborn, and yet unsure of himself. He saw Inanna, frightened, wide-eyed, stunned, and holding onto her man with all her strength.

She did not understand the words, but she picked up on the tone of their voices. What would she do if these two Giants decided she was not wanted here? Banishment from a second home? She tried to remain calm, and fought an urge to run out of the apartment, find her way outside, into the dark where she could hide.

While what he saw did not repulse him, Ionic was uneasy and inclined to send Ogenus and this tribal child away until they had come to their senses. But he was also radical enough to want to keep his own cultural prejudices out of a personal discussion. He determined not to judge others by his standards, despite his feeling of unease. He almost succeeded.

He invited them inside his apartment, seated both in his living room, and offered them refreshment, which they declined. He then sat and stared at them for a long time. No one seemed inclined to speak.

Ionic cleared his throat, "I have some important news for you."

"What?" Ogenus said, happy that Ionic decided to do something besides stare at them. "What is it?"

Ionic shook his head. "Some of it is good news, I guess. It's about the comet. You remember that? We talked about it."

"Of course. You said it was coming toward Earth. Is it going to hit us? That can't be the good news."

Ionic smiled. "No. I believe the comet will miss the Earth." Then the smile faded. "I do not believe, however, that it will miss us on its second pass."

"Second pass?" Ogenus leaned forward. "Is it coming back after the first time? How can you be sure? How close of a miss? And how long do we have before it comes back?"

Ionic ran a hand across his scalp, then sighed. "So many questions. You're worse than some of my students. Stubborn and ignorant and asking too many questions." He looked at Inanna, dipped his head. "I used to be a professor of astrophysics," he said to her. "As a student, Ogenus would have been an arrogant know-it-all who wanted answers to questions without doing any research." He smiled. She smiled and nodded back, her blue eyes expressing total bewilderment. She glanced at Ogenus.

"He is a pompous old fool," Ogenus said to Inanna, "who thinks his viewpoint is the only one worth considering." She smiled at Ogenus and nodded.

"My friend here," Ionic said to the girl, an edge in his voice "is upset at me for doubting his judgment. He can't justify himself, so he gets angry."

Ogenus sat stiffly. "My elder adviser here has no business advising me on my personal life. He sticks his nose where it is not welcome."

Ionic frowned. "My young ignorant associate has no idea what he is getting himself into."

"My esteemed elder has no idea what concerns I've been dealing with."

Inanna tried to follow the whipsaw conversation, but was hopelessly lost. She did, however, sense the growing tension and anger. As Ionic pointed a finger at Ogenus and took a deep breath, Inanna reached out and grasped the digit, pushing his hand down while at the same time, pressing two fingers of her other hand across Ogenus' lips.

Both men stopped with retorts half-formed. Inanna spoke in her tribal language, which neither of the men understood. They had little trouble, however, understanding the meaning of her tone. "Stop," she said in the language of the men, a word she had picked up in her lessons with Ogenus.

Ionic's eyes widened and Ogenus started laughing. He took both of Inanna's hands and pressed them to his cheeks. "You're right," he said to her. Then turning to Ionic. "I'm sorry our conversation became heated."

Ionic shook his head and smiled. "You were absolutely justified, my friend. My nose was out of its mind. I don't intend to judge others, but sometimes..."

"Let's just forget it," Ogenus said, also smiling. He reached out and placed a hand on the elder's shoulder. "What about the comet?"

"Eh? Oh, yes, the comet. It will come fairly close to us this time," Ionic said, taking a deep breath. "If it gets close enough to our gravity field, it might break apart, but that probably won't happen...this time. The next approach will be anywhere from five to twenty-five years from now. And all my calculations tell me it will pass much closer, and there is a real possibility that fragments of it will collide with the Earth. The effects could be, well...worrisome. I believe we will need to prepare for the worst. Fortunately we have plenty of time to get ready."

"What do you mean 'the worst' and what's involved in getting ready?"

Ionic shrugged. "We could see some heavy localized flooding, earthquakes, maybe volcanic eruptions. If our luck is really bad, we could be smacked by one or more of the larger rocks."

Ogenus had a thousand more questions to ask, but he simply sat and looked worried.

"Oannes?" Inanna said softly, staring at him. "Home? Now?"

"She called you Oannes," Ionic said.

"She has trouble with the hard *G* sound."

"Kind of like it," Ionic said.

"Well, now that you mention it, so do I. But I guess we'd better be going," Ogenus said, standing. "Inanna has experienced so many changes. It's easy for her to get overwhelmed. She needs to rest. I want to hear more about that comet when we have time."

Ionic nodded. "Sensory overload," he said, rising. "It's not going to be easy for her." He watched as they left, shaking his head. He was more worried about his friend, and the young woman, than he'd let on.

*

Simple things, such as indoor running water, or even the availability of hot water, were mysteries beyond her comprehension. Inanna had to be taught the simplest functions that city dwellers took for granted. She learned how to use a shower, how to flush a toilet (and why), how to turn lights on and off, accessing entertainment screens (and why), eating utensils and cooking over a stovetop. She learned what kinds of items came in boxes and cans and how to open them (and why). She learned that Giants had small metal ice caves in their homes to keep their food cold or frozen. Amazing!

She learned (just in time) that not everything appearing on the entertainment screen was real. Some were labeled "fantasy," others called "fiction." She had trouble understanding such concepts, and how to distinguish them from similar programs based in reality.

She learned the delight in sleeping next to her man on a soft, comfortable mattress with warm blankets. If the studio room got cold, heat would magically happen. If the studio became hot, coolness would flood the room. Light was everywhere, controlled by a switch or a voice.

The few words of Ogenus' language she had learned during their trek to the City of Giants were woefully inadequate. A whole new vocabulary was necessary. There were grammar rules to learn, and context. That was the hardest, she found. Those who were born and grew up in this environment and culture had that context ingrained as children at the same time they learned spoken language. For Inanna, she had to learn all of that in a short time with no ingrained context. By contrast, hunting and gathering was easy. She spent a lot of her time in frustrated despair.

Then there was the concept of *writing*. The tribes used symbols to mark territory or trails. The Shaman and the Chief employed a few dozen charcoal marks in the execution of their offices. But a written language? A way to take spoken words and make them permanent so that you could look at them later and understand? Inanna almost screamed when it became clear that in addition to a new spoken language, she needed to learn how to write the symbols of that language. She learned to pronounce the hard "G" sound, but continued calling her man Oannes as a term of endearment.

Ogenus remained patient, content to spend as much time with this delightful person as possible. The more time he spent with her, the more deeply he fell in love with her.

Inanna also discovered that the world was a much larger place than she could imagine. As their communication became more complex, Ogenus told her about distant lands and nations, with global population in the billions. At first, she thought he was joking. Tribal territory was expansive when traversed on foot. But it was tiny compared to the size of continents and the world itself. They visited a library, and he showed her a globe of the Earth, pointed out where they were in Kursatta, and where her tribe probably was, and the tiny difference. He explained how maps were flat representations of a round world.

The whole world, Ogenus told Inanna, was home to many individual nations. The citizens of those nations spoke many different languages, yet travelers from far distant lands were able to understand and in many cases speak that foreign language. For some of the major languages, there were magical devices that helped Giants translate words they didn't understand into ones they did. Headache is too mild a word to describe what Inanna experienced during her first few months living in the City of Giants. She often dreamed of her old home, up among the ice and mountains. But she never let herself feel a desire to return.

In her experience, each tribe had its own unique, and rather simple, language. Often that language was similar to those tribes nearby but gibberish to others further away. The primitive tribes were not inclined to learn languages spoken by other tribes. While they maintained uneasy truces, punctuated by periodic conflicts, each tribe in reality saw themselves as civilized and all the others as little more than sub-human. Only at rare conclaves, gatherings of many tribes, were such attitudes set aside and then only for a short time.

Inanna was accustomed to sleeping on the ground, softened with the furs of animals. Toilet was made outside, in the forest, with a guard present. Food, if cooked, was done over an open fire with fuel gathered from the surrounding area. Clothes were made, not bought. The concept of money was beyond her comprehension.

Going places meant walking. Hunting meant the very real possibility of being hunted.

She made tremendous progress, but as months passed, an overwhelming cultural dissonance sent her into a deep depression. Ogenus could feel her mood, and he worried about it, but didn't know what to do.

A knock on the door one evening caused Ogenus to start and Inanna to gasp in panic. "Who is it?" Ogenus asked softly. A voice came from a speaker near the door. "It's Eris. May I come in? Can we talk?"

Ogenus' eyes widened in surprise. The last person he expected a visit from was Eris. They had not spoken since the visit to his old office months ago. What could she possibly want at this late date?

"Open," Ogenus said. He stood as Eris entered. She looked at him, then gazed at Inanna, perched stiffly on the edge of the bed.

Eris shook her head, frowning. "I've heard things," she said softly. "I didn't believe them, until now."

"Why did you come here, Eris?"

She took a deep breath. "I had a couple of reasons. One of them no longer matters. Can we sit?"

He made an unwelcome welcoming gesture with his hand. They sat on the sofa. "I came here to tell you we've had more navigational anomalies. I believe your friend's suspicions about the sun acting up might be right. There was a chance the review board might have been convinced to reassess your hearing and possibly change their decision."

"Was?"

Eris looked flustered. "Ogenus, you're living here with a female child. There's been talk..."

"So what? Let them talk. It's our choice. And she's not a child. She's from a mountain tribe, and I've been studying her, learning her language and culture, and she's learning ours."

"And more, I'm sure."

"That's certainly none of your business. She's free to leave at any time. I won't stop her."

"Ogenus, I'm not here to criticize. I'm here to make sure you don't destroy your future. You were our best navigator. I want you back working for us."

"Can't happen," he said. "I have responsibilities now. I can't be gone for long periods."

"Look," Eris said softly, "can't we work something out? I've always liked you, Ogenus. Send this child back to her tribe, then you and I can, perhaps, develop a relationship. You might have heard that I've left my spouse. Ex-spouse."

"I'm sorry to hear that, but it has no bearing..."

"It has every bearing," she said angrily. "I'm giving you an opportunity here."

Ogenus laughed humorlessly. "Such a grand sacrifice on your part. But it won't work, Eris. She was rejected by her tribe. There are no circumstances where it would be safe for her to return. Like it or not, she is part of my life now, and that's exactly the way I want it."

Eris said nothing, but gazed silently at Ogenus until he became uncomfortable.

"Okay," she said slowly. "How about this. Become my mate, and you and I can adopt this child. We'll give her the best schooling and counseling so that she can learn our language and culture. Eventually she'll be able to fit in."

"An interesting offer," Ogenus said. "But I don't think it would work out." He stood and didn't move until Eris stood as well.

"Can you at least consider my offer?"

Ogenus took her elbow and guided her toward the door. "I'll think about it."

At the door, she turned to look at him. "Think about what's best for her. She deserves to be a child. Obviously she has not had that opportunity within her tribe. You can give her that childhood."

"You see her as a child. I don't," he said.

"Please, just think about it."

"I have thought about it," he said, "I've thought about little else. And, thanks to you, I think I've finally made my decision. Thank you for your visit, and good night, Eris." Ogenus closed the door, then pressed against it for a long moment.

He turned and Inanna came to stand next to him. "That woman," she said, "I do not understand many of her words, but she is angry."

"I'm sorry, Inanna. I understood them all too well. I wish I hadn't."

"Why she is angry about you, about us?"

Ogenus shook his head. "That's hard to answer," he said. He reached out and held her face in his hands, gazing into those brilliant blue eyes, "but you just need to know that I love you, and I'm going to be with you now and for all of my years."

Tears welled up in her eyes. "And I with you, always. Always," she said forcefully.

No matter what, he said to himself. No matter what.

He thought, briefly, of moving them across the sea, to another nation. He quickly discounted that idea. He couldn't bring himself to subject Inanna to another culture shock. And himself as well. While he had visited many nations, he had not lived among them. If alienating his friends and acquaintances was the cost of giving this girl a stable life, then he was willing to pay it. Oceanus had few laws regarding mating. Age of consent was a matter for parents, and for the individuals in question, to decide. Inanna herself didn't know her exact age, but she had been functioning as an adult for several years, being the provider for her family. Other laws might apply, but he was not a practitioner of law, so possible consequences troubled him. While he considered Inanna his mate, because of his doubts, he had not yet taken that final irreversible step to make it so.

Living together, sleeping together, they had been intimate, of course. But he had so far managed to avoid the one activity that would mark them as a mated couple, and, eventually, as parents. It was not for lack of trying on Inanna's part. She proved to be single-minded in her quest to bind them together in a way that would make it almost impossible for Ogenus to choose another mate.

He understood her need. He admired her for her tenacity, and her creativity. Each day it became more and more difficult for him to avoid the inevitable, despite what their imaginations came up with. Eris' visit pushed him to consider the direction of his future, with, or without, Inanna.

*

Ogenus came home from work one evening soon after and found Inanna in tears. He thought she had shown signs of adjustment recently, but obviously was mistaken. "Inanna, are you okay?"

"You are gone all day again. Can't stand to be alone in this," she looked around, "this box."

"I'm sorry," he knelt before her and rested his arms on her knees, reaching up to entwine his fingers with hers. "Look, I'm off the next two days. We'll do something, go somewhere, okay?"

She wiped her eyes. "And you don't love me!"

"What do you mean. Of course I love you. I adore you. I live for you..."

She looked at him with tear-filled eyes. "But we haven't done, you know, what we need to do to make me a mother... and you a father."

"You're right. We haven't done that—yet. But we've had fun in other ways, haven't we?"

A hint of a smile crossed her face, instantly gone. It was time to ask the questions that troubled her, no matter the consequences. "But why not? Is that other woman, Eris, yours? Do you want her, and not me? Do you have other mate, somewhere else?"

Ogenus sighed, then stood and sat next to Inanna. He looked down at his hands. "No. It's not her. Her words also confuse me. And there is no one else. Until I met you, I was alone, and very lonely. I want you to be my mate, but I'm so much older than you, Inanna. And our customs are different here. I'm looked down upon because you're a teenager. If you got pregnant..."

She smiled again. "In my tribe, I am almost too old to find a mate. None would have me. Here I am too young."

"You're right. It's my problem, not yours." He looked her in the eyes, his gaze steady.

He sighed and shook his head. "And I'll solve that problem right away. Actually, we'll solve it together." The wall of his doubts had to be breached, and now was the time.

Inanna's eyes lit up. "You mean...?"

"I mean dinner can wait. If that meets with your approval."

She grabbed him and kissed him deeply. There would be no turning back now. He took a deep breath and set aside his doubts, knowing that his life, and hers, would be changed for-ever. Whatever the future brought, they would face it together.

That night was long, and filled with joy for both of them. Ogenus banished his doubts as thoroughly as Inanna had been banished from her tribe. He allowed himself to commit to her as deeply as she had committed to him one day long ago and deep in the forest.

The next day he decided to take her to the river, near the bridge where they had first seen each other. They woke late, mid-morning. While Ogenus refreshed himself, he took the time to carefully trim his beard. When finished, he gazed at himself in the mirror and noticed a smile on his face.

While Inanna showered, Ogenus laid out the tribal clothes she had worn in the forest. "Put these on," he told her when she reappeared. "Get your spear from the mantle."

Silently, she did as he asked, a small smile on her lips.

Inanna now enjoyed riding in vehicles of the Giants, but she was still a bit apprehensive moving so fast. They stopped beside the bridge. Ogenus let his new mate lead him down to the river. Her old cautions and habits came back as soon as she stepped off the road and onto dirt and rocks.

They stood on the river's bank, rushing water singing to them. "This water," Ogenus said, "is my love for you. See? It fills the ocean, the endless ocean, with my love for you. The ocean will never go dry, nor will my love for you."

Inanna recognized a marriage ceremony in his words. "Oannes, this water connects me with you. The ocean," she stopped, tears running down her cheeks, "the ocean is my love for you. It is deep and endless, and so is my love for you."

They held each other. He softly kissed her forehead and stroked the soft dark curls that framed her face. He looked into her eyes, those mysterious blue eyes, now filled with tears. "If all the world says we should not be together, let that be the strength that binds us together."

"Yes," she said. And that was all she needed to say.

Hand in hand, they walked beside the river for a time. Inanna was about to spear a fish when Ogenus stopped her. "I have a gift for you," he said, reaching into his pouch. He pulled out a large, sharply pointed three-pronged titanium trident that he'd had made to fit the top of her spear. After some effort, he managed to remove the original spear point and attached the new one, made it permanent. He handed the obsidian point to Inanna for her to keep.

Ogenus grasped the spear shaft, hefting it, feeling its power. "May I borrow this, for a short time?"

Inanna nodded, eyes wide in wonderment. Ogenus had brought a weighted belt with him, which he now wrapped around his waist. Their strolling had taken them to a rocky beach where the river spread and emptied into the sea.

"Wait here," he said. "I'll be right back." Tri-tipped spear in his hand, he waded out into the shallow water. He turned and watched her as he backed into deeper water. Then he turned and disappeared beneath the ocean waves. When he appeared again, he was far from shore. He took deep breaths to charge his lungs, then sank beneath the waves. This was new to Inanna, but Ogenus had spent much of his youth exploring coral reefs along this part of the coast. He and his friends would use their weighted belts to drift below the waves and observe various species of sea life and the colorful coral and kelp forests.

Inanna waited patiently. Then she became nervous. After two or three minutes, she panicked and began pacing back and forth in the shallows. She wanted to go after him, but she had never learned to swim. She cursed her imagination; within seconds a thousand death scenarios flashed through her mind.

When she saw his trident slowly rising up out of the water, she gasped in relief. She brought hands to her cheeks as the head of Ogenus appeared. He walked toward her, spear in one hand, a large fish in the other. Smiling, he held the fish up to his head. "I am He-Fish, master of the seas."

Inanna laughed and clapped her hands as he joined her. "Oannes, you are the god of fishes. Give that to me, and I'll clean it."

He dropped the fish on a bed of beach rocks. "Lets both do it. You can teach me how."

She pulled out her knife and knelt beside the fish, then looked up at her new mate. "Who can teach a god," she said, "anything."

*

"I think I'm pregnant," Inanna announced upon Ogenus' return from work one day a few weeks later. She moved up against him and looked up into his eyes. "I'm going to grow you a son."

He smiled, laughed, lifted her off her feet and kissed her. "Not a daughter?" He asked, grinning.

She shook her head. "A son. All of our children will be sons. I've seen it in the stars. Does that make you happy?"

He kissed her again. "I'm happy to be a father to our son. And other sons in the future." Arms linked, they walked over to the windows and gazed out at the sea. "I hope that some-day, he can go to sea with me and learn navigation. Let him succeed where I have failed."

"You have not failed, my love," Inanna said softly, her arm tight around his waist. "Your legacy," she said, using a word she'd just learned, "is not what you have done or did not do at sea. Your legacy is rescuing me and raising my children." She giggled. "Of whom this is the first," she said, patting her belly.

"And what shall his name be?"

Inanna rested a finger against her lips and looked thoughtful. "I think we should call him Iapetos, firstborn of the mighty Oannes, he who walks from the sea with a trident and a fish, founder of many nations, a god, a Giant."

Ogenus took a deep breath. "That's a lot to expect of me. I'm not a god, nor a Giant. I'm just a man. And I haven't founded a single nation."

"You haven't founded a nation...yet. Our time is still young. In the years ahead, who knows?"

He picked her up and gently placed her on the bed. "And you," he said, lying down next to her, "you are my greatest treasure."

*

Nine months and a few days later, Ionic walked into a hospital room, hands filled with flowers. Inanna, looking tired but immeasurably happy, smiled at him from her hospital bed.

"You've come to see our new son?"

"And his beautiful mother," Ionic said.

She accepted the flowers with one hand while displaying a sleeping baby in the other.

"I'll bet the father is proud."

Inanna giggled. "He fainted when he first laid eyes on him."

Ionic laughed. "Sounds like Ogenus. Where is he now?"

Inanna pointed with her chin, "He went to get something to eat. Sit for a moment. Thank you for the flowers."

Ionic perched on the edge of a seat. "Have you named him?"

"Iapetos. He will grow big and strong and make his parents proud."

"I have a feeling they are already bursting with pride. Congratulations and my best wishes to you both."

Inanna shifted her baby to the bed, moving over to make room for him. "I'm glad Oannes brought me here ahead of time, so I could see how everything worked," she said, looking around the hospital room. "I had never seen a hospital before. My people did things differently."

"I'm sure they did. Are you happy with your choice, my dear? Glad you left the mountains and your tribe?"

Inanna was silent for a long moment as she gazed into the past. Her smile faded. "Sometimes," she said softly, "I miss it terribly. I miss my parents and my little brother. He was so small and innocent. I miss the crisp chill of the mountains. I miss the thrill of a successful hunt and the joy of having fresh food. But I don't miss the isolation and the..." She paused and searched for an unfamiliar word. "I guess you'd call it suspicion. I was a female hunter, and they didn't like that. I have blue eyes, and they didn't like that either." She looked away and stared out the window. Her voice became very soft. "Then my family was killed when I was away, and the only comfort offered was banishment from the tribe. When I needed someone the most, I was cast out."

Ionic sat silently. He pretended not to see Inanna wipe away tears. He had not heard her story in detail before. It made him appreciate the monumentally difficult decision Ogenus had made.

"Now," she said with determination, almost to herself, "now I am at last a woman."

"When Ogenus first brought you to my apartment, I thought he had made a terrible mistake, in more ways than one. I believed in bringing you here, he would make your situation even worse. I imagined you sinking into a terminal depression, and Ogenus being torn apart." He reached out and patted her hand. "Thankfully, I was wrong. You are a survivor, my dear. You were strong enough to adapt, and that is most amazing."

"Thank you," she replied. "Oannes held on to me when I needed it. And I needed it so much in those early days. It was hard, very hard. My mate is a good and kind and very patient man."

Ionic smiled. "And he loves you deeply." He tilted his head. "More deeply than I think you can even imagine. I never saw him truly happy until he came home with you. You gave him that, and I am eternally grateful."

The baby stirred and cried briefly before resuming his nap. The door swung open and Ogenus entered with a tray.

"Ionic! My friend! Have you seen him? Isn't he beautiful?" He almost shouted.

"Shhh," Inanna said, "he's sleeping."

"Just now." Ionic couldn't help but laugh.

"Amazing, isn't he?" Ogenus whispered intently. "A whole marvelous human. And I made him," he glanced over at his mate, "with a little help."

Ionic laughed, stood, and slapped Ogenus on the back. "You surely did. And he is, indeed, beautiful."

Ionic's smile drifted away. "Can we have a short talk," he said softly, "out in the hall?"

Ogenus set the tray on a bed table and arranged it so Inanna could reach the food. "Of course. My Angel," he said to Inanna, "we will be right back."

Once in the hallway, Ionic's visage changed from happy to worried. "I've been doing some observations of the comet. You remember, we talked about it a year or so ago?"

"Yes, the one heading toward us. What about it? It's supposed to miss us this time, right?"

Ionic shrugged. "According to my calculations, yes. We're probably okay this time. But we've made enough observations to determine its probable orbit, and what we saw is disturbing. We now know that it's definitely going to return a few years after this pass, on essentially the same orbit."

"When?"

"That we're not so not sure of, exactly. But if our calculations are correct..." Ionic paused for a long time.

"What?"

"I think it's going to pass by very close to Earth the second time, Ogenus."

"How close? Impact?"

"I don't know. Probably not. But, Ogenus..."

"Okay, out with it. What's troubling you?"

"My measurements indicate that it's huge. It's a giant comet, almost the size of a small moon. I've had my figures verified by several observatories and the space telescope. Some of my colleagues think this comet has passed close to earth many times in the past. If so, it's a regular visitor in our skies, even if some of those visits are thousands of years apart."

"But if it's not going to hit us..."

Ionic sighed. "It's a comet, Ogenus. If it were a moon or an asteroid and it passed near us, the effects would be minimal and transitory. Perhaps some tidal anomalies, but little else. But this is a comet. It's made of ice and a bunch of rocks. As it nears the sun, the ice begins to melt. When it passes near Earth, and our gravity pulls at it, it may start to break up, ejecting ice and rocks into our atmosphere. The ice isn't a problem, it will melt long before reaching the surface."

"The rocks?"

Ionic nodded. "Yes, the rocks. Therein lies the problem. They could be huge or small, many or a few. At worst the damage might even alter the Earth's orbit or inclination. We could have floods, earthquakes, volcanic eruptions. The global effects could be catastrophic."

"But maybe not. And you don't know when?"

"If you forced me to answer, I'd say ten years. Maybe twelve. Or fifteen. This comet hasn't been in our skies for several centuries because we have no modern record of it. What it does, or doesn't do is just a guess at this point."

"So what? Anything we can do about it?"

Ionic shrugged. "Not much except pray to the gods. Before it reappears though, I think it might be prudent to store fuel cells in various locations, along with food and fresh water. And something else..."

"Enlighten me."

"I've sent an associate to the east, to the nation of Anadolu. He's going to work with locals and some of my colleagues there to build a series of stone observatories, encoded with information about the comet. The stones will be aligned with various celestial landmarks. If we survive, it can be used to determine orbital changes, if any. And if we don't survive, it will be a monument to our existence, perhaps, a warning to future civilizations."

"A warning?"

"How tenuous and temporary our mighty civilization turned out to be," Ionic said with a soft voice.

"Aren't you being a little melodramatic?"

Ionic sighed. "I hope so," he said. "I do hope so."

*

Weeks later when the comet approached Earth, it was a spectacular sight. Its tail grew, stretching across the sky night after night. "One might think," Ionic said, "that it is a god coming down to Earth."

"That's interesting," Ogenus said. "Your idea?"

Ionic chuckled. "It is very similar to some prehistoric accounts of gods arriving on Earth on flaming chariots. It's understandable; nothing this large has appeared in Earth's sky for perhaps a thousand years. For a while, it will outshine even the Moon. I wouldn't be surprised if some of the tribes aren't worshiping it right now. Unbelievable, isn't it?"

"As long as it leaves us alone," Ogenus said. Silently they

watched the light show in the sky, each busy with their own thoughts.

Ionic was right. Its appearance was almost god-like as it approached the Earth, its effect even on the population of Kursatta was almost spiritual. Ogenus regarded it as a warning from the gods. A warning and, a threat. Yet the comet passed by Earth without effect, rounded the sun, and eventually disappeared from the sky. It headed out into the dark reaches of space. Ogenus hoped it was gone for good.

*

The next few years were the happiest Inanna had known. Her second son, Hammurabi, was born a year after Iapetos, and Shemash two years after that. She had finally left her tribal life behind, fully immersing herself into the culture of the Giants. She now spoke and wrote the language of her adopted home fluently. She could operate all the apartment's voice-actuated conveniences. She even sometimes rode by herself in Giant vehicles, running errands, shopping, or just enjoying the scenery during rare occasions when Ogenus stayed home with the boys.

As they grew from babies to toddlers, Inanna took her sons out into nearby wilderness areas for long hikes. She taught them the ways of the hunter, but emphasized that at this point in time weapons were only for protection, not for bringing down prey. Her sons learned quickly the skills needed to move silently through a forest, how to stalk without themselves being stalked. They learned to make fire, how to catch a fish from icy streams, how to clean and prepare their catch for cooking. They were taught which plants and roots could be eaten, and which were not food. They learned which animals might threaten them, how they hunted, and ways to avoid becoming a meal.

Inanna didn't know if her sons would ever need these skills. But she was determined to make her children aware that they were not just the sons of Giants, but also the offspring of She-Wolf. Iapetos and Shemash had been born with her unusual blue eyes; Hammurabi had his father's dark brown eye color. They grew taller than the typical tribal boy. The eldest and youngest had her dark brown coloring whilst Hammurabi was pasty like this father.

The boys attended school and learned the ways of the Giants. They immersed themselves in the culture of a fully technological civilization. Inanna, however, continued to also educate them in the ways of her tribal customs.

She trained them until they could sneak up on her silently, or fade into the foliage and become virtually invisible. They treated it as a game, Iapetos and Hammurabi playing a more serious version of "hide-and-seek" at first, until Shemash could walk, then the toddler joined them.

They tried playing their games with school friends, but the Giant children had little skill in the wilderness. It was no fun sneaking up on someone who never heard you, or hiding from someone who always made too much noise. So they kept the games to themselves and grew up bi-cultural. Their mother was very proud of them.

At a picnic one day, at their favorite location where the river emptied into the sea, Inanna rested on a blanket. They had just finished a picnic lunch. The weather was calm, warm, and humid. She watched as her mate and three sons splashed and played in gentle waves. She sighed, then smiled at their screaming and laughter.

She had been with her mate for almost five years, and how things had changed during that time! She realized, resting against a water-smoothed log, that she was happy and fulfilled.

Her childhood question had been answered. She knew what it was like to be a Giant, and to be mated to a Giant.

Oannes was more than she could have ever hoped for in a mate, gentle and considerate. He worked at his job judiciously, providing for his family without complaint. He had given up his life at sea, although Inanna sometimes caught him staring wistfully at the endless waters. She knew he was wondering what could have been, if only.

Despite that, their family was a happy one, all of them smiled and laughed frequently. They never worried where their next meal might come from. They never feared attacks by wild animals. They lived a comfortable life, unlike the mountain people. Memories of her time with them grew dim for Inanna. But she kept the tribal culture alive by teaching her sons the ways and language of her past. She showed them her spear, still topped with Oannes' trident. They begged to hold it, and she let them. She wanted them to feel the weight, the power, and the connection it provided to her other life.

She told them stories of her parents and her brother, and how she came to be known as She-Wolf. She left out the sad parts, mostly. If she felt sad in the telling, she would look at her sons and smile.

*

In four years and eight months after the birth of their third son, the comet reappeared once again, slowly growing in size until it blazed in the night sky, tail stretching across the horizon. Ogenus, Inanna, and their three children stood at the edge of the water and gazed out to sea. Shemash, the youngest, held by his father, watched silently while middle brother, Hammurabi, on hands and knees, slapped at the gentle waves of the beach, and turned over rocks looking for baby crabs. Iapetos held his mother's hand.

"Ionic says parts of it will hit the earth in a couple of months," Ogenus said

"What will that do to us?" asked Inanna, a young woman now, well out of her teens.

Ogenus shrugged. "He says it depends on where the fragments impact and how large they are. The bulk of the comet will miss Earth. He thinks it will partially break up at closest approach, some of the rocks will enter our atmosphere. If pieces hit the sea, we'll have tons of water rising into the atmosphere, and there will be a series of tsunamis. If it hits land, earthquakes and volcanoes. And," Ogenus paused and looked at his children, "if it hits the ice caps, they will melt instantly with sea levels rising without warning."

They continued staring at the comet. Its effect was almost hypnotic. "That damned thing looks like a snake," Ogenus said, "stretched across the sky, coming to devour us."

Inanna shuddered. "I'm afraid. This is happening and there's nothing we can do about it."

"Don't be scared, Mama," Iapetos said softly, "we'll protect you."

She looked down at her eldest son. She placed hands on both of his thin shoulders. "I know you will, my son." She hugged him, but her eyes returned to the sky.

Ogenus also gazed at the comet. He wondered if he really could protect his family in the coming days and weeks. Their fun visit to the ocean that day had ended on a somber note. There would be no more such visits.

He'd made what preparations seemed prudent to him. Each had a backpack with food, water, and other supplies. They were stacked together at the entrance to his new, larger two-bedroom apartment. They were prepared to leave at a moment's notice, heading for higher ground. Ogenus looked out the window, at a moonless night and dark ocean. A moment later, the overcast thinned, and a glow appeared over the sea as if someone had flipped a switch. In the sky, comet and tail had grown larger than the moon. It wouldn't be long before Earth's gravity field pulled at the comet, and it responded by flinging pieces of itself at the Earth.

*

Ogenus paced in Ionic's apartment. "You need to tell me exactly what's going to happen when that thing hits us."

"Ogenus, it's not going to hit us. Not directly, at least. And I don't know what's going to happen. You've asked me a thousand times. The answer isn't going to change." Ionic looked worried and very tired. "There are too many variables. You already know as much as I do. An unknown number and size of fragments captured by Earth's gravity are going to impact somewhere on this planet within the next 36 to 48 hours." He threw his tablet on the desk and gazed out the window. Then he turned and looked at his friend.

"There's more bad news."

"How can it get any worse?" Ogenus shouted.

"The comet breaks up and fragments of it hit us. But that's only a small part of the comet. It will continue on, around the sun, in a long, elliptical but somewhat erratic orbit. In five, ten, maybe twenty years from now, our paths will cross again. More fragments will possibly impact Earth. Besides that, some of those rocks will be pulled away and form their own orbit, which may intersect Earth for hundreds of years. Most of those will burn up in the atmosphere, but some may impact. This could happen over and over again until all the fragments are gone or are shifted into orbits away from us. I don't know. I wish I knew more, Ogenus. I've contacted every astronomer I've ever worked with, and we all agree that we don't know enough. And there's something I haven't shared with any of them. I hesitate to share it with you, but I know you can keep your mouth shut for the time being."

Ogenus shook his head. He was about at his limit for bad news.

"I think I mentioned once before that these impacts might affect earth's orbit, possibly its inclination. We could be in some real trouble if that happens."

"How will we know?"

Ionic spread his hands. "Ogenus, once again, too many variables. But we probably won't know, at least not at first, not until our climate begins to change radically. Our technology, while capable of giving us the answers we need, is also very tenuous. These impacts are going to decimate our ability to tell what's happened."

"I have a mate and three sons," Ogenus said. "I don't want bad things to happen to them."

Ionic looked his friend in the eye. "And if there is anything I could do to prevent that, I would. Together with many other scientists, I have spent the last three months telling anyone who would listen to get to higher ground, get out of the cities, find somewhere away from the ice fields, get prepared. Most ignore our warnings and think we're insane. Even some astronomers dispute our findings. Quite a few agree with me, of course, but choose to do nothing. Only a few people will take heed and actually do something. Whether they survive or not, that's another matter. I don't think our civilization is geared for catastrophic survival."

"Couldn't we fire rockets at that thing? Hit it with nuclear warheads?"

"Possibly," Ionic said, "even probably. But the best we could do with the most powerful weapons we have is to break it into even more large pieces. If we happen to push a big chunk into our gravity field, the consequences would be beyond our ability to imagine. Remember what killed off the dinosaurs."

"Then what can we do? I mean 'us' not humanity. *My* mate and *my* children."

"I was getting to that. In a few hours, I'm taking my own advice and moving to the Crecopia. You and your family will come with me. It's far inland and well above sea level. It's basically a giant rock sticking out of the earth, so even if there are earthquakes associated with this comet, we should be okay. We'll be cramped in my flier, but we'll get there."

"Okay, I'll talk to Inanna. When do you want us to be ready?"

"By my rough calculations, the first impact will be in about thirty to forty hours. Can you be ready in twelve hours? That will give us enough time to get there and get settled in."

"Twelve hours," Ogenus nodded, glad they had already made some preparations. "We'll be ready." He turned away, then turned back. "Thanks," he said.

"May the gods protect us," Ionic said softly. But he knew, in his heart, that the gods weren't paying attention this time.

DURING

Ionic's air ship settled on the flat top of the protruding rock the astronomer called the Cecropia. Its flat surface housed an astronomical observatory, living quarters, and a couple of storage buildings. Ogenus and his family exited the flier and watched in dismay as Inanna bent and vomited, a victim of air sickness and stress.

"Sorry," she muttered. Ogenus held her and they followed Ionic to the residence. The electricity was still on, and water flowed from the tap. "Make yourselves at home. Food in the kitchen."

Ogenus and Ionic transferred their belongings from the

flyer to the residence. "Secure everything," Ionic told Inanna, "maybe some of it will still be here...after."

Inanna nodded, then glanced at Ogenus, who shrugged. "Do the best you can," he said.

*

The comet was almost as large as one of Saturn's smaller moons. It filled the Earth's sky, with a tail that stretched east to west across the sky. It would be the stuff of legends for thousands of years, as it had possibly been for thousands of years in the past. Had the impacts been direct, the result would have probably destroyed most life on Earth. The fact that it was a comet, rather than an asteroid, meant that it was a collection of rocks, large and small, held together by ice. As the comet approached the sun, the ice began to melt, and some of the rocks and dust started to detach due to the pull of Earth's gravity.

The comet was sufficiently large that its passing caused the Earth to wobble slightly on its axis. The approach was close enough that some of the detached rocks were pulled into Earth's atmosphere. They came in low and fast at a flat angle, some reaching over 60,000 miles per hour, roaring and burning. The first two, the size of cities, impacted the Arctic ice sheets a few thousand miles apart, turning much of the ice into water instantly, and the remainder into steam. Water temperatures rose to over 2,000 degrees Fahrenheit.

The ice that became meltwater rushed to the sea in whatever way it found possible, changing entire landscapes in the process. That which rose as steam or vapor, saturated the atmosphere, blocking out the sun. Global temperatures quickly increased due to the intense heat generated by impacts.

Human civilizations in what would, thousands of years later, be known as North America, were wiped from the face of the earth as flood waters, massive earthquakes and long-dormant volcanoes erupted, covering hundreds of villages and cities in flood waters, debris, and molten lava. Some of the smaller animals, which could move fast, survived. Those too large to escape died instantly, buried in mud, or in the weeks and months that followed as the environment changed radically, and their food became scarce.

As the comet curled around the Earth, its orbit partially altered by gravity, more, smaller, rocks detached and plowed into the surface. A few impacted the ocean, sending more steam and vapor into the atmosphere. Many more burned up in the atmosphere, while some of the smaller fragments hit land, blasting craters into the planet and flinging tons of material and ash high into the sky.

Further east, more impacts on ice sheets.

Then the comet broke its gravitational connection with Earth, and moved on toward the sun, in a slightly altered orbit, slightly smaller and slightly less cohesive. It also left behind rocks following in Earth's orbit. While this comet had likely been seen in Earth's skies before, it had, with a few notable exceptions, usually passed with minor effects, or none at all. This time...

*

Results of the comet fall had yet to reach the Crecopia. They had minutes, perhaps, to make final preparations. The sun turned red as atmospheric debris quickly spread around the globe.

Ionic touched Ogenus on the shoulder. "Will you accompany me to the observatory?"

Ogenus took another long, worried look at his spouse and children. "You'll be okay?"

Inanna nodded. "You go. We'll be fine. Just be careful."

Ionic, with help from Ogenus, spent quite some time tying down the aircraft. Ogenus suggested his friend was overdoing it a bit, securing the machine with chains to large eyelets sunk deep into the rock.

"You just wait, my friend," Ionic said. "When this is over, you'll appreciate my caution."

After securing the aircraft, they covered it with a thick form-fitting tarp which was, itself, firmly secured to the rock. "There," Ionic said wiping his hands on his pants, "that ought to hold it as well as anything. Time will tell if we succeeded."

Ogenus looked at his friend. "Exactly how bad do you expect this to be?"

Ionic gazed back, then shook his head. "I'm afraid it will be beyond your imagination. I hope I'm wrong." Both men glanced up at the sky. Beyond the far distant horizon there came loud echoing and ominous "*crack!*" It echoed and reverberated off distant mountains and even the clouds overhead. Somewhere nearby a window broke.

Ogenus took one last look at the plane. "Yes, for once let you be wrong," he said softly, then followed Ionic to the observatory.

From the surrounding village, the Cecropia was accessed by a crude set of stairs carved into the rock on the south side. Ionic kept this access blocked so the curious wouldn't tamper with his delicate equipment. He stopped for a moment, looked thoughtful, then unblocked the gate. "Those people, down below in the village, maybe some of them can make it up here, if they hurry."

As Ionic and Ogenus strode to the large, round observatory building, they felt the earth rumble beneath their feet. "May the gods preserve us," Ionic said softly.

A large, well-muscled man emerged from the observatory. "Sir, the telescopes, everything, shaking," he looked back and pointed. His deep voice was filled with panic.

"My assistant, Hercle" Iconic said softly to Ogenus. "Strong as an ox, breaks everything he touches."

"Then why keep him?"

"He's my nephew. My sister's son. He took it hard when she died a dozen years ago. We both did. He's a good man. You can depend on him."

Another sharp shake, followed by an even larger one sent Ionic to his knees. Ogenus steadied himself against the door frame, and used his other hand to help Ionic to his feet. Hercle ducked back into the building in response to a loud crash. A grey pillar of smoke appeared far to the southeast, indicating perhaps a volcanic eruption.

Ionic had just steadied himself when they experienced a massive shake of a magnitude far larger than the previous ones. Part of the observatory building collapsed. Hercle roared and burst from the door followed by debris and dust. Ogenus found himself on the ground, and he held on, trying to make the shaking stop, but it continued for several minutes. Then the ground unexpectedly quieted. Overhead the sky was filling with dark, ominous, rolling clouds. A strong wind kicked up from the north.

Ogenus ran back to the residence to find that half of it had collapsed. "Inanna!" He called. There was no answer, but he heard a child crying. He tried to lift a section of the roof, but found it heavier than he expected. Suddenly the roof rose and was flung to the side. Hercle stood beside Ogenus, shaking the dust from his hands. The electricity had gone out, and the air around the flat top of the mountain became dark from a sudden overcast.

While the ground began to shake again, Ogenus and Hercle extricated Inanna and the three boys. All of the children were crying, but seemed uninjured. Inanna had a cut on her left arm and another above her right eye, and she walked with a slight limp.

Ogenus grabbed her and looked into her eyes. "Are you all right?"

She wiped away blood, then nodded, eyes wide in fear. "How are the boys? Are the boys okay?"

Ogenus looked over to where Hercle was brushing dust and debris off the three children. "They're good," he growled, then went to a knee as the earth lurched again. The air became hot and dust-filled, and very humid.

"Ogenus!" Ionic called from near the observatory, "keep an eye on the south. We're going to have some massive waves coming at us."

"This far inland?" Ogenus asked.

"Easily this far, my friend."

Ionic joined the others. "We're pretty stable up here," he said breathlessly, "but they're really getting hit hard down there," he said, pointing to the small village at the base of the rock. Ogenus followed the end of Ionic's finger. Through the dust, he saw only collapsed buildings. Nothing had survived. He could see tiny figures moving through the rubble. Buildings were ablaze. Hints of screams reached their ears.

Ogenus heard a loud roar and looked up in time to see a fireball blaze across the sky and disappear into the distance, leaving a smoky trail behind. Two more fireballs, further away, marked their passage with trails of fiery smoke.

"The gods!" Hercle shouted from the observatory, pointing, "they come to Earth. This is bad!"

The air became heavy and suffocatingly hot. Ash drifted down as thick as a black blizzard. The shaking went on for another twenty minutes, a steady deep rumble punctuated by sharper shakes.

Then a sudden quiet descended. Quiet enough for Ogenus to hear periodic screams from below, village survivors either injured or fighting to extricate themselves from rubble. The quiet was replaced by a new, soft rumble that steadily grew in volume. It began to rain, and the drops were hot and gritty. He heard the distant roar of another fireball, but the sky was too filled with rain and debris for him to see it.

*

    Inanna had sprained her ankle when the roof fell on her, but she said nothing. Her spouse and Ionic's assistant had rescued her and her children from the collapsed house. The damage was almost total. She went to her knees and tried to hold onto the shaking ground with one arm and her children with the other. They were not near the edge, but debris shook and moved, and larger objects rolled here and there.

    She knew Ogenus and Ionic were speaking but did not hear most of their words, and didn't understand the rest. She looked up when the shaking stopped, and everything became unnaturally quiet. Her tribal instincts told her this wasn't over. The worst was to come. She pulled her boys closer and waited.

*

    To the north, water that had minutes before been sheets of ice roared out of the mountains, flooding the distant river and washing over cultivated land. Ogenus turned around and saw a slight glimmer in the distance to the south. The rumble became louder. He realized it was even more water. A wave front roared toward them from the sea, almost a hundred feet high with a speed that caused their flat mountain to vibrate.

    Walls of water hit both sides of the Crecopia. They were drenched as waves hit and then washed across the top, hundreds of feet higher. But the tsunami itself did not rise above their refuge. It roared past them, fighting with the ice melt, and on and on, back across the cultivated land and small villages, up into the foothills, carrying debris and bodies and sea life with it, only to crash against trees and boulders, uprooting the trees and shifting the house-sized boulders and floating them like pebbles in a storm tide. The twin floods fought each other, swirling back and forth, grinding, destroying everything.

The wave from the sea slowly receded, only to be replaced by a second wave, then a third, and a fourth all equally horrific in size, speed, and power. With the fifth wave, the height and ferocity of each began to diminish slightly. In an hour, the water had calmed considerably. Dry land began to reappear around them, the tops of hills covered in debris.

Then the rain turned from steady drops to a hot raging downpour. There was no wind at first, just the rain, the unending rain so heavy that one could barely breathe in it.

Then the wind returned with a vengeance, blew strongly, then began to howl, threatening to fling the humans off the now slippery flat surface. Ionic and Hercle urged everyone back into the remnants of the observatory. The building's base was mortared stone and had largely withstood the quakes. Behind these curved walls, exhausted and shaken humans sat with their backs to the stone, holding each other as the ferocity of rainfall drowned out any attempt to converse. The wails of three terrified boys was overcome by the roar of water falling.

Ogenus sat near Ionic. He leaned over and shouted into the older man's ear. "So much water. Where?"

"Ice," Ionic shouted back. "Fragments impacted the ice sheets. Tons of water vapor saturating the atmosphere. Ocean levels rising, almost instantly." The wind paused and rain lessened to an overpowering roar. "Most of the largest cities of Earth's nations are at or near sea level. Within hours, most will have sunk beneath the sea. All but the very tops of buildings and some further inland. But, as you can see from our vantage, few inhabitants will survive."

Ogenus shook his head. "Are you sure the effects were global? Maybe the impacts were just nearby."

"I would wish it were so," Ionic shouted into the wind. "But my calculations showed a far north entry and impact for the largest fragments. No, I fear what we are suffering is mainly due to major impacts in the far north, almost to the Arctic region. All that ice melted in a flash. Much of it became water, the rest steam."

Ogenus shook his head, "So Earth is done for."

Ionic patted his friend on the shoulder. "The Earth will survive, as it has for millions of years. And we're still alive, my friend. At least for the moment."

Rain continued to pour, the wind blew. Dark surrounded them.

At the end of the comet storm, none of them could have said how many hours they huddled behind the rock wall. More than thirty-two hours, Ionic estimated. There was no dawn, but light finally illuminated the sky enough to see beyond the Crecopia. They'd had nothing to eat or drink during that time. Ogenus had swallowed some of the rain and found it to be salty and gritty.

Slowly, the wind died down, and rain diminished to a steady downpour.

Ionic stood and strode to the edge of their refuge. Down below the deluge was still draining to the south. As he looked down, he searched for the village in vain. It was gone. No foundations, no walls, very little debris. The village had been sucked into the sea by the barrage of tsunami waves and meltwater.

He looked back to see Ogenus and his family, along with Hercle, assessing what remained of his observatory and other buildings. Amazingly, they found Ionic's flier still chained down. It appeared to have suffered little damage. The covering tarp had been ripped away sometime during the storm, and two of the chains had snapped. One cockpit window had suffered a crack and the entire machine was covered in mud, ash, and debris.

The house had completely collapsed, and much of it literally blown away. The observatory's large telescope housing was totally gone. Inanna and Ogenus retrieved emergency rations kept in hollowed-out housings secured with iron covers. Everything inside was covered in water and ash, but the protective coverings had, mostly, done their job. They found some food and a limited amount of fresh water sealed in containers. Seven people sat, exhausted, at a broken laboratory table to eat a survival meal.

"When we're sure the worst is over," Ionic said, munching a cracker, "you and I," he pointed at Ogenus, "will take the airship and do an inspection run. See how bad things are in Kursatta."

"If there's even anything left," Ogenus said, cleaning Hammurabi's face. The child, usually happy and outgoing, was quiet and almost unresponsive. Neither Inanna nor the children ate much.

*

The next morning, a feeble sun broke through persistent clouds. Rain fell periodically. The reawakened volcano south of them continued pouring ash and smoke into air that was already saturated. Water that recently swirled around the Crecopia had drained away, leaving puddles, mud, and debris. Global sea levels had risen significantly, Ionic told them. The lingering ice age had come to an abrupt end. Temperatures were now almost tropical.

They endured two more days of frequent rain and wind, as well as the occasional rumble and shake from deep within the Earth. They slept fitfully, lying against the observatory's wall. A tarp kept some of the rain off. Finally, faint sunlight cast subdued rays sufficient to make shadows.

Ogenus walked with Inanna away from the children. "We'll be gone for only a short time," he said softly. "We're

109

not planning to land anywhere unless there is a good reason to do so. We should be back before dark."

"I don't want you to go. It's too dangerous out there." Inanna paused. "But I understand your need. Has anybody except us survived? We need to know. Can we go home? If not, where are we going to live? I'm afraid I already know the answers to those questions, but you need to be sure."

Ogenus hugged his spouse, held her tightly. "You're the smartest person I've ever known," he said, his lips caressing her hair. "Because of you I have no doubts we'll survive."

"Don't say that. I'm a savage from the mountain people. I know nothing."

Ogenus looked at her, their eyes locked. "You know much more than you think," he said. "If we manage to survive this disaster, I firmly believe it will be because of you. Believe it or not, you are an expert on survival. When it comes time, you will lead us and keep us all alive."

Inanna shook her head. "Go now. Come back quickly, my love."

*

With Ionic at the controls, the airship rose into falling rain. Ogenus was the only other occupant. Hercle stayed behind and was told to work with Inanna and do what they could to devise some kind of shelter. They didn't expect any intruders, but it was possible, if unlikely, that some survivors might be able to climb the steep stairs of the Crecopia.

The flight south took a couple of hours. Ogenus was amazed at the changes. Much farm land they flew over was now under water, and what remained above the waves had been transformed into a group of small islands, one of them the source of a massive volcanic eruption. In order to avoid it, they flew in a wide curve to the west, then back south.

Where the city of Kursatta had been located, only a large island remained. Of the city itself, all but a very few buildings had collapsed and fallen into the sea, or burned until only the steel sub-structure remained. Each of the few intact buildings still standing had been severely damaged.

Looking for their former home, Ogenus and Ionic had to circle the island twice before they recognized their apartment high rise. The building had partially burned but still stood, wisps of smoke drifting into the sky.

"Think you can land on the top?" Ogenus asked.

Ionic looked down as his flier circled, and studied the roof. It was only partially intact, but there were several potential landing spots. "Probably," he said. "It will be risky. Why?"

"I'd like to get something from my apartment, if it's still there. Something…sentimental. Didn't think about it when we left, and there wasn't room anyway."

"A few things I'd like to retrieve in my residence, as well," Ionic said softly.

Ionic flew closer and circled the damaged building. "All we can do is try." Slowly, he brought the craft down. Unburnt portions of the roof appeared to be structurally sound. He lowered the landing gear and as gently as possible, brought the craft in for a landing. The roof held and both men let out a sigh of relief.

They got out and stood on a rubble-strewn surface. There were cracks and fissures in the concrete, and the building seemed to shudder from time-to-time.

"Okay, let's go. Get what we need and get out of here. There may be more earthquakes, especially with that volcano over there," Ionic pointed north where they could see a black cloud of smoke.

They entered the building by prying one of the locked access doors open. Ionic's residence was on the top floor;

Ogenus' apartment several floors below that. As they entered the staircase, they noticed that the building was far from silent. There were creaks and pops and an underlying muted noise that neither could place. The stairwell reeked of fire and smoke. They hoped any toxic fumes had dissipated in the storm that followed.

Ogenus left Ionic to rummage through the mess that was his residence. He carefully made his way down the stairs until he reached the floor above his. There, a wall had collapsed blocking the stairwell. He moved as much debris out of the way as he could, then used his handheld beam to cut away enough pieces so that he could squeeze through.

Once in his apartment, Ogenus was appalled at the destruction. His floor-to-ceiling windows were gone. The kitchen had collapsed. The bed for their two older boys was hanging out the window of their room, teetering, ready to fall 72 stories. He vowed to keep this to himself, but he thanked the gods Ionic had talked them into leaving. On the wall above his bed he found, still attached, what he had come for: Inanna's long spear, topped with his trident. He reached up and lifted it down, hefting it.

As he turned to leave, he saw movement. A man poked his head into the apartment, followed by two more with some women in the hall. "Ogenus?" one of the men said, hesitantly, as if he'd seen a ghost.

"Marban? Harrow?" Those were the two he knew.

"How did you get here?" Marban asked, "the elevators don't work and the stairs are blocked. Three floors below this one, there's nothing but substructure. We've been trapped here. There isn't any water, no electricity."

"We flew in, parked up on the roof," Ogenus said. Unconsciously, he had been holding the spear at the ready. He settled its pike on the ground and tried to relax.

"Can you help us?" Harrow asked. "Can you get us out of this building?"

"How many of you are there?"

"Seven. Us three, two women and two children."

"The flier doesn't belong to me, but I'm sure Ionic will agree to ferry you to the ground."

"Ionic!" Marban said. "He wouldn't help his own mother. That arrogant..."

"Let's just go find out, shall we?" Ogenus led them up the stairs to Ionic's flat. After a short argument and some thought, Ionic reluctantly agreed to transport the refugees off the building. "But no more than that," he said firmly.

It took three trips to get all the refugees on the ground. As Ogenus turned to re-board the flier, Harrow grasped him by the shoulder. "So, you're just going to leave us here?"

Ogenus turned. "What else do you expect us to do? We haven't enough fuel to transport all of you to somewhere else. And, quite frankly, there isn't a 'somewhere else' left."

"But we're stuck here on what is now an island with no facilities, no way off."

"It's like that everywhere," Ogenus replied.

Harrow pulled a kitchen knife from inside his shirt. "We need that flier more than you do. Tell Ionic to get out."

Ogenus looked at the other man for a moment. Then he angrily knocked the knife out of the other's hand with the pike of his spear. "No! We have our own agenda and our own priorities. We got you out of the building, and that's all we're going to do. Got it? There's enough stuff around here to build a raft. You can find food, enough to sustain you for a few days. Rain falls every couple of hours, you can collect that for drinking. Build a decent raft and that should get you to the mainland if you're careful."

Harrow stepped back, looked at the others. None of them seemed inclined to join the argument. "C'mon, Harrow," one of the women said, "we're out of the building thanks to them. Let's start looking for food and supplies. The children are hungry."

Harrow glanced at the flier. "We wouldn't all fit in there at the same time anyway." Then he and the rest of the survivors turned almost as one and walked off, picking their way slowly through the debris. One of the children, with a smudged, dirty face, turned to look back at Ogenus. Her sad eyes burned into his brain, and he almost called them back. Then the group disappeared around a corner and were gone.

Ogenus backed his way to the passenger's side of the flier, but kept his eyes moving in case there were more refugees. "Get ready to depart as soon as I get in," he said to Ionic. He stowed the spear and jumped into his seat as quickly as he could. Ionic had them in the air almost as the hatch was closed. Ogenus struggled to fasten his belt while the flier gained altitude.

"We're going to need more fuel," Ionic said when Ogenus was fastened in. "If it's still there, I know where we can find a supply."

*

Eris had taken Ionic's warnings seriously. While she did not know the scientist personally, she trusted his judgment and decided to heed his warnings. Thus when the first rumblings of the catastrophic upheaval began she had already exited the Maritime Association building and was seeking higher open ground. Her backpack contained survival supplies and equipment. When she reached the street, others who were just beginning to panic looked at her strangely as she struggled to maintain balance with the large pack.

More intense temblors hit, making her steps more of a drunken stumble. Eris dropped the pack in her vehicle and quickly, but carefully, drove to the highest point she could find among the area's modest hills. The roads were beginning to buckle, some parts collapsing and other areas being shoved higher. She found a possible refuge, paradoxically, on a hill near the sea. Partway up the hill were storage containers for fuel cells, located far enough from the city that an accidental explosion would cause little damage. At the very top of the hill, mounted to one of the storage tanks, was a broadcast antenna tower with a platform several hundred feet up.

Eris found a steel ladder attached to the tank's side. She grasped a rung and looked up. She shook her head and began climbing. As the ground shakes became more violent, Eris hung on for her life. During periods of relative calm, she climbed as quickly as she could.

Eris survived the first effects of the comet's passing atop the tank, clinging to a small access door near the antenna's base. But when she saw the approaching tsunami waves, she knew immediately that the elevation of the hill and tank wouldn't provide enough height for safety. She gazed up at the antenna platform and sighed. It was either up there with no supplies, or drown. While it had swayed as a result of the earthquakes and wind, the tower still looked sturdy. At least it was upright.

She took some water and enough food for a couple of days and began to climb. The rumble and shaking of the approaching waves provided motivation to climb the antenna ladder as quickly as possible, despite her fear of heights. From her vantage, she could see much of Kursatta. Buildings were on fire, and many others had collapsed. This was not going to be pretty.

How she survived the tsunami waves, the torrential rains, the shaking, she would never know. The tower and the high platform upon which she collapsed after her climb, somehow remained standing. It shook and swayed and groaned and popped, but did not fall. When the rains subsided, she slept. It was dark as night and pouring rain when she closed her eyes; filtered sunlight when she awoke. She waited several more hours, watching as the sea slowly retreated.

Carefully and hesitantly, she made her way down the tower and stepped off onto the storage tank. The ground surrounding it was still awash in sea water. Of the city to the south, she could see only a few remnants of towering buildings. She gasped at the realization that the entire city of Kursatta had been destroyed, damaged, or sunk below the waves.

For two days, she lived on top of the tank, subsisting on her meager rations. She saw not another living human, although she observed many bodies floating in the water.

On the third day, sunlight broke through thick clouds for a brief moment. After another endless day and night, Eris became very hungry and thirsty. She kept waiting for more of the flood water to drain away, but while the level dropped somewhat, it remained much higher than before the cataclysm. She found herself stranded on an island. She almost gave up hope, and then a speck appeared in the sky.

*

As Ionic and Ogenus approached the storage tanks, they were stunned to see an individual standing upon one of them, waving frantically. Ionic slowly swung around the tank, making sure the survivor was alone and appeared unarmed.

Ogenus looked closely, then looked again "Eris?" he said softly. Then he turned to Ionic, "Go ahead and land. I know her."

"You have friends in very strange places," Ionic said.

The airship settled upon the tank.

"Thank the gods," Eris shouted, running forward. Then she stopped abruptly and stared as two men exited the machine. "Ogenus? Where? How?"

"Eris, are you alone up here? How did you…?"

The woman grabbed his arms and held on. "You're alive! You survived."

The men hadn't brought a lot of food and water with them, but Eris appreciated every last drop and crumb.

While Eris and Ogenus caught up, Ionic unlatched an access port on the tank's roof. "Help me get this off," he said. Ogenus and Eris lent their strength to lift the heavy cover. Darkness and a descending ladder awaited them, along with, ominously, the slosh of water. Ogenus went down into the tank and began carrying fuel cells up, one box at a time. Ionic and Eris moved them to the flier's cargo space.

"Most of those fuel cells are going to be ruined by water," Ionic said. "These tanks are be packed with fuel cells. I had hoped we could continue using them for quite some time, but now it doesn't look good."

After an hour of loading, Ionic declared the small cargo space filled. They used some to refuel the flier itself, then all three boarded the machine and Ionic guided his craft into cloudy skies. "Sluggish," Ionic said, "we're a bit overloaded, but we'll make it."

They drifted off over a devastated landscape. They saw only a few living humans, forlornly looking up at them from various newly-formed islands. The flier slowly gained altitude as they headed north. During their flight, Ogenus and Eris recounted their respective experiences.

"I assume you're still with that tribal child?" Eris asked.

Ogenus sighed. "Her name is Inanna. And, yes, we're still together. She's not a child, Eris, she's a mother. We have three sons now."

"I'm glad things worked out for you." She gazed at him steadily for a long moment, but said nothing more.

*

Two hours later, they circled the Cecropia, upon which Ionic had pinned his hopes for surviving the cataclysm. From their aerial approach, he could see that he'd been only partially successful. Wind, waves, earthquakes, and ash had caused substantial damage. Still, it seemed to remain the best option after their assessment. Just about every place else they'd seen had fared much worse.

Ogenus gazed out his window and saw Inanna and the boys going through motions. His spouse had a long knife and the boys brandished shorter ones. They were dressed not in the colorful clothes of his civilization, but the muted leathers and cloths patterned after those of Inanna's tribe.

Upon landing, Ogenus was first on the ground. He gazed at Inanna and realized how much he had missed her, and that she was as stunningly beautiful now as the day he had first seen her.

"What are you doing?" he asked.

Inanna and the boys stopped their exercising. She caught her breath. "Oannes, I'm teaching my boys how to survive." She walked up to him and gazed into his eyes.

"We won't..." Ogenus paused. "I don't think we will have to live a primitive life. There are other nations, other civilizations. The comet couldn't have destroyed them all. Somewhere..."

"Don't fool yourself," Inanna said angrily. "The gods have looked upon your civilization and found you to be arrogant and pompous, lovers of things rather than people." She waved a hand toward the south. "The gods have destroyed your great empires for daring to reach for the heavens. They will grind your magic to dust, along with your towers. All that you know, all that you've built will become nothing more than legends and myths, handed down in place of wisdom from generation to generation for all of time. Someday, others will point to the legends and myths and declare they are the new giants. And the gods will once again become angry."

"But..." Ogenus looked at the sweating boys.

She followed his glance. "They will need to survive in this new world. It will be very similar to the world I left behind when I," she paused, gazed into his eyes, "became yours. They will not die as weaklings, unprepared. I have already shown them how to survive. Now they will know my ways of dealing with the wildest animals known: men facing death. When we leave this rock, we will face the world I knew, and if it's up to me, we will live." Her words were defiant, and she expected a heated argument.

Ogenus opened his mouth, then closed it. He held up a finger, then turned back to the flier and rummaged around inside for a moment. When he exited the machine, he held Inanna's spear with its trident. "Then you'll need this," he said softly.

Inanna stared at the weapon, then reached out and took it in her hands, looking it up and down.

There were tears in her eyes as she looked at Ogenus. Silently she came to him and lay her head against his chest. "Thank you," she whispered.

*

"Okay," Eris said to Ionic. "Show me around. What are your plans from this point? What do we do?"

Ionic looked at the woman with distaste. "Do? We do nothing at the moment, my dear. First, we rest and have a bite to eat. Then we talk. We have much to discuss. Decisions need to be made, and for that we need knowledge."

While Ionic and Ogenus were gone, Hercle had cleaned up an undamaged portion of the observatory. He repaired another table and set up enough chairs for the small group. While not protected against wind, a roof of sorts at least kept the frequent rains off. It was where they ate, and now it would serve as a meeting place where decisions would be made.

Inanna greeted Eris with a neutral "nice to see you again." Eris returned the greeting, but seemed preoccupied. Thereafter, Eris largely ignored the young woman. Eris' attitude was familiar to Inanna, reawakening memories of her tribal days.

Ionic introduced his nephew, Hercle, to Eris. "Five years ago, he almost single-handedly dredged a deepwater channel between the boot, where the nation of Torrea is located—or was located—and the island it seemed to be kicking. That made it possible for ships to traverse our ocean and connect with the Great Sea to the west without waiting for high tide. Hercle worked underwater using a breathing apparatus designed by some engineer friends of mine. Used some explosives and some underwater dredging equipment, and a lot of muscle."

"Hah!" Hercle exclaimed, flexing. "I used muscle, lots of muscle."

Ionic smiled. "He even erected iron pillars on each side of the channel at the narrowest point. Called them the 'Pillars of Hercle.' One of them fell down last year."

Hercle looked sad. "Now both under water. Sea level too high now. No one will remember my Pillars."

Ionic asked the others to sit. He stood at the table's head and postulated. "We've suffered a catastrophic event. Let's face it, our civilization has been all but destroyed. I would suggest that most, but hopefully not all, of Earth's major nations have been similarly affected, either destroyed or heavily damaged."

"But we *can* rebuild," said Ogenus.

Ionic shook a finger at his friend. "Ah, yes, perhaps we could. But that won't happen soon, perhaps not for ages. Unfortunately, the comet isn't finished with us yet."

Ogenus frowned. "What do you mean by that, exactly?"

"Look, when the comet passed near Earth, parts of it broke off, some of those objects entered the atmosphere and impacted the planet. But only a small percentage of them. The primary mass of the comet itself has continued on its orbit, somewhat altered, around the sun. However, the pieces that were torn away and did not enter Earth's atmosphere are still out there, now in an orbit intersecting with Earth's." Ionic paused and ran a hand through his thin hair. "I expect that the orbits of that mass of rocks, or the comet itself, will meet with us again some time in the near future, and one way or another, we'll get hit. And it may happen over and over, until the largest rocks are depleted, or the comet's orbit has been altered sufficiently that it no longer comes close to our planet." He looked at each of the others. Their grim faces told him they had no doubts about his predictions.

"That's not the only problem," Ionic said sadly. "Our planet was hit hard. It's possible that Earth may have been knocked out of its orbit, or that the obliquity, or inclination of our planet may have been altered."

"So what," Eris asked. "What's that got to do with our survival?"

Ionic looked at the woman. "Everything, actually. If our orbit has changed, we may face much hotter summers or much colder winters. If the obliquity has changed, once again, our seasons may be modified, may become more extreme. If both happened..." He spread the fingers of his hands and looked at them silently.

"So what do we do about it?" Eris asked.

Ionic sighed. "Before this catastrophe, we could have easily taken astronomical measurements. Our satellite GPS and orbital mapping systems would have provided accurate data. As you can see, my observatory is no longer functional. Most of the observatories and receivers on the Earth are probably damaged and inoperable, or gone completely. While many of our satellites are probably still in orbit, it takes specialized equipment and power to receive the data. That equipment is now gone."

"So what do you propose," Ogenus asked.

"We have many thousands of fuel cells available if we can get at them. That gives us access to portable power for engineering equipment. I propose we use that equipment to build astronomical alignment facilities all over Earth. With those alignments, we can detect possible changes that may have occurred as a result of these current strikes, and any that may happen in the future."

"Won't they be damaged, or knocked out of alignment, if we get hit by more comet fragments?" Ogenus asked.

Ionic smiled. "Not," he said slowly, "if we build them of stone, and we build them large and heavy and stable. And," he spread his fingers, "not if we build them all over the globe in varying places and different styles. We'll align them to the magnetic poles, to various celestial objects, constellations, and stars. Even if some of them are damaged, others will survive, and they'll give us the information we need. I and several colleagues in nearby nations began work on just such a project before the comet hit. We had crews working at several locations northeast of us in Anadolu. I don't know how far they got as we no longer have any means to communicate with them. Once all this moisture and junk filters out of the atmosphere, we may be able to use satellite phones to communicate, as long as we can power them."

"And how does this help us," Eris said, "put food in front of our children, care for the injured, and rebuild functioning cities?"

"It won't," Ionic replied, impatience in his voice, "not in the short term. Of course we have to meet the needs of our people now. But we also must plan for the future. There are things we need to know for the benefit of any nations or cultures that will arise from the ashes of ours. If we do it right, our stones will survive for thousands of years. Certainly long enough for another advanced civilization to develop. We'll use these stones to tell them what happened to us, we'll warn them. We'll send a message to the future." He slammed his fist on the table, and gazed at each person with a challenging look. "We'll tell them that we were as advanced as they. We will make sure they don't forget us."

"Maybe it is best they do forget us," Inanna said softly. "How many have died because of this...this war with the gods?"

Ionic shook his head. "Impossible to tell. Before all of this happened, Earth had a population of about four-point-two billion people. While we here were hit hard, some nations and areas will have escaped the worst of it, at least for now. As a rough estimate, I would guess that at least two-and-a-half billion may have perished in the last several days. More are going perish in the coming weeks as they dig out of the rubble of their homes and discover they are ill-equipped to survive. We've lost...just about everything."

Eris agreed. "It doesn't take much to shake off the coat of civilization. We all need to understand that we're not here to be civil; we're here to survive. In a civilized society, we could appeal to a higher authority. We no longer have that society, and there is no authority to hear our appeals. And that means we must be ready to kill, if necessary, to protect ourselves."

"I don't particularly agree with your kill-or-be-killed philosophy," Ogenus said. He held up a hand when Eris started to speak. "But it's something we will have to be prepared for, as a last resort, if it comes to that."

The group was silent for a moment, each thinking their own thoughts.

Ogenus glanced over at Inanna, then back to Ionic. "So how long do we have? When will the comet hit us again?"

Ionic shrugged. "No way to tell without precise measurements. I would guess five or ten years, maybe a little longer. We may intersect with one or two fragments, or numerous ones if the comet itself comes close. We can no longer tell. And until those fragments have been used up, so to speak, we might have hits or near misses again and again for centuries to come."

*

Ogenus and Inanna walked, hand in hand, to the southern edge of the Crecopia. They gazed down at a view of utter destruction, remnants of the small city, now littered with bodies and debris. Sea birds swirled around the bounty, screaming at each other. Remaining waters were rapidly draining back into the much larger sea. They could see water glistening in the sun, left over from the flooding. A new shoreline of the sea was now no more than half-an-hour away by air, whereas before it had been a two-hour flight to Kursatta, which had been built at the water's edge.

"Ionic thinks we'll suffer another ice age, and that sea levels will eventually drop back almost to what they were before all this happened. But if we get hit again, there will be more global flooding, perhaps even worse. This cycle might happen several times. Eventually, when things settle down, sea levels will remain about where they are now."

"I don't know what to think about that at this moment," Inanna said. She looked up at him. "What I do think is that we should consider visiting my old tribe."

"Why? Giving up on me? On our boys?"

"Never, my love. But we need food, real food, not just these boxed rations. We need to learn what my people can teach us about survival. And they need to learn what we can teach them about civilization, about growing crops and raising farm animals, and getting along with other tribes. We need to be able to communicate. I know much of your language and I know mine. You know some of mine and yours. Together we can reach out and share what each of us needs."

Ogenus shook his head. None of that had occurred to him. It was more evidence that his spouse was much wiser than he, and more practical too. "You're right. We'll do that, just as soon as we can. We need to get organized here first. Ionic's plans are important as well." He sighed. "We're all going to be very busy for a long time to come, I'm afraid. Once the water recedes, survivors will begin to gather here, and we'll have to deal with them one way or another."

"Yet, in spite of it all, we will survive," Inanna said firmly.

They wandered back to the observatory and re-joined the others.

Eris raised a hand for attention. "Ionic has done an excellent job of thinking things through. Although I don't completely agree with all of his ideas, we certainly have plenty to keep us busy. What we need to do now is select a leader. Someone who can organize the few of us here, prioritize tasks, and get us moving. We also need to search for other survivors whose expertise can assist us with our tasks."

Ogenus looked skeptical. "You have any idea who that leader should be?"

Eris smiled coyly. "It should be by vote, of course. Select a couple of candidates, and we all vote for them. The one with the most support is elected. Simple."

Hercle slammed the table, causing everything on it to jump. "We need to choose the smartest person, the best thinker," he said in his deep voice.

"That's a very subjective criterion," Eris said to the large man. "I believe if we all vote, we'll make the right choice."

"In my opinion," Ogenus said softly, "I think we ought to wait..."

"For what?" Eris interrupted.

"There are only five adults here," he looked around. "We are all, I believe, capable and competent. But I think we have to bring in more voices, more options. When we have fifteen, perhaps twenty people, we'll have a better representation. We can then select a leader, perhaps someone who isn't even here right now."

"I second that idea," Ionic said.

Eris looked at them for a moment. "Okay. Maybe you're right. Maybe that's a good idea. There's no shortage of critical tasks." She nodded. "Choosing a leader can wait, for a little while at least."

*

"With your permission, we want to take your flier for a day or two," Ogenus said to Ionic.

"Who is 'we'?"

"Myself, Inanna and our boys."

"And where do you propose to take it?"

"Inanna wants to visit her old tribe, make contact."

"For what purpose?"

"Look, Ionic, I'm sure you realize that life is going to be difficult for us. We are surviving right now on the remnants of our former civilization. What happens when those remnants are gone?"

Ionic shrugged and looked thoughtful. "I suppose our bad situation will become even worse."

"Exactly. We want to contact the various mountain tribes, the hunter-gatherers. Get to know them, communicate with them. These people know how to survive on very little. You mentioned the possibility that the larger fauna will have fared poorly in this catastrophic environment. Many of them, I believe you said, may go extinct. So these tribal people will also need our help. We can at least show and teach them how to grow crops and raise domesticated animals. We can show them how to build primitive village structures out of stone rather than grass and sticks. And they can help us with the stone marker program you've proposed."

"What can they do to help with that? It takes techno-logical engineering and planning."

"It also takes muscle. You're going to need tens of thousands of stone blocks, aren't you?"

Ionic nodded. "Probably millions. We have laser cutters, but they require a lot of power. Our fuel cells won't last long. So we'll need to develop other methods for cutting and dressing stone. And," Ionic sighed, "yes, it's going to take muscle and many bodies."

"That's what we're after. An exchange of knowledge with the tribes, and perhaps their help as well."

Ionic was silent for a time. "I'd like to disagree with you, Ogenus, but I have a suspicion you are right. The tribes will have suffered, but not nearly as badly as we have suffered. Go ahead, make your contact. Just be sure you come back."

Ogenus nodded and turned away, took a few steps, then turned back. "Do you think…?"

"What?"

"Did every nation on Earth suffer the same fate as us? Were all of them destroyed?"

Ionic took a while to answer. He looked around at the devastation surrounding them and as far into the distance as he could see. "Without a visual assessment, I can't really tell. As I said earlier, I believe at least parts of some nations might have survived. Dravidia had several cities at higher elevations. Egena as well, might have come through with less than total destruction. Anadolu is fairly close to us and had cities a distance from the sea. I think the best bet, though, might be

Jiahu, in the far east. It's a very large country with many cities. I expect some of them survived. I've tried making contact by satellite phone, but haven't gotten any response so far. Too much junk in the air." The old scientist shook his head. "If none did survive, I fear we are in for a long era of night, an eon of darkness."

*

As the flier rose into a cloudy morning sky, it further revealed the extent of destruction. Tsunami waves had reached far into the foothills, destroying farms and ranches. Debris and quickly rotting bodies of humans and animals littered the muddy ground. Many trees had been uprooted. Flooding from the melting ice sheets delivered destruction from the heights. Giant boulders uprooted by meltwater had been moved down to the foothills and valleys, as water washing down had met water rising up.

Most of the tribal villages were located at much higher elevations, up near where the ice had once been. Hopefully, they had survived better than had the advanced civilizations near sea level.

Inanna observed the destruction silently. Their sons chattered among themselves and pointed out things to see. She could not have found her way back to her old home on foot. All trails and paths had been destroyed. Tribal signs and markers were gone; rivers, creeks, and waterfalls obliterated.

"It's hard to understand how angry the gods must be with us to smash us so," she muttered to Ogenus.

He glanced from piloting the flier to see tears on her cheeks. "Had it been the gods who sent the comet, they must have seen some hope in us. We're still alive. A direct hit might have torn the whole world asunder."

She managed a weak smile.

They rose higher into the mountains.

*

From out of the sky came a vehicle of the gods. It settled, with noise and rising dust, before the hut of the Chief. Tribal members stood, weapons at the ready, and watched the hatch open. Out stepped one of the Giants, followed by someone they recognized, then three children. Weapons were raised.

Out of the Chief's hut came a slender young man Inanna recognized. "Rabbit?" She said softly.

A gesture from the Chief caused weapons to lower. "Not Rabbit," said the young man emphatically, "Imkotep. I did not expect to ever see you again, She-Wolf."

"Not 'She-Wolf' but now Inanna, mate of the Giant Oannes."

"We've come to speak with the Chief," said the Giant in poor but understandable language of the tribe. This caused a stir of muted exclamations.

"You stand before the Chief," said Imkotep, "As I am known at the great conclave as 'One Who Hunts With the Wolf.'"

"Your father?" Inanna said.

Imkotep shook his head. "His ashes are with the ashes of former chiefs. Since two summers ago. Why are you here? Have you come from the gods to punish us further?"

"We, ourselves, have been punished as well," Inanna said. "The Giant cities are gone, destroyed. Of the Giants, only a few remain. We have come to you for help, and to offer help in return."

Imkotep stared at Inanna for a long moment. "You are no longer the angry, lonely child who befriended me. You have grown well."

Inanna smiled at her former friend. "And you, once my only friend, are now a Chief." Inanna encircled her sons, "and these are my boys. I'm now a mother."

"Surely you did not bring them here to rejoin this tribe? We have too little even for those of us who remain."

The woman shook her head. "As I said, we are here to see if we can help each other. We are merely survivors..."

Imkotep frowned. "We, too, felt the wrath of the gods. Many of us died or were injured. Half the village was swept away when the gods touched ice and it became water." He raised a hand toward the lowlands. "We find few prey, and we grow hungry. The only thing that has saved us is there are so few of us remaining to be fed. We fear the gods will come again and strike us down to the last man."

"Perhaps they will, in time," Inanna said. "Perhaps even worse in the future. I have seen the sea flood an entire city, washing away most of its inhabitants. I have seen fire rain from the sky. I've seen smoke erupt from the center of the Earth."

Imkotep frowned. "If the Giants can't stand before the gods and survive, what hope is there for us? We are simple people. We cannot fly." He seemed angry.

"I understand," Inanna said softly, "but perhaps together we can find a way back..."

"Our medicine man gave me this," said Ogenus, in the halting speech of the tribe. He held up a large bag, flat with a curved handle, yet bulging with contents. "Inside is knowledge for growing food, raising animals, and building in stone to withstand further upheavals. Inside are seeds, and we will show you how to grow them and how to turn the results into food."

"Messages from the gods?"

"Messages from the Giants," Inanna said firmly. She touched Imkotep's hand which held the bag. "A gift. Perhaps a future."

*

Imkotep examined the contents of the Giants' bag. He was not quite ready to negotiate an alliance with those who flew down from the sky, even if their spokesperson was a former member of his own tribe.

A war with the Giants, however, was not a viable option. With his tribe depleted, injured, hungry, and scared, a war would mean the extermination of all his people. As he thumbed through the various papers, the words meaningless, he was nevertheless heartened by their proposals. Pictures provided some encouraging information, and there were drawings on how to build structures to withstand further cataclysms. At the bottom, a clear bag of seeds. He replaced the papers.

If they told him how to grow crops and domesticate animals, the knowledge would need to be imparted to him, as a child learning from its parents. Imkotep grimaced at the thought. Yet did he have a choice?

The drawings of stone structures included in the handbag of the Giants were a different matter. Some of them intrigued him, especially those with the sloping sides, looking like huge artificial stone mountains. One, in particular, depicted such a mountain with a tiny stick figure of a human for scale.

He showed the drawing to Ogenus. "Are you saying such a mountain could be built?"

Ogenus nodded. "We would need to find a flat plain, near a large river. Our airships," he indicated the flier, "are not large enough to transport the size of stone blocks needed for this construction. We would float them down a river on barges. Tens of thousands upon thousands of stone blocks."

Imkotep looked from Ogenus to Inanna. The man spoke, and his woman translated the words into tribal tongue. "Once built," Ogenus said, "such a structure would be impervious to upheavals and earthquakes. It would stand for thousands of years. Its placement would echo our civilization down through the ages."

Imkotep looked bleak. "Your civilization, Giant, not ours. We have little to do with ages, or civilizations."

"Perhaps," Ogenus replied. "Yet maybe the gods are looking for new civilizations, built by new giants."

Imkotep was unconvinced, yet his eyes kept returning to the drawings. "How would one cut and prepare so many stone blocks?"

"We have tools, powerful enough to cut through stone, as long as they have power and continue to work. After that, we have other, more primitive methods that will take time and many hands, but it can be done."

"I would be interested in building such a structure." He swept a hand to encompass the village. "I will meet with my elders and see if my people will agree to do this. I assume this means we will need to move from our home to another place? We have done so before, but not beyond these mountains. This will need much talk and thought. If we decide to do this, some of the other tribes may choose to join us, once I have spoken to them. We will consider this on one condition."

Ogenus frowned. "And that is?"

"You must assure that we have sufficient food and supplies. Once we have cast our lot with you, we will no longer be hunters. We will grow your seeds and make the land feed us, raise rather than hunt animals." He held up the bag, "Just as this promises. We hold you to that promise. You will show us how to do these things."

Ogenus nodded. "I will agree to that, so long as it is in our power to do so. We can move your people over the sea to a new home. The nation of Esna occupied the land upon which we will build the mountain. They have been impacted by the wrath as well. If your tribes join with them, you can, together, accomplish many new wonders. Our medicine man needs to know if the Earth has been altered by the impacts that caused all of the destruction. If it has, it could mean a slow, evil death for us all. Building the mountain as he designs it will aid in gathering that knowledge."

Imkotep stared at Ogenus for a long moment. Then he nodded. "I will call for a conclave of tribes. Some, I am sure, will join with us. Others will not."

"I fear," Ogenus said softly, translated equally softly by Inanna, "that those who do not will soon perish. We will, of course, try to help them."

"If they do not choose to join us," Imkotep said, "I do not believe they will accept your help either. Perhaps they will die, perhaps not. You will be surprised at the ability of my brothers to survive on land that hoards its treasures."

Imkotep was silent for a period, thinking. "Today we have eaten of your tree of knowledge, be it good or evil. Our decision may allow us to survive, or it may be a futile attempt to postpone our extinction. We will meet, then, and let the gods guide us."

Ogenus bowed his head. "We believe you will make a right and proper decision. You are wise beyond your years, Chief Imkotep."

The Chief invited the family to dinner. It was a sparse meal, but he showed interest in Inanna and her sons. Imkotep related his story to the boys. They were amazed to learn that their mother had once killed one of the large-toothed cats, and had presented the pelt to Imkotep's father. They stared at her with renewed respect and not a little awe. Imkotep explained that his wolf had left him two seasons ago, gone off to die. Before that, his wolf spirit had mated and thereafter had presented his cubs to Imkotep. These had been raised by chosen members of the tribe and were now companions of many hunters.

Imkotep's reputation as a Wolf-Walker spread far and wide. When he wore the long-tooth cat pelt at multi-tribe conclaves, his reputation was enhanced even more. Among the nearby tribes were none who would dare challenge him.

He smiled at the boys, then pointed to the wall behind them, "That is the very pelt your mother presented to the Chief. It became his source of power, and it is now my source. It was his prized possession, but he never knew from whence it came."

"As I requested," Inanna said. "It was an apology to the old Chief, and my ultimate statement of independence from this tribe. It gave power to the Chief and freed me."

At one point, Ogenus left the tent and strolled through what remained of the camp. He saw damaged huts and several places where ice melt and mud had washed away portions of the village. Mountains, now free of ice except at the very top, rose above him, bare rocks exposed to the sky. Already temperatures were dropping, the sun, when it shone, was feeble and weak. Most of the time, skies were overcast with uniform gray clouds. Once atmospheric moisture was back to normal levels, snow and ice would return to the mountains, and over the next few years, build up thicker and thicker. This warm interlude, he decided, would be brief. The coming winter was just one more thing to worry about.

He suddenly realized that more than one of the tribe's sentries were watching him with intense caution and wariness. He quickly terminated his walk and made his way back to the Chief's hut.

Several rounds of negotiations, confrontational at times, resulted in an agreement. Imkotep would lead his tribe, and any other nearby groups who wished to join them, down the mountains and set up a temporary camp at the Crecopia's base. From there, they would be transported to land between Esna and what remained of the Kingdom of Naqada in small groups by flier if possible, by boat if not. In the meantime, Ogenus promised shipments of food. He was not quite sure where that food would come from, but he knew the search was already on for a source.

*

Flying back to the flat-topped mountain, Ogenus sighed. "We have more tasks to accomplish," he said to Inanna. "Ionic's global network of stone is needed; we need to find food and a source of fresh water. We need to find refugees who survived and provide them with assistance. We need boats." He shook his head. "We need, need, need. It's almost overwhelming."

Inanna was silent for most of the flight, her attitude solemn. "This," she said, "is the world in which I have been tasked to raise my sons." She looked at her mate with a wan smile. "It is not as I had imagined."

Ogenus took her in his arms and gently stroked her hair. "Not as I would have wished it, either, my love. But we will live, and they will live. And perhaps, someday, legends will be told of our efforts."

The three boys, listening from the back seat, placed hands on their mother, the older two making comforting sounds. "We won't let you down, Mother," Iapetos said softly.

"I know you won't, my son. My sons." She turned in her seat and looked at her boys. "We will face the future together whatever it holds."

Inanna was happy her boys were close to each other. They quarreled, certainly, but their shared culture had set them apart from their Giant playmates. This had drawn them even closer together; they looked out for one another. They were intelligent and spirited, Inanna thought, growing tall and strong.

*

Upon arrival back at the Crecopia, they found a growing community of survivors. Hercle had cleared access to the top, and weary and hungry survivors began arriving singly and in small groups. Injuries and sickness were common, but food and clean water helped. While fresh water often fell from the skies and could be collected, food was another matter. It took time and effort to locate packaged foods fit to eat, or live animals that could be captured and slaughtered.

Ogenus found Eris busily organizing groups, most of which were tasked with retrieving food and medical supplies. Others were designated hunters, some on search parties looking for other survivors. Still others with specific training were working on restoring technological resources or providing medical treatment to injured survivors. Several fliers, including large passenger ships, were now parked on the Crecopia's flat top or at the bottom near its base.

"I wondered where you had gotten to," Eris told Ogenus when he reported his agreement with the tribes. "Your friend Ionic was not very forthcoming with details."

"I asked him to be discreet until we'd made contact with the tribes."

Eris almost screamed when Ogenus told her he had promised food to Imkotep and his people. Fortunately, they had recently located a cargo ship filled with processed and packaged food. It had ended up far inland from the sea, flung there by the tsunamis, but otherwise only lightly damaged. An expedition was there now, salvaging food and anything else of use.

After consulting with Eris, Ogenus sought out Ionic, who was, with Hercle, cleaning and repairing his observatory. "This will never again serve to study the stars and planets," Ionic said, tossing a cracked lens into a pile of refuge. "But I can still claim the space for other scientific endeavors." He looked up

136

at Ogenus. "How did your excursion go, my friend? I see the tribes didn't eat you."

The other sighed. "The tribe we visited had suffered almost as badly as we in terms of lost life. With temperatures dropping and the ice returning to the high mountains, Chief Imkotep agreed to relocate his tribe, and any others he could convince, to the southern continent, near Esna. We will teach them, and they will raise animals and grow crops, and begin working on your stone mountains."

"Good. We have no time to waste. My colleagues are beginning their building projects in other locations as well. If we can site the major constructions in line with each other, we will have a global network observatory. The entire planet will tell us what is happening to itself. Among all the other tasks, we need to get that completed as soon as possible."

"I agree. The tribes will be here in a couple of weeks."

"We could have sent a flier for them," Ionic said. "We have a couple of the larger passenger vehicles here now, and enough power cells to keep them going for a while. We can get them moved, organized, and over the sea, much quicker."

"Imkotep was reluctant to have his people ride in an eagle of the Giants," Ogenus said. "It's going to take him a bit of effort to convince his medicine man to allow it. When they reach the Crecopia, we will take a few up at a time, get them used to the idea."

Ionic shook his head. "If it must be that way, okay. But I still hate to waste any more time than we have to."

"I agree. This has to be our top priority."

"Unfortunately, our leader, Eris, has other ideas."

Ogenus' eyes opened wide, but he said nothing and followed Ionic through the damaged building. He picked up and discarded various bent and ruined electronics. When they were alone, he spoke softly to the scientist. "She is now the leader? When did this happen?"

"Elected in your absence. I urged her to wait, but time, as she said, is always our enemy." Ionic rubbed his eyes and swept dust off papers. He glanced at the words, then tossed them on the refuse pile. "I just can't convince her that my priorities should take precedence."

"I don't necessarily disagree with her, Ionic. We need to eat, we need to seek out other survivors, treat the injured. Any technological finds will benefit you as well."

Ionic looked out over the ravaged landscape. "You're right, of course. And she is as well. But in a decade, perhaps two, we get hit again. And maybe again. I want those underground cities in stable geologic areas finished. People there can ride out the coming cataclysms in relative safety. We can't build those overnight. Everything I'm proposing takes time, even if we can secure enough power equipment to make it work, and get crews to the locations. We also have to convince the remaining citizens of the other nations to follow their scientists and engineers and take similar actions. That won't be easy."

"How many underground cities are you talking about?"

"At least half-dozen, in places that are located above projected sea levels, if we have time to build them. I want them big enough to hold, say, 20,000 people each, plus livestock."

"Ionic, that's huge. It would take hundreds of years to build something underground like that."

Ionic sighed. "You're right, but we don't have hundreds of years. We'll use explosives, laser cutters, and drills as long as we can find power cells." Ionic's eyes brightened. "We can take the rubble that's removed from construction in Anadolu and ship it to Imkotep in Esna. He can use it as cement to help build his mountains. Even the dust and powder can be used to make permanent bonding material where precision is required."

"And how do you make sure these subterranean cities, as you call them, won't be overrun with refugees once the fireballs start falling from the sky."

Ionic thought for a moment. "Well, they'll have to identify those who are chosen ahead of time, then get them in well before the projectiles start to fall. Once that happens, anyone nearby will be desperate to get inside. They'll have to plug up the entrances. Plug them up tight with huge stones that are too big and too heavy to move from outside."

Ogenus replied gently, "That's going to leave a lot of people stranded and at the mercy of the gods. And they're mostly going to die, aren't they, Ionic?"

The scientist looked at his friend for a long moment. "Yes, they'll likely die. But those people inside will need to remain underground, possibly for several months. If the maximum population density is exceeded, everyone in there may die. We have to save what, and who, we can."

"Who is going to be in charge of building these highly unlikely underground cities?"

"My colleagues in Anadolu have made plans for several such cities. I'm going to send Hercle and a couple of our engineers there in a few weeks to confirm the locations and begin construction. You're right, it's not going to be easy," Ionic repeated.

Ogenus sighed. These days, it seemed, nothing was ever easy.

*

Stairs to the Crecopia had been erratically guarded by one or two volunteers from among those too injured for other work. They were not armed as there were few survivors around, and those who made it to the top were accepted and assigned various tasks, or treated for injuries. Ionic's food, water, and energy cells that he had secreted on the Crecopia were almost all the supplies that had been available to the growing community, until other sources were retrieved.

Local search parties were sent out to find additional food, water and anything else that might prove useful. Other than those salvaging the cargo ship, those search parties often came back empty-handed.

Two weeks after Ogenus, Inanna, and the boys returned from their tribal contact, the stair guard noticed a group of twenty or more men gathered down at the base. They started up, gaining stairs at a fast pace, moving almost at a run. As they got closer, the guard saw they wielded primitive weapons.

He rang the warning bell. As the intruders gained the top, their leader jabbed his sword into the guard and with a quick flip of his wrist flung his body over the Crecopia's edge. It happened so fast, the other guard had no time to react. He stood, unarmed, with a sword pointed at his midsection.

Eris and several other people came running up, stopping quickly when confronted by a group of large, well-armed men. None of those responding was armed.

"Who are you?" Eris asked. "What is the reason for this violence?"

The leader of the invaders stepped forward. "The reason is to take what food and supplies you have, and maybe some slaves. As for us, we are the Lacedeaemon warriors. We come from the east. We have very little time and even less patience. Pile your food and water here. Those who refuse will die."

Eris shook her head defiantly. "No." Two other Crecopia dwellers stood beside her, although they were also unarmed.

The leader of the invaders stepped forward and shouted "I am Lelex, king of the Lacedaemons. Those who disobey me die." He flung the two guards aside and grabbed Eris by her neck with one large hand. He lifted her off the ground. She struggled and gasped for air.

Ogenus arrived at a run. He had a beam weapon at his side, but the safety was on. He estimated his chances of employing the weapon, removing the safety, aiming and firing before he was disemboweled. If he moved slowly at first...

"Stop!" A loud roar emanated from the ruined observatory building. Hercle burst from the building where he had been working. By the time he confronted Lelex, Eris had reached out with both hands, grasping the arm and pulling, to little effect. She made gurgling, choking sounds.

Hercle grasped the same arm and slowly but steadily twisted until Lelex grunted and dropped the woman. "You are not welcome here," Hercle said. "You have only this one chance to leave."

"And you have very little time to decide," said Ogenus, stepping up to stand beside Hercle. He pointed his beam weapon at Lelex. His warriors moved up to stand beside their leader, weapons ready.

Fearless, Lelex roared and started toward Ogenus. From behind the crowded warriors, a black shaft silently arched up from the stairs a step below, its tip a three-pronged trident. The spear struck Lelex in the back just as Ogenus' beam caught him in the chest. The warrior king's eyes widened, and he dropped, his battle cry cut off, sword clattering to the ground. As the remainder of Lacedaemons moved to battle, a commotion below them on the stairs got their attention. Inanna, along with Imkotep and hunters of his tribe exploded onto the Cecopia and gave battle. The intruders, although better armed and trained, were surrounded and disorganized, and were easily defeated with only a few deaths and some injuries among them. They finally dropped their weapons and surrendered, expecting to be cut down to the last man.

Eris slowly regained her feet, rubbing her neck. She cleared her throat and pointed. "You, listen to me! If you ever come back here again, you will all die. Do you understand?"

One of the warriors, perhaps the new leader, bowed curtly. After relieving them of their weapons, Eris ordered the invaders off the Crecopia, and had them escorted well to the east, back where they came.

Inanna retrieved her spear, then fell into Ogenus' arms trembling. "I thought he was going to kill you."

Ogenus smiled weakly and held up his beamer, small even in his hands. "Not a chance," he said.

She stepped back and spoke to all, "Looks like we got here just in time. We saw them from a distance, arriving and climbing the stairs, but thankfully they didn't see us."

Just then, the three boys ran up, Iapetos carrying Shemash, who was crying. "Mom, are you okay?"

Inanna ruffled his hair. "I'm fine, boys."

"I'm fine, too, boys," Ogenus said, with a slight tone of petulance in his voice.

"Hercle, also, is good," said the large man, checking out various limbs and muscles.

Eris was still rubbing her neck, which had begun turning from red to purple. "It looks like we're all okay, thanks to Inanna's timely return with her people. They likely saved us all." She stopped, took a deep breath. "I need to sit down."

*

A month later, a large passenger flier settled on a dusty plateau. It landed near the location where Imkotep's tribe had set up its camp on the great southern continent. They had chosen a plateau near the mighty river. Earlier Inanna and Ogenus worked with Imkotep to prepare tribal members to move themselves and their meager belongings onto the airship. It had taken much work to convince what were superstitious hunters and gatherers that entering the ship was not cursed, nor was it an affront to the gods. Small groups had been lifted for brief excursions to accustom them to the sensation of flight.

"It is merely a machine that travels in the air," Inanna had told those who were reluctant, "just as a spear travels through the air. The air bird is launched and controlled by people like you and me, just as a spear is launched and controlled by you. The spear is a machine to help you feed and clothe your family. This flier is a machine to move you over the sea to a new and safer home."

The Chief and several of his counselors were flown to a hastily convened multi-tribal conclave. The flight experiences were then related to leaders of the other tribes. There were, of course, a few groups who wanted nothing to do with the Giants, or their flying machines. They would remain, they said, and maintain the traditional ways. It would take time to rebuild their numbers, but they would do it, and they would do it without interference. Leaders of other tribes were more daring, willing to risk the unknown for a chance to improve the lives of all their people.

Over the next several weeks, Ogenus and Ionic transported members of various tribes to the land of Esna, near the wide river that ran south to north at the edge of the mighty southern continent.

Ogenus knew little of the verdant interior of that land. He knew there were many kingdoms and primitive tribes, as well as nations equally advanced as those in the north. As a navigator on trade ships, he knew intimately the many ports and cities on the western and southern areas of this continent; however, the interior was largely unknown to him.

Ogenus, Ionic, and Inanna transported the last of many tribes in a large passenger craft. They settled the flier at a new village near the plateau where Ionic wanted Imkotep to build his premier stone structure, the artificial mountain. Imkotep had expressed a desire to build smaller structures nearby to work out his engineering and construction process. "I want my main structures to be smooth-sided, brightly polished, so that all can see the accomplishments of this primitive tribe," he told Ionic via Inanna. "If we have time, we'll add the others you asked for, each one married to a star in the night sky."

"You are the engineer," Ionic replied. "Design as you wish, but build the placement, size, and measurements as I have indicated. If you succeed, ten thousand years from now, your name shall still be known."

Imkotep smiled shyly. "Not my name, Ionic, but my son's name. His name, similar to mine, Imhotep, shall live on down through many generations. My name shall be buried by gentle waters and covered over with the flowing mud."

"But..."

"That is as I would wish it," Imkotep said. "I am a leader of my people, not a god. Those who come after will be seen as both."

"You are a wise man," Ionic said. "Your knowledge will help define our future. I'll supply you with power cells and laser cutting saws, drills, and other machines. There are good sources of stone up the river. I'll go with you and train your people how to use our tools. We also need to build boats. The Esna Nation has a number of them, but we will need more." Ionic had gathered a few former teachers and farmers who were now impressed to teach Imkotep's people how to farm and raise domesticated animals. Inanna spent a lot of her time translating, an unwelcome task that took her away from her boys and Ogenus.

*

Imkotep and his tribe members met with leaders from the Esna nation. The Esna peoples had not quite reached the technological levels of many other nations, but they were far from a primitive hunter-gatherer culture. There were artists and architects there who had built their own impressive

144

buildings in stone and stone-like concrete, in just the style Ionic envisioned.

One was a giant representation of a jackal's head atop a lion's body resting, gazing at the rising sun. Ionic looked up at it and smiled. "This is what I'm talking about," he said to Imkotep. "No amount of upheavals can move those eyes from their task of pointing to the rising sun each equinox. If Earth's orbit were to shift, this monument," he patted the stone side of the jackal, "would tell us. The ones we are going to build will give us equally important knowledge."

The fact that there were already large structures here was one reason Ionic had chosen these people and this location for an alliance. Imkotep had a good imagination, but he needed to see the scale of Ionic's plans. While the meetings were constructive, there were tensions. Ionic worked hard to facilitate a harmonious relationship between the two cultures. He spent time logically (if not accurately) merging various religious and spiritual beliefs of the two groups. It turned out to be a bit easier than he had expected. The arrival of these strange newcomers via air transport convinced both groups that the gods were behind the merger.

Eventually, Ionic also traveled over the Great Sea to the far western continent. Among his goals at Mokaya Land was one a bit more personal. Earlier he had not been free to see in person the intact and non-fossilized feathered dinosaur that had been discovered by paleontologists from Mokaya Land. Scientists of that nation housed the specimen in a climate-and-temperature controlled glass case in the national museum. Ionic learned that the catastrophe had caused much of the museum building to collapse. The portion that housed their feathered serpent had sunk into floodwaters, and there it remained.

Along with his nephew Hercle, Ionic assisted with the retrieval of the prehistoric exhibit and its return to dry land. It had been visually damaged during its time in the water, although the protective case had maintained its integrity. Temperatures above freezing had caused some deterioration, but the animal was still intact, and to Ionic's eyes, a unique and magnificent find.

Ionic stroked his newly-grown beard and stared at the restored exhibit. "Incredible," he exclaimed. The Mokaya Land scientists were appreciative of his assistance. In fact, they began calling him the father of the feathered serpent, named Gukumatz.

While similarly devastated, nations of the western continent had maintained some of their technology. Ionic shared with scientists and engineers of even more nations his plans to build monuments of stone. He asked each nation to consider joining others in building the stone mountains that would withstand anything but a direct hit, and would last for centuries, if not eons. These nations, too, had some remaining technology that could be used to cut and dress the many giant stones needed. He provided each nation with his pouches containing plans and details along with measurements and alignments needed to achieve his goals. Also included were methods for stone building after scarce fuel cells had been exhausted. Construction needed to be completed within a decade, Ionic said. After that, further impacts could happen at any time.

Ionic's aerial assessment of the western continent was almost as bleak as that of his own land. Everywhere he flew, refugees were searching for food and shelter. In several locations, small villages were under construction, attesting to minimally organized groups. He hoped those groups would expand and grow. What humanity needed now, more than ever, was a period of stability.

It was a strange world, Ionic found. Some nations maintained a fairly high level of technology while others had lost nearly everything. Some sought to increase their territory and influence, while others were content to care for their current citizens. He later realized that trend should have been a warning.

Two months after Ionic's return to the Cecropia, Eris urgently called Ionic and Ogenus into a private conference. Her face was ashen. "I just learned that war has broken out in several areas."

"What?" both men shouted simultaneously.

"War? What do you mean by war? How can there be a war? And who's involved?" Ogenus asked.

She shook her head. "Not one war, but a series of conflicts, executed by those who managed to maintain some tactical technology. So far as I have been able to determine, Dravidia, Jiahu, and to a limited extent, Caral-Supe and a few others are involved."

Ogenus took a deep breath. "How bad is it?"

Eris took a moment to reply, gazing steadily at the two men. "Before we lost communication, it was confirmed that conflicts were nuclear between Dravidia and Jiahu. Air raids between them all. Dravidia has used laser beam weapons as well. I'm afraid, Ionic, some of the preliminary construction you have commissioned might have been destroyed or partially damaged."

"Gods preserve us!" Ionic shouted. "Wasn't the comet strike enough? Weren't the tsunamis enough? Wasn't the return of the ice enough?"

Ogenus rested a hand on his friend's shoulder. "It won't last long. It can't. There aren't enough military assets still remaining to allow for a long war. When it's over, we'll assess the damage and get back to work."

Ionic jerked away. "The fools used *nuclear weapons?* Are they trying to turn Earth into one giant desert? We work to the bone just to feed ourselves, we search the rubble for working pieces of our technology. And for what? So that these fools can blow themselves up?"

"We have work to do," Eris said quietly. "Let's focus on our own survival, shall we?"

"There isn't enough time," Ionic said hotly. "We're running out of *time*."

"We have all the time there is," Ogenus said. "But I agree with you. It's a waste, such a stupid waste. Perhaps the gods were right. Perhaps we are not competent to inhabit this planet."

The incongruity of that statement caused Ionic to pause and take a deep breath. "Forgive me, my friend. I'm an old man, and my patience is dying faster than I am."

Ogenus chuckled, then frowned. "They called us Giants. But we are not Giants; we are only foolish humans," he said.

According to reports that were eventually received from a few remaining communication sources, a Dravidian city was hit with one bomb in the interior of the country. A near miss struck Jaihu's far north with little damage, and several bombs detonated on the northwestern area of the great southern continent, effectively destroying several smaller nations and causing survivors to migrate south or east toward Esna. More bombs were dropped on the far western continent, destroying cities and farmland. As a result, no nation could claim victory. For most, the gain in territory was minimal. The damage rendered most remaining technology useless. Areas that had heretofore been lush and productive were rendered uninhabitable deserts.

Reports from survivors of the nearest nation, Dravidia, described vast destruction caused by a nuclear detonation and air wars with lasers and missiles. Descriptions of inhabitants of affected cities suffering radiation sickness appalled both men.

"How will the surviving primitive cultures view this war a thousand years from now?" Ionic speculated. "Will they see it as a war between gods, rather than the last gasp of stupid, foolish men?"

Ogenus and Ionic stood at the edge of the Crecopia and looked out over land and sea that had so recently been a mighty nation. Neither could imagine things getting worse, and both were afraid that they might.

*

She-Wolf crouched behind a fallen log, silent as the night, watching and waiting. A deer entered a small clearing near her hiding place. She held her breath as the animal moved closer, foraging on grass and bushes. She-Wolf stood and let herself be seen. The deer's head jerked up; its eyes locked on the woman's. Then it jumped and sped back across the meadow. As the deer approached trees and safety, two spears arched up from either side, following the fleeing animal. Both spears struck it, one on each side, and the deer fell, bleating in pain, kicking slightly, then died. Iapetos and Hammurabi ran from their hiding place and met their mother. They looked down at the deer.

"Well done, my sons. Now, sadly, you are hunters."

"I don't like killing animals," Hammurabi said softly. "They're too beautiful to kill."

"But we have to eat," Iapetos said, placing a hand on his little brother's shoulder.

"Yes," said Inanna, "and in order to eat we have to carry our food back to the Crecopia. Food for another few days."

Inanna and her two oldest boys then hunted every couple of days. Game was scarce and skittish, but the boys learned fast, having watched their mother hunt and make kills. Soon they were hunting on their own, providing most of the fresh food for the Crecopian survivors.

As they hunted and learned from their mother, their skills grew. Inanna didn't like killing animals either. Most "civilized" people didn't. But those same people didn't mind eating them, especially when hunger gnawed at their insides, and their children cried for food.

*

"I want the comet and its aftermath carved into rocks and the global stone structures," Ionic said.

"But why? It adds to the work that must be done," Ogenus protested.

"Quite so," Ionic replied. "But I'm determined to leave our message down through time. This," he swept his hand across the horizon, where tall structures once stood, now mere sticks pointing to the sky, "was once our civilization. Now it's gone. Our story, our fate, must be remembered." He shook his head, "It doesn't matter if the story is told as myth or legend. Our far distant ancestors must remember us in one way or another. We were here. We accomplished much. We weren't stupid. The gods aren't finished with us yet." Ionic looked at his friend. "We have a long way to go. We may not survive; the odds are against us. Our legacy may very well be buried in a day and a night; It will be as if we never existed. That is, unless we take measures to leave our story in places where it cannot be erased by either cataclysm or time. Our stone structures must have a dual purpose: to exist as a record of our time here on Earth, and to measure possible changes to our planet. We cannot favor one over the other. We must do both. You understand?"

Ogenus thought for a moment, then nodded. "But how do you carve a comet into stone?"

Ionic smiled. "I've thought about that. I think I might have found a way, a symbol that will, hopefully, be familiar to anyone who has actually seen a comet."

*

Across the globe, survivors of various nations worked on the grand plan Ionic and his colleagues from many nations had set into motion. Artificial mountains were slowly erected, each aligned to various types of celestial bodies, to Earth's magnetic poles, or both. Other stone structures were matched with Earth's movement around the sun. Still others, entire cities, were built underground to protect vulnerable populations and their livestock, food and water supplies, in preparation for the comet's eventual return. Work progressed despite periodic flare- ups of local wars and battles. Nuclear weapons and those dependent on higher technology had been spent in the earlier war, and battles became personal, with smaller weapons and hand-to-hand combat. Humans, devastated by nature, strove almost successfully, to drive themselves into oblivion.

Once power cells were exhausted, Ionic developed and taught other methods for working with giant stones, including precisely-directed explosives and various types of acids, and the creation and use of stone cement. Steel blades were used until the steel wore out. Some of the methods worked better than others, but the work continued.

Many of the tribal cultures flourished. Hunter-Gatherer groups expanded their populations as they were more suited to survive in the new post-catastrophic world. Legends began as oral tales, of gleaming cities and gods who came from the skies, civilizations that sank beneath the seas, of a golden age now gone. Primitive civilizations grew up as a result of contact with survivors of the old advanced civilizations. These survivors taught agriculture and farming, law and mathematics, hygiene and medicine, and dozens of other things former hunter-gatherers needed to know.

Eventually, new cities rose, primitive cities made of stone and wood, mud and adobe. Ogenus and Inanna and their three sons joined a growing village near the Crecopia's base. New structures were built where once stood an earlier, more advanced village. That village had been destroyed during the comet fall, its remnants washed away during the flooding and tsunamis that followed.

Ogenus and his boys found plenty of building material strewn about. They used stone, wood, and sun-cured mud bricks and ended up with a large home with a central courtyard. While the new home did not have the luxuries or technology of his Kursatta apartment, Ogenus and his family were happy and fulfilled. They helped construct the village's streets and parks, temples, and schools.

Slowly, the Earth and its surviving inhabitants returned to normal. A new normal, to be sure, but life settled down. Farms and domesticated animals solved much of the hunger crisis, but there remained areas where people struggled to feed themselves. The globe-spanning wars were over. Sea levels receded somewhat as ice returned to higher elevations.

The new civilizations tended to avoid ruins of the old cities, seeing them as cursed by the gods. They built new, much smaller and more primitive cities in new locations. What technology remained became suspect. Many came to believe that the cause of the cataclysm derived not from the comet itself, but from the electronics, computers, and observational equipment that tracked the celestial objects. Thus, technology, what little there was left of it, came to rest in the hands of scientists, who hid themselves and their marvelous, magical machines away in secret and protected locations. Eventually, most of those advanced machines wore out, or lacked fuel cells to keep them going.

Land near the Crecopia was cultivated, pens built for domesticated animals. Slowly, former city dwellers learned to farm and tend to animals. They learned to butcher livestock and turn wheat into bread. At higher elevations, small hunter-gatherer groups continued on much as before.

Earth's human population had been depleted but rebounded somewhat in the coming years. Global trade ceased, but new regional trade routes formed. Ships that plied oceans were replaced by smaller boats that kept much closer to sea coasts. Languages began to diversify as nations with similar tongues no longer interacted. Over time, they found it increasingly difficult to understand each other. Written languages, when they survived at all, faced similar diversification. Even similar written words gained differing pronunciations and modified meanings. In many places, however, writing fell out of use. Paper was quickly used up and computer screens no longer worked. There was insufficient time or skill to make adequate substitutes. Children learned how to kill prey, grow crops, and tend animals, so no time remained to learn reading and writing.

New nations arose, kings crowned, slaves taken, territory increased or shrunk, alliances created and shifted. A new generation grew up not knowing giant cities and technology. Tales of their parents and grandparents were regarded as fantasy tales or legends of the gods.

Then, one day, the comet returned, as Ionic had predicted, reappearing in the sky almost a dozen years after the last approach, as an ominous and glorious speck that slowly grew in size.

The now quite elderly scientist had lost credibility when the comet failed to return as early as he had originally predicted. Ionic maintained that his calculations had been flawed due to insufficient measurements, but he insisted that the comet would return. And its effects would be just as devastating as its original appearance, if not worse.

"From what I can tell, this time we may have more water hits than land," Ionic told Ogenus and Eris. His estimate for the day and time of the impact was not exact. Preparations were made, and those nations who had built underground facilities began planning the moving of citizens, supplies, and livestock into them, after which they would be sealed from the inside. Others were urged to find high ground, build boats and put out to sea, or, at the very least move inland, as far from the seas as possible, despite the dangers from melting ice. Many gazed at the speck in the sky and dismissed it, proclaiming it simply a new star.

"I'm afraid," Ionic said, "that this time, as the Earth's temperature rises, water from melting ice caps will be met with tsunamis even worse than last time, which were rather localized then. We happened to get hit here, but flooding largely spared Esna, Dravidia, and Anadolu. This time we might be facing a global flood."

Ogenus gazed at the sky, and something inside him broke, something that had been bottled up for many years. He fell to his knees and cried out in frustration and fear. "We had *everything!* We had the world in our grasp. And in a moment, it was all taken from us!" He looked up at Inanna, tears in his eyes. "And the gods continue to punish us! Why? *Why?*"

Inanna knelt in front of him and gently held his head. "The gods punish arrogance. But they cannot punish love. All they can do is be jealous." She kissed his forehead. "So let us continue to live and use our love to punish the gods."

They sat quietly for a very long time, holding each other.

Later, Ogenus presented his plans. He and Inanna and their sons would face the comet's effects, not in high mountains, but on the open sea. "I'm going to build us a boat. No engine, no sails, no technology, just something that will stay afloat. We'll put our supplies and livestock aboard. Where and when it comes to rest, we'll make our new home."

"And if it sinks?" Inanna said dryly.

"Then we die together and the Earth will have to abide without us."

"And our sons will die as well," Inanna pointed out gently.

Ogenus gazed at his mate. "Losing you and our sons would be my greatest regret," he said softly, "but I know the sea, and I think I can build a boat that will keep us alive."

He gazed at his family, looking at each individual boy, now teenagers, in the eyes. "If we make it, we will be no better off than those who lived where your mother was born," he said. "But we have the advantage," he said as he looked at Inanna, "because she did live that life. She-Wolf will lead us. She will teach us how to survive on barren land."

"What kind of a boat, Father?" Hammarabi asked.

"I've discussed this with Imkotep and Ionic. We all think a boat that's round in shape has the best chance for survival on unpredictable ocean currents. We don't need to steer it; navigation will be impossible. This is a very poor design for getting from one place to another. It's a much better design for the type of sailing we plan to do." He spread his design drawings out for the boys to examine.

"I'm scared," said Shemash, a tall and thin sixteen-year-old.

Ogenus looked at his youngest son. "You and me both," he said.

They set to work. First, they needed to gather sufficient building materials. Ogenus sketched plans for the individual sections. He designed his boat to be large enough for the family and their animals, which now grazed a few hundred yards from the Crecopia's base. It needed to be large enough to withstand massive waves and rough seas. Its navigation ability would be minimal.

Ogenus met with Ionic to learn more. His friend had grown old, yet still exuded a spirit of youth and energy. "What can we expect? How long will these effects last?"

"There's no way to tell, Ogenus. It all depends on how many comet fragments are out there, and how many are pulled into Earth's atmosphere. It also depends on where the fragments hit. Last time we suffered mostly land hits, in the north, on ice. This time, based on observations made before all this happened, I believe we will see a majority of ocean hits. After all, oceans cover most of the planet. There will be more rocks this time. Some of those that were pulled off the comet last time weren't captured by Earth's gravity field. But they might this time. And as the comet approaches, more material will be ejected, and some of that will impact Earth as well."

"And after? If we survive the wrath of the gods, how much will the sea levels recede after the flooding?"

Ionic shook his head, "Only the gods know for sure. I believe this will kick us into a permanent warmer climate. As we discussed years ago, the solar minimum is transitioning to a maximum, which is already causing some warming. The ice will rebuild on the poles and at higher elevations, but I don't believe our oceans will return to the lower levels any time soon, if at all. When sea levels stabilize, they will remain at that level for the foreseeable future."

"So," Ogenus said, "we can begin rebuilding our cities and villages near the sea..."

"But not too near," Ionic said, holding up a warning hand. "If there are more comet fragments in the same orbit, we could get hit again maybe a year after this one, even if the comet leaves us alone. The fewer fragments remaining, the less impact they will have. But we need to be prepared."

"What about your global stone alignment project?"

Ionic shrugged. "Just about every nation on Earth has built or is working on some form of giant structure, some very highly engineered and designed, others more primitive. Some of them won't survive, of course, but I believe most of them will, and hopefully there will be sufficient knowledge among the survivors to read and understand results of the measurements. When this is all over, we'll just have to go back to work. This is information we need to know, and we don't have technology any more to know it any other way."

"So where are you going when the comet hits?"

"Going?" Ionic replied. "I'm not going anywhere. The Crecopia has been my home for many years now. It withstood the last comet fall; I believe it will withstand this one as well."

"How can you be sure?" Ogenus asked, looking around at the busy encampment.

Ionic shrugged, "How can one be sure of anything, my friend? All we can do is plan, prepare, and trust in the gods."

"You mean those same gods who seem to be trying to crush and drown and pound us into the Earth?"

"Yes, those gods. Those very gods."

"You recall we almost perished on the top of this thing the last time," Ogenus said.

"What else can one do? Some of your fellow villagers will join us, others plan a relocation to higher elevations. Many don't believe me and plan to stay right where they are." Ionic shook his head. "You go ahead, build your boat. We'll prepare here as best we can. We'll be fine."

"Come with us," Ogenus urged. "There's going to be plenty of room."

Ionic smiled sadly. "I'm subject to seasickness. I'd never make it. Were I 20 years younger...but I'm not. Now go. As usual, we're running out of time."

*

Ogenus looked up into the night sky. Somewhere out there, a comet was hurtling toward Earth, and Earth was hurtling toward a cloud of fragments. He wondered if he and his family would survive. He wondered if Earth itself would survive.

He moved his family near their original home in Kursatta, using a flier to navigate over the wetlands where once dry land reigned. The former island volcano continued to smoke and rumble. Lava flow had built a large mountain at its center.

An hour later, they settled near their old home. Where once-mighty structures stood, now only a few pillars pointed to the sky. They made camp at the sea's edge and lived in tents. Fresh water was scarce as the river that originally emptied into the sea had been obliterated by tsunamis and sea-level rise. Water from the mountains had carved a new riverbed several miles north of their camp.

This required frequent trips by his sons and mate to secure and return with water. After attempting to begin construction on his boat, Ogenus eventually abandoned the plan as the building materials he needed were also inconveniently distant.

He moved his family further east, near a smaller river. He looked for a smooth area upon which to work, but the land was uneven. The family eventually settled at the mouth of the river and took their chances that an unusually high tide or an early impact wave might ruin all their work, or send the boat out to sea before they were aboard.

Earth's climate had seemed to return to normal, with warm days, cool nights, and infrequent storms. But that could change in an instant.

Fortunately, there was a forest of young trees along the river. Most were small and flexible, ideal for constructing his round boat. They found a partially damaged warehouse nearby filled with a large supply of bitumen imported from the southern continent. This material would be used to seal the boat and make it water tight. Before power cells became scarce, Ogenus had flown to Esna and consulted with Imkotep, who had become not only a leader, but a gifted engineer. They went over plans for building the ship. Imkotep was skeptical, but exceedingly helpful. He made several suggestions for improvements. "Your chances for survival are small," he said, handing over the sketches he had made.

"I'm aware of that," Ogenus said, "but I lived much of my life on the sea. I believe it is calling me to return."

"May the gods bless your voyage," Imkotep said softly.

"As with you," Ogenus said. "Before the stones fall from the sky, I would recommend you move your people far to the south, along the great river, but not too near it."

"And of our work here?"

"You have built well. When you return, the foundation of your mountains will still be here, even if the sea completely inundates the area temporarily. You can then resume your work, just as the rest of us will."

Imkotep looked at the underlying beginning of his stone mountain, rising jaggedly into the sky. "It will be here," he said, looking at Ogenus. "We will finish our work when the gods stop shaking our world."

Ogenus ushered Inanna and his boys into the flier, and they returned to the Crecopia where Eris flew them back to their camp at the edge of the sea. There, the skeletal frame of their boat awaited them.

His plans called for a round ship with living quarters for his family at the top, and stalls below for their domesticated animals. Those animals were their share of ones penned up near the Crecopia. Ham and Shemash had flown back with Eris to herd the animals overland to their new, temporary pens.

Ogenus, Inanna and Iapetos spent weeks gathering materials for the ship they would build. They watched the sky often as the comet's glow and the tiny invisible companions that traveled with it began to grow larger.

Construction of the ship went slower than Ogenus anticipated. They built the bottom first, working halfway up its round sides before starting to insert the six-level flooring. The top level would house the humans and some supplies. There would be a bridge and several cabins that would, in the event of their survival, be used for housing when they reached dry land. The next three levels were constructed to house the livestock and more of their supplies. The fifth level would contain items to assist in rebuilding their lives where ever it might be that they came to rest. The bottom level was ballast with hand pumps to purge water that might enter the ship as the result of waves, leaks, or rain.

Bitumen was used to seal the thin branches, layer after layer of the small trees woven together into a massive thick hull.

The boat rested at the sea's edge. Before construction began on the ship, Ogenus and his sons had laid down log rollers, from the beach down into low-tide sea levels. Their ship was then built upon these rollers. Two large vertical support logs secured the vessel and would be knocked away when they were ready to launch. As the days passed and thousands upon thousands of young branches were woven together and sealed, it began to resemble a craft of some sort.

All the while, the light in the sky grew and began to show a tail. As the ship neared completion, Ionic and Eris paid a surprise visit, using a flier powered by a stash of recently unearthed fuel cells.

The whole family stopped work to greet their visitors. Inanna took Eris up the ladder and inside the ship to show her the work that had been done.

Once they were alone, Eris chose to be frank. "You don't have to go in this, this death trap, Inanna. You and your boys are welcome to stay with us on top of the rock."

"What are you saying?"

"Let Ogenus float in his boat by himself, if he insists. It's not likely he will survive. Just look at this thing," Eris glanced at the walls curving up around them. "Only a fool would trust this on the open sea."

"I'm sorry," said Inanna. "Ogenus is my mate. My place is with him. That is final."

"But...okay, okay," Eris said soothingly. "It had to be said. Please consider leaving your sons with us. At least they deserve a chance to survive."

Inanna sighed. "I know you mean well, Eris. But our family stays together. You may not have much faith in Ogenus, but my trust in him will last until this ship sinks into the sea or we come to rest on land, alive and safe."

Eris laid a hand on Inanna's shoulder. "I thought that would be your decision. You realize that even if you do survive, you will probably be a long way from here? You, Inanna, have almost single-handedly, saved everyone on the Crecopia and those living nearby. We owe you for that."

Inanna smiled. "We only did what we had to do."

Eris didn't smile. "Without you, all of us would most likely be dead by now. When this comet incident is over, you would be even more valuable to us. Yet we don't even know if we'll ever see you again," she looked around, "even if this silly thing doesn't sink."

Inanna smiled and shook her head. "You'll always be in our memories. And, maybe, life won't be as bad as we fear."

"Ionic expects to die," Eris said bluntly. She smiled, which turned into a sob. "And I do, too."

*

"How are you coming along?" Ionic said to Ogenus, leaning on his wooden cane. Walking was more difficult for him now.

"We're almost finished," Ogenus said. "We could launch any time now, but I'd kill for another couple of months to prepare and check our sealant." Ogenus looked out over calm waters. "It would have been nice to do a trial run. We have all our eggs," he said, looking up at the round side of his ship, "and chickens in this one basket. It seems almost criminal not to test it."

Ionic shook his head. "No time, my friend. Death and destruction are upon us, once again. By my calculations, which at this point are nothing more than somewhat educated guesses, comet fragments will begin entering Earth's atmosphere within two or three weeks. After that..." he shrugged and his voice trailed off.

"I know," Ogenus said. "Are you prepared?"

"As best we could. We're going to move everyone we can convince, and most of the animals, to the top of the Crecopia. We've fortified our new buildings. We have stored supplies. That's the best we can do."

"How about other areas? Other nations?"

Ionic shrugged. "We've sent messages. We used the last of our power cells to deliver warnings, in person where necessary. I've heard that you aren't the only one planning to brave the comet in a boat. There are probably dozens of others with the same hair-brained idea. We've urged people to move to higher ground. Or for those who can, to move into the underground survival areas they've been building. Almost all of them are at elevations above projected sea levels. The area where we're standing will probably be inundated at first, then become an island again. This time it will likely be permanent. The warming will maintain and perhaps even rise. The long ice age ends for good this time."

Ogenus shook his head. "We saw so many changes after the last comet fall, I can't imagine what will happen this time."

Ionic looked into the distance, where the stark remnants and skeletons of Kursatta still stood. "I'm afraid the sea will grind our former cities into rubble. It will be as if they never existed. Our technology is all but gone. Our land will be under water. Earth's orbit may be altered. I don't know." He paused, "I just don't know."

Ogenus put a hand on his friend's shoulder. "But we will survive, you and I. And we'll build again. Our cities will rise out of ruins and be great again."

"I wish I could be as optimistic. The infrastructure that built our cities no longer exists. What we will build for the benefit of coming generations, those few who survive, will look nothing like what was. We'll build from wood and stone, mud and sticks. When it gets dark, fire will be our only light. Once we recover, we'll farm, of course, and raise animals. We'll work our way up to forging steel once again, someday, but who knows how long it will take? We'll be able to work with bronze in a short time. Iron will take longer, maybe copper next, then, eventually, steel." Ionic looked sad.

"Sure it's going to be hard work," Ogenus said, "but we can do it. We did it before. Our peoples lived through thousands of years developing and refining and inventing."

"Yes, of course. But do you know the impetus for most of that advancement?"

"Scientific curiosity? Social necessity?"

Ionic snorted and barked a laugh. "If only it were that simple." He looked skyward, as if he could see through the marine layer, and above it the blue sky of day, at the rushing comet. "I'm afraid the Mother of invention is not curiosity, nor necessity, but war. Build a better weapon, conquer more land. Destroy your enemies, take more slaves." He shook his head. "I fear for the world in which your sons and their mates and their children will grow up. Endless ages of war and strife, pushing us toward more and better means of killing each other. Our ancestors, as did our forebearers, will write their history in wars and battles, in death and destruction, in rivers of blood. Earth, and the universe, angered by this will chime in with periodic comet falls. We made it all the way to atomic weapons, and look what we did with them." The old man shook his head, wiped his eyes. "Forgive me, my friend. I grow old and in doing so, become soft and weak and pessimistic. We must go now. So much still left to do before time once again becomes our mortal enemy."

Ogenus, Inanna and the boys saw Ionic and Eris to their flier, and watched as the machine, one of the remaining few, lifted off, gained altitude, and sailed north, eventually disappearing in the distance.

The five watched, each deep in thought. "Back to work," Inanna said, urging her family to the giant ocean ship that would be their fate, one way or another.

Supplies for various species of animals were loaded, last-minute work finished, most of the food and water stored. Ogenus racked his brain to make sure they weren't forgetting something essential. If they didn't take it with them, they'd have to make it later using the most primitive of methods, or do without.

As the days passed and time for departure approached, Inanna asked Ogenus for a private conference, away from the boys. When she told him why, his eyes widened and he looked at his sons in a way he had not done before. He had a tendency to see them as children still, when actually they were young men grown tall, their voices deep, except for Shemash who was almost at that point. This realization startled Ogenus.

"There is a small village a couple of miles to the east," Inanna said softly. "It's a poor village, not much there. But still, we should go to visit. Warn them, if nothing else."

Ogenus thought for a moment, then nodded. "Sons!" he called, "Come with us. We're going to take a short hike."

"What for, Dad?" Iapetos asked. "We've got more loading to do."

"Just come along. We'll finish loading later. We need to do this now."

"Shouldn't we leave one of us here to guard the ship?" Hammurabi asked, running up.

Ogenus laughed. "Everyone thinks we're fools for building it; who's going to steal it?"

"Do what?" Shemash asked, joining the group.

"You'll find out," Inanna said, a small smile on her face masking the worry she felt.

They hiked for several hours, carrying packs of food, water, and supplies just in case their task took longer than expected. There was another reason as well.

They were not warmly welcomed at the primitive village, but their gifts of food and water dampened the suspicion. Some of these people, who had once lived in great cities, had once been rich beyond measure. Now they had virtually nothing and were barely producing enough food to feed themselves. Those still alive had learned to get along in harsh conditions, but even so their lives were hard and dangerous. The oldest members sat around in small groups, bewildered and defeated. The adults and older children busied themselves with various and urgent tasks of daily life. There seemed to be very few babies or small children.

Their buildings were primitive, made of dried mud and stones. Homes were little more than square boxes with thatched roofs. Those more talented incorporated small windows. Wood was scarce and used for cooking fires and warmth, so doors were made from animal skins or thatched grass. The older adults had grown up in a world where plentiful water was heated or chilled as necessary by electricity and machines. Their children were thankful for enough water to drink. Food? Sometimes, but often not enough.

Ogenus sought out the leaders. "We're going to be hit by the comet again," he said. "We expect flooding, possibly on a massive scale. You should move your people to higher ground, high into the hills if possible."

One of the women shook her head. "Our old people could never make such a journey. And we don't have enough supplies to sustain us. And besides, this is our home now."

Very softly, Ogenus said, "You may need to abandon your elderly if any of you are to survive." He held up his hands as her face clouded in anger. "I agree, it is a horrible, terrible, unthinkable choice. But you must choose, save the able-bodied and your children, or risk everyone." They looked at each other for a long moment, but no further words passed between them. Her eyes no longer looked angry, just defeated.

"I can't choose for you," Ogenus said, breaking an uncomfortable silence. "You must do that yourselves. However, I might have a solution to your supply problem." He continued speaking for several minutes, quietly explaining his plan, leading up to Inanna's goal which, when he dropped that bomb, led to more shouting and emphatic gestures.

Ogenus withstood the onslaught silently. Finally, the leaders ceased objecting and stood silently, gazing at each other, knowing the answer they had to reach but not wanting to admit it.

"I understand your position," Ogenus said. "I'm offering you a choice that is only slightly less repulsive than what your own choices will soon be. I can't fault you, whatever you choose to do. You are faced with an impossible situation."

The village chieftain, a woman named Samantara, pulled Ogenus aside and spoke with thinly veiled hate. "And if you're wrong about the comet?"

Ogenus didn't answer. He simply turned around and looked into the afternoon sky. There, the comet and its tail blazed brightly. They could almost see it hurtling toward Earth.

Samantara dropped her head in her hands and sobbed. After a few moments, she wiped her eyes, then moved off to confer with the other leaders of her village. That discussion also often grew heated, and more than one of them turned and glared at Ogenus and his family. He glanced over his shoulder at his mate and his sons. Iapetos held Inanna's spear at rest, and the boys stood near their mother, ready to protect her if necessary. They still could not fathom what all the shouting was about, and neither parent had told them anything.

One of the male leaders confronted Ogenus. "You're the fool who thinks he can survive by building a stupid boat."

"I am," Ogenus said.

"Because you think there's going to be a flood?"

Ogenus nodded, "I do."

"Well, I don't think there's going to be any flood. I think you're a fool."

Ogenus smiled slightly. "You may be right. Fool though I may be, we must do what we think is right."

The other looked at the three boys. "You'll never get a child of mine on that crazy looking thing. I've seen it from a distance a couple of times. It will never float."

"I think it will, but again, you may be right."

Inanna watched the drama with apprehension. She didn't expect violence, but these were desperate people. Ogenus' warnings and demands did not help the matter.

Samantara rejoined them and broke up the confrontation. She pulled Ogenus aside and spoke to him quietly. He nodded and walked over to his family. "Now we wait," he said as he approached.

"Why?" Iapetos said.

"I'm hungry," said Shemash.

"We need to get back to the boat," Hammurabi muttered. "The comet is getting too close. We need to go."

Ogenus placed a hand on his middle son's shoulder. "You're right. But be a little patient. We'll be leaving soon. And except for loading the animals, we've done almost everything we can do to get ready."

The wait was considerably longer than "soon." In fact, Iapetos began to wonder if they would spend the night in this hostile environment. They had brought their own food, but not enough for an extended stay.

As the sun dipped below sea level, torches and fires were lit, but Ogenus and his family were not invited to share the light and warmth. And still they waited. Finally, out of the darkness, Samantara emerged. Following her were three teenage girls and their mothers. There was much weeping and protesting. Hammurabi's eyes widened as he caught a clue as to why they were there. He started to speak, but Inanna shook her head and put a finger to her lips.

Samantara shouted for quiet. "This must be done!" She looked at the three girls. "If he," she pointed to Ogenus, "is right, our chances for survival here are very small, microscopic. Even if we decide to move to higher ground, the distance is simply too far away, and there isn't enough time. You must go with them, and carry our legacy into the future. Your chances are so much greater than ours, but only if you obey the wishes of your families. They want you to go. You'll be well treated and eventually mated to those three boys."

The protests grew louder, objections stronger, and tears flowed.

Ogenus stepped forward. "I'm sorry. We must go. We're quickly running out of time."

Iapetos leaned close to Inanna and whispered, "Mother, do you seriously intend for us to mate with those girls? Are we bringing them with us?"

Inanna smiled briefly. "Son, the answer is 'yes' to both questions. Once our ship launches, we may not see other humans for many years. We'll probably be on our own. You and Hammurabi are ready for mates now, Shemash in a couple of years. This is the only way to ensure our family continues."

"But mother..." Iapetos' voice was drowned by his brothers expressing objections and asking questions. They asked far more questions than she could answer, even if she had the answers.

Ogenus stepped forward and gathered the three girls, and, almost dragging them, brought them to his family.

"Iapetos," he said softly, "this is Adante. She is a year younger than you." His voice grew tense, "She will be your mate if we survive." The two looked at each other. The girl glanced over at her mother and she shook her head violently. Her mother responded silently, but with an equally intense gesture, "Go!" her wordless reply said.

Ogenus looked at the second girl, and she stepped forward at his gesture. Her cheeks were wet with tears, but she looked at neither Hammurabi nor at her mother. "Ham," Ogenus said, "this is Zeda Nabu. Within a year, should we be alive, she will be your mate."

The third girl, the youngest, stepped forward on her own. She glared at Ogenus, then shifted her glare to Shemash. "Son, this is Nala. She will be your mate a few years from now. Until then you will consider her as you would a sister, and protect her as such."

Nala glanced at Ogenus, then at Inanna, then glared at Shemash. "I will *not* be his mate," she said forcefully. "I won't have him, ever."

"Fine," Shemash said hotly, turning red. "I wouldn't want you for a mate. You're too skinny. And you're ugly." His reply, while heated, was not entirely accurate.

Nala spit a laugh. "Well, you're spindly and stupid."

"Yeah, well..." his reply was cut off with a word from Inanna.

Each girl carried a small bundle of clothes and belongings. "Boys," Ogenus said, "carry their things for them. We need to go, now."

169

Iapetos and Hammurabi took the bundles. Shemash tried, but Nala snatched it away, determined to carry it herself. He shrugged and took charge of Inanna's spear.

Before they left, Ogenus asked his boys to leave their food and water supplies. "We have enough in the boat, and they're going to need everything they can get."

Into the dark of night, this small party of eight began their trek back to the boat. "A lot of my people think you're wrong," Nala said, "and I do too. I don't want to go on your stupid boat. I want to go *home!*"

"Your home," Inanna said softly, "will not be there soon. It will be washed away, along with any of your people who don't move quickly to higher ground."

Adante stopped. "I want to go back. If they're going to die, I want to be with them."

Inanna turned and looked at Adante. She spoke softly. "They made a horrific decision to give you a chance to live," she said. "You dishonor them if you don't do as they wish."

Nala said, "I need to be with my little sister. I don't *have* to listen to you!"

Inanna had taken her spear from Shemash. Walking in the dark over strange territory, she felt more comfortable carrying it. She stopped, confronted Nala, holding the spear upright, and loomed over the girl. "I'm sorry. I understand your urge, but it would only end in a foolish death. You've been torn away from your family, and you'll never see them again. I am your parent now. One of them." She pointed to Ogenus, "You will do what we say, when we say it. Don't make a mistake, little girl. This is not a vacation we are on; it's a fight for our lives. And if you want to fight us, you'll lose. You'll be tied up and carried aboard the ship." They stared at each other for a long moment, then Shemash took the girl's hand and pulled her away. Nala looked to see who had her hand, then jerked it back, glaring. But she walked beside him, not too close, but still…

Inanna glanced at Adante, who stood looking over her shoulder back the way they had come. The oldest of the three young women shook her head, then turned and joined the others. Inanna gave a small sigh of relief, then resumed her place beside Ogenus. It was a long walk back to their boat. While prospective mates walked with each other, there was little talk between them. An overwhelming sense of sadness and shock permeated the group. Major surgery was never painless.

*

They walked through the night, their way lit by an almost full moon and glare of the fast-approaching comet. Both rotated away from their view as a brilliant morning glow appeared on the horizon. A few hours later, Ogenus' ship rose out of the morning mist on the horizon before them. It took another hour walking along the water's edge to arrive at the massive round ship, an indication of just how big their vessel was. Despite their fear and shock, the young women expressed amazement at the ship's size and height.

"My father," said Adante, "said you were fools. But he never actually saw your ship."

"What do you think of it?" Iapetos asked.

The girl hugged herself. "It scares me. I don't want to do this."

"Yeah, well neither do we, really. If there was another possibility…"

They ate, then resumed the task of preparing for departure. "We load the animals last," said Ogenus, pointing to a series of enclosures nearby, each filled with a varying number of domesticated animals that would accompany them. He designated Adante and Zeda Nabu to feed and water the livestock. Everyone else finished loading the last few supplies onto the ship.

Hammurabi stood beside the vessel, looking up at its curved side. He could only see part way. "Have you decided to name the ship, Father?"

Ogenus set down a bundle and wiped his hands. "I was going to name it *The Ionic* after our old friend. But he suggested, somewhat facetiously, that we name it after a crazy sailor who once tried to circumnavigate the entire world in a tiny ship."

"What happened to him? Did he make it?"

Ogenus shrugged. "No one ever heard from him again. But I agreed to Ionic's suggestion. Our ship is named the *Noah*, the lord of foolhardy mariners. May his name go down in history."

That night, just before retiring for sleep, Ogenus declared the ship fully ready. Earlier that afternoon, animals were herded aboard and secured in their pens. Last of the supplies were on board. At sunrise, at high tide, the *Noah* would put out to sea with its human and animal cargo, to survive or perish as the gods would decree.

Ogenus woke with a start. It was still dark, and he wondered why there was a flicker of light. Then he smelled smoke. He jerked to his feet and saw fire near the ship. Someone had piled brush at the boat's base and lit it. Someone, holding a torch, stood near the flames and watched.

"Boys!" Ogenus shouted as he ran toward his burning ship. He heard shouting behind him, and Shemash shot past him at a full run. He grabbed the wielder of the torch, and there was a short struggle. At the same time, Ogenus, Iapetos, and Hammurabi stomped on the flames and kicked the burning twigs away from the *Noah*. Inanna joined them and doused most of the flames with a vessel of water.

Holding another torch, Ogenus strode to where Shemash held the culprit and shoved the torch to reveal Adante. Her hair was mussed and her face red. "Let go of me!" she shouted at Shemash, jerking her arm out of his grasp.

"Why did you do this?" Ogenus asked.

Adante was silent.

"Answer him!" Inanna said forcibly. Adante glared back.

Iapetos stepped out of the shadows to stand before his mate-to-be. "Speak!" he said.

Adante took a shuddering breath. "I did it because..."

"Yes?"

She pointed to the ship. "This boat, it's a stupid idea. We can't survive in that thing. We'll be swept away into the sea, and we'll all drown." She burst into tears and sank to the ground. Zeda Nabu joined her and glared at her adoptive family. "I want to go *home*!" Adante wailed.

Ogenus looked at his sons. "Let's take a look at the damage, boys." All three moved off, and the women gathered to speak in quiet voices that their men couldn't hear. Ogenus and his boys examined the area burnt by the fire. "Not too bad," Ogenus said, running a hand over blackened and still warm wood. "We'll have to reseal it and wait for it to cure."

"There isn't enough time, Father. We have to go now!" Hammurabi looked into the sky.

According to Ionic's imprecise calculations, the comet fragments were due to enter Earth's atmosphere sometime within the next 12 hours.

"We'll wait as long as we can. Now let's get this damage repaired."

By torch light, they quickly cleaned and re-sealed the damaged area. Ogenus used his beam weapon's last few moments of power to heat and cure the bitumen. He had been hoarding the weapon's power cell, but now, when the blue beam sputtered and stopped, he looked at the small weapon, then tossed it away. Morning had arrived.

"Okay," He said, "everybody aboard. We launch at the peak of high tide." He ushered his family and the three girls aboard the *Noah*. He and Iapetos were about to pull the doorway closed when a group of men from the girls' village appeared. They began looking around the abandoned camp. They did not look happy.

"We left our extra supplies over by the corrals," Ogenus called out. "Some of the livestock we didn't have room for are there as well. You're welcome to it all."

One of the men grunted. Another shouted, "You're a fool Ogenus. You're going to your death."

Ogenus nodded to Iapetos and together they pulled the large hatch shut. They secured it, sliding two rows of wooden pegs from the ship into the door's receiving holes, then sealed the whole thing with bitumen. When they were finished, they climbed up stairs to the top level. There, Hammurabi and Shemash stood on each side of the cabin, each with a rope in their hands. Ogenus checked the tide, then waved to his boys. The ropes were pulled, and the upright logs holding their ship dropped to the ground with a loud crash.

At first, the *Noah* didn't move. Then they felt it tilt slightly as high tide washed in and lifted the boat. A log began to roll, then the next, sliding their ship gently into the tide. The boat lifted on higher water, and the logs rolled it slowly and majestically into the ocean.

It took a few minutes as the boat rocked gently near shore, but the vessel at last got completely under weigh. After floating beside the coast for a while, outgoing tide caused the round craft to begin moving into deeper water. Ogenus could hear, and smell, the livestock below, noisy and moving, unaccustomed to the boat's rocking motion. Without motor or sails, or even a bow, movement of the *Noah* through water was silent except for the occasional splash. It rotated this way and that as the tide and waves took it.

Inanna and Zeta Nabu joined everyone else in the pilot cabin. "So far, no leaks," Inanna said. "We'll keep checking, but it looks like we're water tight."

Almost silently, their huge round ship floated on the outgoing tide into deeper and deeper water. By noon the coast was almost lost to sight.

*

"Any time now," Ogenus said, as he and Iapetos watched the night skies. It was a clear, calm, night filled with brilliant stars. The others were below trying to get some rest, although Ogenus suspected none of them were actually asleep.

Something bright and glowing roared overhead, leaving a trail of sparks and fire behind. It disappeared toward the east. "On your feet everyone!" Ogenus shouted. "Prepare yourselves."

The next step in Earth's destruction had begun.

Comet fragments plunged into Earth's atmosphere at tens of thousands of miles per hour. Most of the giant rocks hit Earth's oceans at oblique angles, but with unimaginable kinetic energy and incandescently hot. Trillions of gallons of water were instantly vaporized. Sea water was shoved into the depths where it was compressed from two sides, above and below. When it could take no more, the water exploded back, creating gigantic tsunamis such as the world had not seen since the dinosaur killer. The *Noah* was sucked south, then back north. Without rudder, engines or sails, it spun, tipped, tilted, but remained afloat.

Elsewhere on Earth, many smaller rocks peppered the resurgent ice sheets, melting them instantly.

Earth's atmosphere became super-saturated with water vapor. A global rain began, in some regions with water hot enough to scald. Rain fell in sheets while the seas of Earth sloshed in their basins and roared onto land, flooding every lowland area, and far into higher elevations. At the South Pole, impact effects were slightly slower as the large, thick ice cap melted. Giant, continent-sized icebergs broke off, and within hours, the Antarctic was virtually ice free.

Sea levels rose 200 feet in less than a day, and still the rain came down.

Every human habitation on Earth was affected. Small villages simply washed away along with their inhabitants as flood waters moved landward. Larger cities, and the rusting remains of the old cities such as Kursatta, were inundated, and virtually all of the remaining tall skeletons of the old buildings were toppled, then ground into the sloshing mud. The remnants of once-mighty civilizations sank beneath the sea. Mud, rocks, and sand covered most of that, completely erasing any trace.

The partially-built artificial mountains Imkotep and his people had been working on were quickly flooded under hundreds of feet of water. In most cases, strong foundations withstood the onslaught; in others, stone works broke apart and drifted in all directions, crushed against each other or thrown around like pebbles.

The same scenario occurred the world over. Most villages humans had built over the past decade and longer were simply washed away, inundated, sunk beneath gigantic waves. Most of the few remaining larger animal species, unable to move quickly to higher ground, were overwhelmed. Earthquakes became rampant, and volcanoes old and new brought forth heat, smoke, and burning lava which further spiked global temperatures.

Rarely, a large comet fragment, entering the atmosphere at an oblique angle, hit the ground, leaving oblong craters of various sizes. In other instances, a fragment would reach the lower atmosphere, then explode. One such detonated above a high elevation plateau in the southern part of the western continent, demolishing a partly-built stone city, scattering pieces in all directions. Most of the workers were killed instantly; others died shortly thereafter when a nearby lake sloshed out of its basin and flooded the plateau. Earth rang like a warbling bell. In other areas, large boulders virtually melted from the heat of explosions from fragments large and small.

In space, the comet and most of its accompanying rocks silently moved on around the Sun.

*

Aboard the *Noah*, humans and animals were tossed to and fro, many of their supplies smashed, and the boat began leaking. Nala suffered a sprained arm, Iapetos was knocked unconscious and dislocated his shoulder. Inanna and Zeda Nabu suffered cuts and bruises. Shemash found Nala screaming in pain next to one of the animal pens. He gathered her up, but could do nothing to bind her arm as the ship heaved up and down, spun, and rocked violently. He wedged himself into a corner of an animal pen and held onto the girl as tightly as he could.

All eight passengers became violently ill. Their ship was tossed about like a cork in a washing machine. Its unique shape prevented it from capsizing, but just barely. Day became almost dark as night. Rain continued to flush into the sea, and wind howled as if in pain.

While the fall of comet fire lasted only hours, the rain and howling wind continued for many unending days as Earth's skies worked to stabilize and rid itself of excess moisture.

When morning came days later, the sun's glow produced only a faint grayness as the superheated water rose to great heights, cooled, and fell back as driving rain.

Somehow, the mariners aboard *Noah* survived. Beaten, broken, bruised, shaken, and exhausted, they managed to find food and drink, and sometimes kept it down. They fed the animals that had survived, and tended to their complaints when possible. Inanna set Nala's arm and bound it in a cast. Other injuries were treated to the extent possible. Above all, the wind howled and rain fell in a drenching burst of endless water.

"If this storm doesn't abate soon, we'll all be dead, us and the animals," Ogenus said as he and Iapetos gazed bleakly on the carcass of a sheep that had its neck broken. Someone was constantly at the hand pumps, trying to remove water as fast as it came in, an impossible task. Leaks were repaired when possible. The ship began floating lower in the water. However, the additional weight of water in the lowest level gave *Noah* additional needed ballast, steadying it against the massive waves.

Eventually, the sea began to calm, the howl of wind reduced to a pitiful cry, and rain fell as drops rather than drenching sheets.

Later, when everyone compared experiences, they were never able to determine if the storm lasted a week, two weeks, or even a month or more. Rain continued to fall almost constantly.

One day, the steady downpour turned to showers. The wind died down, and crashing waves reduced to relative calm. Gray skies became brighter, but just barely. They could not determine their whereabouts as there was nothing to provide a visual reference. Once, Hammurabi thought he saw a ship in the distance, but repeated tries to find it again proved unsuccessful.

At least now those aboard the *Noah* could see, but all they could see was water from horizon to horizon.

"Father," Shemash asked, "where did all the land go?"

"It's out there. When things settle down, we'll find it."

"But how? We can't even steer this ship."

"I don't know, my son. If the gods will it, we will be all right."

"And if they don't?"

Ogenus rested a hand on his youngest son's shoulder and gazed into his eyes. "They will. Trust me, they will. And we're still alive, aren't we?"

"Barely! And we've lost a lot of our livestock."

"Hopefully, the worst is over," said Ogenus.

Another week passed, by Ogenus' reckoning, and they saw a seabird flying. A second one landed on the edge of their boat and rested for a while.

"Don't get excited," he told his family. "These birds don't indicate land nearby."

Storms came and went, but none of them were as violent as the ones before. The sky became increasingly brighter, but still no sun penetrated the cloud cover. Shadows were muted. Rain fell much of the time.

Several days later, a crow flew over. "That," Ogenus said, pointing, "is a land bird. We must be getting somewhat close to land."

They initiated a daytime watch. Those not busy caring for animals or themselves kept watch for any sign of land.

Just after sunrise one day, Iapetos began shouting. "*Land!*" He yelled, pointing. Everyone ran to the ship's small bridge. "Look! Over there!"

Zeda Nabu shaded her eyes with a hand. "Where? I don't see anything."

"I do!" Nala said, "very far in the distance. See? Right over there."

Inanna was the next to make out a hazy difference at the edge of an endless sea. Taking turns, they watched all that day.

The land seemed to grow somewhat closer, but it was still very, very far away.

The next morning, they could make out features of craggy mountain peaks in the far distance. The sea became even calmer, and days significantly brighter.

"We made it," Nala whispered to Shemash. "We're going to live!"

"Looks like it." He looked at her and smiled. They hugged each other.

Their traumatic experience had drawn the two youngest closer together. It seemed to Inanna that they might be holding a mating ceremony for the youngest first. Iapetos and Adante spoke frequently, but maintained a distance from each other. Hammurabi smiled at Zeda Nabu, and spoke to her, but she fairly ignored him for the most part. This was a source of mild concern for the boys' mother.

Inanna spent considerable time observing the interactions between her boys and the three girls. Since the sea had calmed, she had plenty of time to watch and think. Interactions between the six younger people were interesting and somewhat fluid, but in the end she determined that if the extended family were to be isolated for any length of time, their impromptu group would be okay. Extraordinary events required innovative and sometimes extreme solutions, and Inanna knew her cobbled-together family could easily self-destruct. She kept a close watch on the young people, ready to provide a gentle shove in the right direction, if it were needed.

Next morning, they could see that the land they'd been drifting toward had recently been the tops of mountains. As they got closer, foothills appeared. Since sea levels had not been this high before, there was no beach, just grass and some trees sticking out of the water. They floated well off shore until the tide changed, and waves, gentle now, began swirling them toward land.

That afternoon, the ship made a grinding noise and tilted slightly. They had made landfall. Ogenus wondered if they'd stay where they were, or if high tide would wash them back out to sea. They could certainly extricate themselves from the boat any time now, but they needed the boat itself. They had to unload their animals and supplies, for one thing. And the wood contained in the boat's construction held a source of building material that would certainly make their lives easier.

Ogenus determined that the water level was dropping slowly and, barring any additional heavy rainfall or storms, the boat would soon be resting completely on dry land.

"Sea level should continue to recede," he said to his family. "But just to be sure, I want us to remain in the boat until tomorrow morning."

He ignored groans and protests. Humans and animals had been cooped up in the ship for many weeks without proper facilities. The smell was almost overwhelming. A steady breeze helped some, and while the boat tilted slightly, it no longer rocked on the waves. That fact alone provided all eight a sound sleep that night.

Ogenus prepared his extended family to disembark on a new and unknown land. The world itself would have changed, perhaps beyond recognition. He sent Iapetos down to unseal the hatch and prepare it for opening. The young man pulled pegs back into the wall, releasing the hatch. He then used his knife to cut the bitumen seal. He kicked at the hatch, but it didn't budge. Next, he rammed his shoulder into the barrier, the instantly regretted it as pain shot through his back. But the hatch cracked and opened an inch or two, and light shone around it. Another hard shove and the door fell open and became a ramp.

"It's open!" he shouted back up to the bridge.

Still, Ogenus waited until high tide to make sure the water level was below where the boat now rested. As sea level continued to slowly drop he gave the signal to abandon ship. Six of the occupants stepped gingerly off the boat onto hard ground. Ogenus had left Shemash and Nala on the bridge as a precaution, just in case things were not as they looked.

There were no animals about, just a large flock of sea birds feasting on carcasses of fish and other sea creatures that had been left high and dry when flood levels receded.

The wet ground squished as they walked. Nearby foothills had all been submerged until recently. Everyone took deep breaths of clean fresh air, and some of the tension began to fade.

"How about it, Father?" Shemash called from the top level, his voice echoing and sending birds squawking and flying to a less intrusive environment.

"Come on down," Ogenus called back. During the few moments they had been on land, the water level dropped several more inches.

Shemash and Nala joined the others, just as a brilliant sun broke through the overcast. It was the first time any of them had seen sunlight since their aquatic adventure had begun.

Zeda Nabu pointed toward the ocean. "Look, there, it's a rainbow!"

"A good omen," said Inanna. "The gods may be looking upon us kindly."

"Perhaps," said Ogenus. "But we still have a lot of work to do. We need to build shelter for all of us, and pens for the animals. We need to find a place to cultivate the land and plant our seeds. It's not going to rain forever so we need a source of fresh water. Finally, it would be nice to know exactly where we landed."

"And I need to pee," said Hammurabi. "I'll be right back. Don't nobody look." He walked over toward the water and disappeared around the *Noah*. Everybody laughed, and it went on longer than necessary. Partially it was a laugh of humor, but it also expressed relief and a growing awareness that they were still alive and unharmed. Their chances of further survival were much better now. They were on dry land. The sea had delivered them here safely.

"Where will we get building materials?" Shemash asked, "there aren't any trees here."

Ogenus looked up at his boat. "We'll take the *Noah* apart, of course. She will provide us with what we need, for a while at least." He looked at his family and smiled wanly, "I'm afraid it won't be anything like Kursatta. No electricity, no vehicles, no computers, no technology of any kind."

"More like our time at the Crecopia," Hammurabi said.

Pulling some supplies from the boat, they made themselves a celebration meal. Inanna started a fire using logs stored on the ship's fifth floor for just such a purpose, and they were able to cook some of their food. They laughed and sang, and smiled at each other in realization that they were still alive and well.

Work for the next several weeks was long and hard. They built pens for animals, set up tents for themselves, and started breaking apart the giant ship. Ogenus and Iapetos took overnight hikes looking for a source of fresh water. They started off east and north but didn't find anything, and finished toward the south and west. There, they saw in the far distance, mountains with a few streaks of snow clinging to the highest peaks. They found a small stream fairly close to their encampment, and Ogenus heaved a sigh of relief. While they had planned for most contingencies, fresh water was a necessity, and they couldn't rely on continued rainfall.

While the two men were gone, Inanna kept watch over the rest of their group. She noted that afternoon Adante had finished feeding and caring for the sheep and wandered back toward the boat. The girl seemed to be quietly trailing after Hammurabi in a roundabout way. She stopped, looked around, then noticed Inanna watching. Adante turned quickly and stepped up the ramp and into the *Noah*.

Minutes later, Hammurabi reappeared around the opposite side of the boat. It was enough to give Inanna pause. Adante then stepped back down from the ramp and joined her middle son in quiet conversation.

Before Inanna could think of what to do about the situation, if anything, she heard Ogenus and Iapetos shouting from a distance. They carried full water bags and Inanna almost sobbed. Their own fresh water supplies were virtually depleted despite the rain capture.

"You found water!" she called. She dreamed of heating enough water for a good warm bath. But that probably wasn't going to happen any time soon.

Iapetos held up his water bag, and the six at camp began cheering.

*

Later, Adante sought out Ogenus. "Ogenus?" she said shyly.

He looked up. "Yes, Adante?"

"I heard a beeping from up in the bridge. Something was beeping. I couldn't find out where it was coming from."

Ogenus looked startled, then strode toward the ramp with the young woman following. "It must be Ionic. Last time he visited us, he gave me a satellite phone. He said we should only use it for urgent communications. Hopefully, this will confirm he and others on the Crecopia have survived."

They rapidly climbed five levels to the top of the ship. Inside the main cabin he opened a drawer and drew out a large handheld satellite phone unit. A periodic flash of light and a sharp "beep" emanated from the device.

"Ogenus here, hello. Anyone there? Ionic?" he said, transmitting.

For a while all he heard was static. Then a scratchy, barely audible voice came back. "Ionic here, Ogenus."

"You survived!"

"...portant...age."

"You're breaking up. Hang on." Ogenus hurried down from the ship and out into open air in the hopes of getting a better signal. That seemed to work as the voice became louder, although the static continued.

"Ogenus?"

"Yes. I can hear you better now. I'm happy to hear you survived."

"Indeed we did, but just barely. I have an important message for you."

"Okay, go ahead."

"Eris and I took the last working long-range flier after the flooding stopped," he said, his voice loud over the static. "I anticipated that the southern pole continent might have been rendered ice free during this event."

"Yes?" He considered for a moment how ironic it was that he could no longer call someone nearby, but was able to communicate with someone half-way across the planet.

"I was right. We just finished flying over the Pole. I was able to map the continent sans ice. I'm going to se...it to you ...lectronically via this phone. Prepare to rece..."

Ogenus made the adjustment. "Ready to receive."

A green light on the radio flashed for several minutes, then remained steady.

"...get it?"

"Yes, I got it."

"Good. You'll need to re-draw it by hand, transfer it to paper. When the battery dies on your phone, it will be gone. Draw it. Keep it. Ice is already starting to re-form...nce in a lifetime chance."

"You can draw it too, once you return to the Crecopia."

"...copia surface badly damaged. Few survivors...we...n't make it back. Not enough fuel....sing altitude. I'm afraid this is goodbye my friend. We're happy you...ade it. Very few humans left alive...p to you. I'm..."

The signal went dead. Ogenus stared at the radio for a long moment, then turned it to standby to preserve its remaining battery charge. He didn't know anyone else who might call him on the radio, but if someone did, he wanted to be able to answer it, for a while at least. He'd draw the map Ionic and Eris had apparently given their lives for. He wondered briefly why it was so important.

While he was talking, Inanna joined Ogenus and Adante. He turned toward his mate, his eyes wide. "They're gone," he said softly.

"What?"

"Ionic and Eris. They're gone."

Inanna stepped up to him, and held him. He was shaking. He glanced over toward the horizon. He and his family were certainly refugees now, and perhaps they were alone on whatever continent the gods had placed them. Here, they would make their stand, to live or to die.

AFTER

Sounds of the *Noah* being cut apart echoed back from nearby hills. First, they removed material from the ship's upper sides and built pens for their livestock. Later, they stored some of the lower curved sides for future use, and worked to free up and lower the top level living quarters to the ground. With some modifications, these pre-constructed buildings would become their homes and shelters, especially from the still frequent downpours.

It was likely, Ogenus thought, these might be their homes for years to come. He did not believe much of humanity had survived the onslaught of celestial rocks. Civilization would need to be built up again, from the bedrock of Earth. Higher sea levels meant less land upon which to construct villages and, eventually, cities. He remembered during the first comet-fall that the land Kursatta occupied had become an island. Most of the land from Kursatta to the Crecopia had become a series of small islands. No doubt this would now be a permanent change. He wondered what new cultures and civilizations might emerge in the future, and what legends might result from the misfortune of his doomed civilization.

Ogenus and his family appreciated what little sunshine that graced them, but while its appearance was more frequent every day, rain dominated the weather. Sea level continued to drop for several weeks, then stopped. The boat's resting place was now well back from lapping waves. They captured as much rain water as they could, which reduced the number of trips to the stream and saved them valuable time.

Until they could finish lowering the living quarters, they slept in tents which quickly became saturated. They used some of the boat's tightly-woven and sealed siding as temporary shelters, leaning sections against the exposed framework, and pitching their tents under them. It helped, a little.

Once the living quarters were removed from the ship, the family worked to build and level stone foundations and a floor upon which the wooden structures would eventually rest.

While their food and water were adequate for eight people, their undamaged possessions were few. Most of those were packed away and wouldn't be available until more urgent tasks had been completed.

A month or so after their landing, Iapetos, Hammurabi, Adante and Zeda Nabu sought out Inanna.

"Mother, we'd like to have a few words with you, if you have a moment," Iapetos said, tilting his head toward the other three.

Inanna put down her work and looked around. Ogenus, Shemash, and Nala were on the other side of the ship.

"Okay," she said, wiping her hands on her pants. "What is it? Trouble"

"Not really," Iapetos said. He seemed hesitant to speak, then the words came out in a rush. "Adante and Hammurabi want to become mates."

Inanna looked at the four young people. "That's not the way we planned it. Have you thought about what this means?"

"Well, they are more suited to each other," Iapetos said, looking uneasily around. "That leaves me and Zeda Nabu. While we are friendly, we don't feel like mates."

"I like him well enough," Zeda Nabu said. "He's like a brother to me. But not a mate."

"And obviously you didn't find Hammurabi suitable."

Zeda Nabu shrugged. "Adante obviously prefers Ham, and I don't want to stand in their way."

""So what is it you expect me to do? I can't create mates for you two out of thin air."

"We know that, Mother," Hammurabi said. "But we're bound to run into other humans sooner or later. We'd like your permission for Iapetos and Zeda Nabu to remain un-attached for a while, until we can see if there are others nearby."

Inanna gazed at the young people for a long moment. She asked Iapetos, "Are you and Zeda Nabu okay with waiting?"

"Sure, Mother. We'd both rather find someone more suited to us, even if it takes a while."

"I'll speak to your father, but I don't see a problem." She hesitated until she had their attention. "But if our circum-stances require it, we expect you to make a practical decision rather than an emotional one. The future of our family depends on you. Do you understand, Iapetos?"

He glanced at Zeda Nabu and his brother. "I understand, Mother."

"And you, Zeda Nabu. Do you understand our situation and your responsibility?"

The teenager glanced at Iapetos, then she smiled. "I understand. If necessary we will do what is required of us, of course."

"We'll do what we can to locate other people. It's better for all of us if we were to form a...a tribe, or a village. To do that, we need more bodies. If we find other survivors, we may have cause to hope, and you may find your solution."

*

Inanna found Ogenus and Shemash engaged in dragging sections of the ship up a hill. They dropped one section with a clatter and wiped sweat from their foreheads. The weather was warm and humid. Ogenus looked around, saw Inanna, and smiled.

"May I speak with you for a moment?"

Ogenus motioned her to join him. "Of course. I need a break anyway. Shemash, see if you can detach the next section by yourself. I'll join you in a few minutes."

"Yes, Father."

Inanna told her mate of the meeting with her two oldest boys and the two girls.

"What do you think?" she asked.

He rested a hand on her shoulder. "You handled it exactly as I would have. Except without a lot screaming and yelling and anger."

Inanna smiled. "Our sons are not stupid. They came to me first."

*

A few days later, Ogenus got around to fulfilling Ionic's last request. He secured a large sheet of parchment and located where they'd stored a few bottles of ink. He sat in what had been the ship's bridge, now relocated to the ground and leveled, purposed as a home for Inanna and himself. He turned on the satellite phone and brought up the map Ionic had sent. He noticed a second icon, but decided to come back to it later.

Drawing a map of the southern continent and its nearby islands took a few hours. The device's screen was small, and the original document itself was large. Ogenus needed to scroll frequently, then check his work. He wanted to make sure his rendition was as accurate as possible.

When finished, he had a large map of the southern pole continent sans ice cap, drawn with a very stable ink that should last a couple of centuries. He rolled the map and inserted it into a metal tube, then used a hand pump to extract as much air as he could, an inefficient and only partially successful method to store the document in an inert atmosphere.

That task completed, Ogenus took a look at the second icon. It was an audio letter, from Ionic to him that had been downloaded at the same time as the map. He stared at it for a while before pressing the "Play" button.

*

"My dear friend and colleague, Ogenus. I know you're wondering why Eris and I would abandon the few survivors on the Crecopia and undertake such a dangerous mission for the sole purpose of mapping a continent, especially during such trying times. I'm sure you must have guessed that this was not the only reason for our final journey.

"We surveyed the southern pole continent because it has not been ice-free for tens of thousands of years, and will probably not be so again for thousands more. It is, in and of itself, worthy of our journey from a scientific standpoint. So copy it, my friend, and try to find some way to preserve it for the future.

"The Crecopia was almost wiped clean during comet strikes and the resulting floods and storms. I'm afraid we did not fare as well as last time. When the storm finally broke, more than half the residents who had joined our little community were nowhere to be found, presumably blown off or washed away by giant waves, higher and more frightening than last time. Of the remainder, many were dead or dying. Of those who survived unscathed, only a few are equipped for long-term survival under such conditions as they now find themselves.

"We lost almost all of our supplies. Indeed, almost all of the buildings regardless of our attempts to fortify them, were summarily swept from the Crecopia. Two of the fleet of fliers remained, a smaller one damaged beyond use. The second, a large passenger craft, was in good shape and required only a few minor repairs. Eris and I loaded its passenger area with power cells and took off before any of the remaining survivors could lodge a protest. I felt bad leaving them as we were fully expecting not to return. We had sufficient power to carry out the goals of our flight, but not enough to make it back unless by some chance we are fortunate enough to discover a supply of power cells. I do not believe the chances of that are good. My colleagues and I, world-wide, committed to securing what little technology remained in various underground locations so that it would be available to us following this second catastrophic event. The devastation has been so complete that I do not believe many of these caches of technology remain both hidden and undamaged. Water levels of this event were even higher than I had anticipated.

"Our goals for this last flight were two-fold. We needed to see the extent of the damage across our globe, a quick and unscientific assessment of humankind. Would we find any cities still standing? The only method left to us is a visual inspection, an inefficient endeavor at best. As we flew across our ocean toward Naqada and Esna, we were hopeful. Your friend Imkotep had, as you know, promised to lead his people south, along the great river, then into whatever high ground they could find. We followed that greatly-swollen river south, then searched both east and west for a sign of that great nation. We eventually found remnants clinging to a range of hills west of the river. While many had been killed, they fared much better than I had reason to believe. They had fresh water, food, and were busy constructing dwellings, with plans to re-populate the north as soon as possible. Imkotep inquired about you and Inanna. I told him you had successfully finished your boat, and he laughed. 'They will survive,' he said, 'they are survivors.' He told us that as soon as the inundation retreated, many of his people would migrate back north and resume work on their artificial mountain, as well as the other tasks which we have asked of him and his people.

"After leaving Imkotep we moved on to survey as many coastal areas of that continent as our fuel would allow. We found no cities intact, and few survivors. In fact, much of the northern section of that continent was buried under massive mud flows. It was impossible to fathom such destruction.

After our Arctic survey, we ventured over a swollen great sea toward the western continent. Unfortunately, we haven't enough fuel to make landfall. But that is of little concern.

I must confess that the results of our comet fall were as I had suspected, although worse. Much of the Earth was flooded, violently. Only the higher elevations and mountain ranges were spared. Unfortunately, there were few human settlements at these higher elevations. While some number of individuals were fortunate enough to find high ground, the cities and villages in which they lived were swept away by waves, or sunk beneath much higher sea levels. Many of those cities met the same fate as Kutsatta; destroyed in the first comet fall, then ground to powder and sunk under water during the second. Should a visitor from another solar system visit Earth at this particular point in time, he would be hard-pressed to find any semblance of an advanced civilization.

"I fear that, with few exceptions, virtually every city on Earth is gone. Almost every one of our proud nations are no more. Most, as you know, were either destroyed or severely damaged during our first encounter with the comet. After this second encounter, I can say with sadness that our once great global civilization is now extinct, Ogenus. It's all gone. I urge you to do whatever you can to make sure that some of the stone structures we planned are repaired and completed. It is more important now than ever that we know if Earth's orbit or inclination has been altered. We also need to leave a message for those in the far distant future that we existed. All we have done cannot disappear without a trace. Something of what we've accomplished must live on. I hope you agree.

"I ask you to take any paper books, documents, and any scientific equipment that might be available to you, working or not, and store them in a secure location, somewhere that will, hopefully, last for centuries. Along with stone alignments, this will be the record of our knowledge and our technology. I'm giving you yet another almost impossible task, I know, as the fastest mode of transportation left to you is by foot. And for years to come your main concern will be survival. Yet, do not let this task pass from you. Keep it in your mind as something to do when the time is right, and you have found a suitable location in which to store these records.

"Those who are best able to survive are the primitive tribes and cultures. They have skills and temperament to live in such meager conditions. It's up to you to contact those nearby and teach them the rudiments of civilization beyond that of uneducated tribal chieftains. It is the melding of their knowledge with your knowledge that will lead humanity back to a functioning civilization.

"Eris and I believe the water level will recede a bit more as the typical weather pattern reasserts itself and the ice caps build. But the sea will remain at much higher levels than before. The land south of us on the great southern continent, west of Esna, was heavily damaged by both the recent war and our celestial cataclysm, and I believe much of it will largely cease to be a lush jungle land with rivers and lakes, as the entire area may become much drier than before.

"You must also be aware that there is a small chance that some civilizations may have survived more or less intact. The area northeast of us had built their massive underground cities. If they were able to move members of their populations and supplies into those cities before the comet struck, they may have a head start in recreating a functioning civilization. There may be others in other areas who heeded our warnings and took action. Do not be surprised by this. You may even find some advanced technology. Our flier survived and others might have as well. Their use, however, will be temporary as fuel cells and repair parts become depleted.

"Unfortunately, most people will be in the same situation as yourself and your family, and I suspect, worse. You must help those you find. While they have learned much since the first comet fall, many still need knowledge of how to raise livestock, how to build with wood, stone, and brick. Members of primitive tribes won't even know these things. Even such esoteric skills as government, law, negotiation, mathematics, astronomy, medicine, accounting, metallurgy will be foreign to them. Leadership and government must replace or at least augment survival of the fittest. I'm afraid the concept of written language might well disappear, at least in the short term. Try to preserve your written language whenever you can, even if you have to carve words into stone.

"We must not fall into the tribal flaw of seeing all others as sub-human or enemies. Humans need to work together to pull out of this pit we have been shoved into. Ogenus, great nations can arise again, but it will take time, my friend, probably centuries. And you must always keep in mind that our battered Earth may, some time in the future, once again tangle with that cursed comet, or the remainder of its pieces. In a dozen years or a thousand, our orbits may once again intersect, and Earth may pay another terrible price for being in the wrong place at the wrong time. I believe we have seen the worst of it for now, but the danger remains just the same. May the gods be with you.

"And now, it is time for me to say goodbye. I would wish for the opportunity of seeing you and your family again, but that is not possible. I'm overjoyed that you all survived. That was your doing, Ogenus. You succeeded where most humans have failed.

"Now I must excuse myself. I need to step into the control room and confess to Eris that our fuel is virtually exhausted, and there is no land for many hundreds of miles. Although I am sure she is fully aware of our situation, I want to leave no doubt. We shall crash into the sea and be no more. Farewell, my brother. I'm proud of you and Inanna. It has been my privilege to know you both."

There, the message ended. Ogenus rubbed his eyes and took a deep breath. He shuddered and briefly held his head in his hands before getting up and heading out once more into the dim sunlight, into a new day and a new world. He was tired. Very, very tired.

*

Two weeks later, the small encampment was a going concern. The sound of hammering and sawing and happy voices of his family gave Ogenus a much-needed lift. The eight humans had shelter, animals were well fed and comfortable in their pens. A small plot of land had been prepared for the planting of wheat and a few other staple crops.

Ogenus hoped that flowing ice meltwater had diluted the sea water flung up by the series of tsunamis. Otherwise, the ground may have absorbed too much salt, and crops might fail to thrive. They had no way to test the salinity except to actually grow crops and see what happened. Fresh water was an ongoing concern, but the small stream of pure cold water coming out of high mountains continued to flow.

They were far enough up from the littered beach that air was fresh, and the sun continued to burn through a persistent cloud cover. Rain showers and rainbows were frequent. Sea level would not return to its previous low levels since much of the upland ice had melted and would not reform. The pitiful remnants of those once-mighty cities that had been swallowed up by the flood would remain below sea levels, buried in mud and sand, perhaps forever.

*

One morning, Ogenus was pondering how best to cure and waterproof treated mud bricks despite frequent showers, when he looked up and saw three men coming over a distant hill.

"Inanna!" he called, but not too loudly.

His mate looked up from her food preparation and joined him. "We have visitors coming," he said, nodding toward the newcomers.

"They're armed," she replied softly.

"I would expect them to be," Ogenus said. "We're not in the city anymore. Everyone is struggling."

"Yes, but compared to others, we may seem to be very wealthy," she said, looking around at their camp.

They watched as the three men made their way closer.

Inanna turned suddenly. "Boys!" she called, but no louder than needed. Her three sons joined them, and she quietly indicated the approaching visitors. "Get the girls outside, get them moving around."

"Why, Mother," Hammurabi asked.

"I want our visitors to be unsure the size of our group."

Their youngest son ran to the huts and returned with three perplexed women.

Ogenus also gave Inanna a quizzical look, but said nothing.

"You three," Inanna commanded the attention of her sons, and she spoke very softly "I want you to go that way, in the opposite direction. Don't let those men see you. Go down through that culvert and keep low. I want you to double back over those hills and look for others in hiding."

"Why these elaborate arrangements, my love?" Ogenus said. "Surely they are here to make friendly contact. After all, there are only three of them."

"Only three that we can see." She turned her attention back to her sons. "They may have men surrounding us just out of sight," she said. "Keep that in mind, Iapetos. Don't let them see you. If you find watchers, incapacitate them if you can, if there aren't too many. If you can't," she paused and lifted her knife half out of its sheath, "make sure they don't sound an alarm. If there are a lot of them, if they've brought an army, don't do anything, just stay hidden. If they don't kill us outright, they'll take us as slaves. If so, follow at a distance. Take your time, assess the situation. Don't get caught. Watch and listen, and eventually you'll find a way to set us free."

"Could it be that bad, Mother?" Shemash asked.

Inanna squeezed his shoulder. "I don't think so. If there are others, I don't think there will be many of them. But just in case, be ready."

"Yes Mother," Iapetos said. He looked at his brothers, and the three moved off at a trot in the opposite direction of their visitors, ducking into a dip in the terrain. Once out of sight, they curved around and worked their way behind the others, watching for additional men in hiding.

A while later, Shemash stopped. "Look," he whispered to his brothers, pointing, "over there, behind those rocks."

Ogenus felt a bit frustrated. "And if they're only visitors and want to be friendly?"

Inanna smiled, a predatory smile lacking any humor. "Then there is no harm done. If they haven't surrounded us, our sons will re-join us and make nice."

Ogenus looked at his mate. "You are very suspicious," he said. "Why do you think they would surround us?"

"Because that's what I would do if I needed food and water, and" she glanced over at Adante, Zeda Nabu and Nala, "females. Excuse me, I need to speak with the girls before those three arrive."

Before Ogenus could reply, Inanna strode off and spoke quietly to the three young women who were gathered near their buildings. As she spoke, they glanced nervously toward the three men. Their unease was easy to see, but Inanna said something and they relaxed.

Inanna rejoined Ogenus, While she was armed with her knife, she did not have her spear. Ogenus cocked an eyebrow, and, sensing his question, Inanna tilted her head toward the structure in which they slept. Zeda Nabu was just exiting, carrying the spear. She remained still while the other two girls continued to move about.

Ogenus opened his mouth, then closed it. He sighed and looked toward the visitors who were close enough now that he could see smiles on their faces. He was convinced that Inanna's complex precautions were completely unnecessary. He sincerely hoped she was wrong.

As they entered the camp area, the leader raised a hand, "Hail!" he called. "Can we join you and talk?" He spoke a language very similar to Ogenus' own, but with a heavy accent.

Ogenus half bowed and swept his hand toward the camp. "You are welcome. Join us."

The three men entered the camp, still smiling. "I'm Hayuk," said the leader. "We have a small village about five miles east of you. Some of our scouts have seen your boat and reported this to me. I thought it best we make contact." He glanced around their camp, looked up at the few remaining wooden ribs of the *Noah*. Inanna noted Hayuk's assessment was both quick and complete, but he asked no questions.

"I'm Ogenus, and this is my mate, Inanna."

"And you've got young women, I see," Hayuk commented, glancing at his two companions. He looked in the other direction. "You have animals, and it looks like you're planting fields. You've done a lot of work. How did you get here?"

Ogenus began to sense some of Inanna's suspicion. "During the flood, we floated here on my boat," he nodded toward the remnants.

Hayuk shook his head. "You're either a great fool or a very brave man."

"Probably both. And you? Where are you from?"

"We lived in a city down there," he ducked his head toward the receding water. "Some of us, a few, made it into the mountains before the world came apart."

"I'm happy to hear that there are other people nearby," Ogenus said. "Hopefully we can help each other from time to time." The three men were all large specimens, and the other two seemed to have scowls painted on their faces.

Hayuk's smile, too, faded. "Well, you see, that's the problem. We can't help you much because we have very little. Some of our people are injured or sick, and we don't have enough food and water. It looks like you have plenty of both." He made a gesture to his three companions, and they drew their knives.

"My friends and I are here to take what we need, your animals, your food, and...those girls."

"That's not going to happen," Ogenus said. "Our girls will fight with us, and there are only three of you."

Hayuk shook his head. "I'm sorry." He glanced toward the hills. "We have you surrounded." He nodded his head toward the north and east. "More of my men are hiding out there, waiting for my signal. We don't want to kill any of you, but we will if you force us to. Now, move aside, if you please."

Ogenus and Inanna stood their ground. "You may not have us as surrounded as you think," Inanna said. She had seen something that Hayuk or his men had not: her three boys coming up behind the intruders.

Hayuk finally caught the meaning of her words and spun around. When he turned back, both Ogenus and Inanna had drawn their weapons. The three young women moved in from the other side, Zeda Nabu leading the way with Inanna's spear.

The leader of the invaders took a deep breath. His shoulders relaxed. He reluctantly dropped his weapon. Following suit, the other two also dropped their knives, which were picked up by Shemash as he and his brothers entered the camp. Iapetos and Hammurabi escorted the three forward.

"Sentries?" Inanna asked.

"Four of them, Mother," Hammurabi said. "Tied up."

"One saw us and almost gave the alarm," Shemash said, dropping three knives at his father's feet.

"What did you do?" Ogenus asked.

Shemash smiled and fingered his own knife.

200

"You killed him?" Ogenus asked.

"*No!*" Iapetos said emphatically, glaring at his younger brother, then smiled. "We gagged him with his own socks."

"Good work, boys," Inanna said. "Now what are we going to do with them? Obviously they outnumber us. If they have a village, there will be women, children."

"All that and more," Hayuk said sadly. "We are also responsible for our elderly and injured. All I told you is true." He was silent for a long moment, looking at each of the others. "I'm sorry we confronted you as we did, but we're desperate. We're out of food, very little water." He looked at his two companions. "We're not thinking clearly. If you kill us..." He spread the fingers of his hands.

Ogenus took a deep breath. "Boys, go untie the other four, bring them here."

"Okay," Shemash said dubiously, "but that one with the sock in his mouth isn't going to be happy with us."

Both Ogenus and Hayuk barked laughs. "Do it anyway," Ogenus said.

When everyone was gathered and seated around a fire, Ogenus pushed a log around with his knife. A quick meal was prepared for the visitors, who had not eaten recently. "We have access to water," he said slowly, "a small stream over that way," he pointed to the west. "You're welcome to as much of it as you can carry, as often as you need. It's a bit of a trek for you, but there's enough for all of us."

"Thank you," Hayuk said humbly.

"We have more animals than we need for our own use. We brought enough to ensure we had breeding stock. We can help you move some of our excess to your encampment. We have some extra food supplies. Not much, but we are willing to share. We need friends much more than we need enemies."

Tears welled up in Hayuk's eyes as he gazed at the flames. "We don't know how to thank you," he said, looking up. "I don't know how. We're not bad people. We just don't know how to survive." He glanced at his companions. "Many years ago we were office workers, accountants, storekeepers, government officials." He smiled sadly. "Took us forever to learn how to start a fire."

One of the others spoke up. "How did you do it? How did you," he looked around, "how did you plan all this? How did you survive?"

Ogenus looked at Inanna. "We had lots of help. Most especially my mate," he reached out and took Inanna's hand, "who is an expert at survival."

"Perhaps she can help teach us?"

"I will do what I can, of course," Inanna said softly.

The intruders were given food and water, and more supplies to carry back to their village.

As they said goodbye, Ogenus told Hayuk they would be along in a couple of days, herding a few animals, a couple of which would give the refugees immediate food and others for breeding.

"Today was a good day," Inanna said after their visitors were gone. "We made some new friends. By giving up some of what we have," she said, looking at her sons, "we may get much more in return."

*

Several days later, Ogenus and his group guided a small herd of animals to the village of their new friends. There, the villagers had already built primitive pens for them. The settlement consisted of almost fifty individuals, many of them old or injured, but also a few children and teens. From time-to-time, refugees would wander into the village, increasing their number slowly, and until now growing their peril by stretching scarce supplies even thinner.

Ogenus and his family were welcomed as heroes, and a celebratory meal was concocted for the visitors. Inanna met with the men and some older women to answer questions relating to their long-term survival. She drew Ogenus in to discuss the care of livestock and techniques for preparing and planting crops. Ogenus shared some of his seeds. "These will grow wheat," he said.

Hayuk dismissed the seeds with a wave of his hand. "Wheat is a terrible crop. When you try to harvest it, the seeds separate and blow away. Too much work, not enough reward."

"I understand, and agree with you in general" Ogenus said, "however, this particular variety of wheat has been genetically modified by gene scientists. When this crop is ready for harvest, the wheat will remain with the chaff until you can gather and separate it manually. I was told that this domesticated wheat could not easily survive in the wild for the very reason that it makes an excellent crop for food. So take it, give it a try. You'll need it."

Hayuk shrugged and accepted the small packet of seeds. "I bow to your wisdom and superior knowledge."

Ogenus laughed. "My wisdom, as you put it, was the fortune of being friends with one of the genetic scientists. A mutual friend, Ionic, put together these bags," Ogenus held up his pouch, "with planting and growing instructions, then passed them out to anyone who would take them before the comet strike."

Inanna's boys and the three girls mixed with younger members of the village, sharing stories of survival and peril. Just before beginning the trek back to their own camp, Zeda Nabu found Inanna. "I want to stay here," she said, "there's a young man here who interests me."

"You haven't forgotten that you're part of our family now?" Inanna asked.

"I know," Zeda Nabu said, "but maybe we can work something out. Would you please come with me?"

Inanna frowned, then followed the teenager to a small group of young people.

"Do you have her?" Zeda Nabu asked a tall young man.

He ducked into a tent from which emanated some shouting and a scream. When he came out, he grasped the wrist of a tall, thin, young woman with night-black skin. Her eyes were fiery and her lips curled in anger. "This," the boy said, shoving the girl to the ground at Inanna's feet, "is Sabra. She doesn't speak our language, but we think she is Nubian or from one of the night-skinned nations on the western coast of the Great Southern Continent. She wandered in one day from who knows where. She doesn't like it here and has been giving us trouble. You can take her if you allow Zeda Nabu to stay."

Inanna knelt before the woman and gazed into her eyes. In the wildness she saw there, Inanna recognized a little bit of the person she had once been, many years ago. She reached out and touched Sabra's cheek. The other moved her head away, but she calmed a bit.

"What's going on here?" Ogenus said as he approached from behind Inanna.

"We're being offered a trade. Her," she pointed to Sabra, "for Zeda Nabu."

"How does Iapetos feel about this?"

"I don't know." She turned to Shemash, "Go find your brothers and bring them here."

"Right, Mother. I'll be right back."

Inanna reached out, took one of Sabra's hands, and pulled the girl to her feet. She smiled, but the other woman broke out with a string of words Inanna didn't understand, but were certainly laced with anger.

Ogenus looked surprised and stepped forward. He listened intently to Sabra as she spoke rapidly and intently for several minutes. Ogenus then responded, haltingly, in the same language. Sabra replied again, and Ogenus nodded.

"You understand her?" Inanna asked in surprise.

"It's a language spoken by a people in the southwest area of the southern continent. I was there many times, back when I was a navigator. Learned to understand their language fairly well, and speak it horribly. It's used by many nations in that area. Or at least it was."

"What's she saying?"

"Complaining about her treatment here, how she was a princess back home, how she was captured and enslaved, how nasty these people have been to her, and how it is our responsibility to get her back home to her people before these villagers decide to eat her. I told her if she comes with us, she will be treated better and that we can discuss her situation in detail. She's thinking about it."

"Tell her we certainly won't eat her," Inanna said. Ogenus smiled and related the information.

The three boys gathered with the group. "What's up, Father," Hammurabi asked.

Ogenus told them what had transpired.

Iapetos stepped forward and studied Sabra closely. She looked back at him defiantly, but said nothing. "Mother, did you tell her what this exchange entails?"

Inanna shook her head. "We've simply offered her a home with us."

Iapetos continued to stare at the young woman. Finally, he nodded. "She looks healthy and strong. I'm willing to see what might happen. We could certainly give her a better home," he said, glancing at his father.

Sabra looked at Ogenus, then at Inanna. For a long moment she gazed at Iapetos. She said some more words, then nodded.

"She'll come with us," Ogenus said, "but makes no promises."

Zeda Nabu told them she and her young man would be along in a day or two for her small bundle of belongings.

Ogenus welcomed Hayuk and his villagers to come visit. Then the small group gathered their things, as well as Sabra's bundle of clothes, and began their trek back home.

Once they arrived, Inanna and Ogenus took Sabra aside. Ogenus translated.

"This is our home. If you wish, it will also be your home. Here you are free, but if you choose to stay, you will have responsibilities and work to do. None of us here is a princess. We all work and we're all treated the same. If it so happens that you are attracted to our son, Iapetos, and choose to become his mate, we welcome you into our family. That is your choice, and you may remain here with us regardless of your choice. We cannot return you to your people. We have no means of transportation, and it is likely your people have suffered the same fate as us. All, or most, have probably perished. Whatever city you may have called home is gone. If you wish to leave us, you are welcome to do so. We will give you food and water, as much as you can carry. But you will not be allowed to return. Stay or go, it is your choice."

Sabra's gaze began with a defiant look, but she said nothing. Then her face softened, and she looked down. Her shoulders slumped. "I have little choice but to accept your offer." She looked up at Inanna, her eyes steady, "I accept all of the conditions."

Sabra raised her hand and offered it to Inanna, who took it and pulled the girl to her in a warm hug. Sabra burst into tears and shook violently while Inanna held her. "It's over," she whispered, "you're home now," and heard the words translated softly by Ogenus.

"I must learn her language quickly," she told Ogenus. "We need to speak together without a man involved."

Ogenus laughed. "It would be my pleasure to teach you, my love. I don't believe it will be difficult for you."

*

Two months later, their small village was growing. Two or more acres were planted in wheat and other crops, most of the animals were alive and flourishing, and it looked as if some baby animals would be joining them soon. Within a span of two weeks, Ogenus and Inanna had held three solemn mating ceremonies for their three sons and Adante, Nala and Sabra. The *Noah* had been fully dismantled and made into three additional dwellings as well as a primitive boat used for fishing. They were on good terms with their neighbors, the original ones and a couple of slightly more distant settlements.

Humans were few, at least in this area, but so was food and fresh water. Earth still shook occasionally, and it rained often, but both were returning to a slightly altered normal.

A month later, Shemash sought out his mother. "Can I speak with you?"

"Of course, my son," Inanna replied.

"Privately?"

Inanna's eyebrows rose. There were few secrets among the group. She led him to the cabin used by herself and Ogenus. Once inside, she closed the door. "Okay, what is it?"

"Nala," he said, then hesitated. "She's..."

"She's what?"

"She's...going to, well, she's going to present you with a grandchild."

Inanna's mouth opened, but no words came out. Then she laughed and pulled her youngest son into an embrace. "That's good news, my son. Very good news."

"But, Mother, who here knows how to birth a child?"

Inanna stopped smiling and looked concerned. "That's a good question. Isn't there a medicine man, excuse me, doctor, among those in the village?"

"I hope so," Shemash said. "Nala is so very happy, but also scared. And so am I."

"You need to reassure her, my son. Growing a baby is stressful enough as it is. Now let's go to the others, all smiles, and tell them the good news. We've got months before we'll need that...doctor."

"I love you, Mother," Shemash said, hugging Inanna. "You always have the right answer."

"There is only ever one right answer," she said firmly.

"And that is?"

"Love."

That night there was a celebration of the news that Nala and Shemash would be adding to their small community's population. They sang and laughed. The night sky cleared for once, and they could see many brilliant stars. As they gazed overhead, they saw a tiny star with a small reverse tail. The comet had rounded the sun and was headed out into the solar system's deep dark expanse, where the King of Earth rested on his throne and sometimes threw comets at them.

As the party wound down, Adante urged Hammurabi to their hut. "I'm going to be next," she said with a smile.

"Next what?" Hammurabi asked.

"I'm going to give our mother her second grandchild. So hurry, we have no time to waste."

"My pleasure," laughed Hammurabi.

"It's not pleasure," Adante said, "it's work. And Iapetos and Sabra are probably working toward the same goal. We need to announce our child-to-be first."

Hammurabi bowed. "Yes, boss."

*

Not long after, Ogenus was plowing a new field when he heard his name shouted from a distance. He looked up, tried to see who it was. The voice sounded somewhat familiar, but he couldn't place it. Then he saw someone top a distant hill. It was a large man, waving frantically, calling "Ogenus!"

Ogenus waved, thinking it must be one of the men from Hayuk's village. But it wasn't. As he got closer, his size became apparent.

Ogenus broke out in a wide grin. "*Hercle!*" he shouted and began running toward the other man.

"Ogenus!" Hercle called. "At last, I have found you!"

They met and hugged, pounding each other on the back, to Ogenus' detriment. "How did you find us?" Ogenus asked, shaking his head.

The big man laughed, and they began walking to the settlement, where everyone had gathered to see what the shouting was all about.

"I keep asking people, 'have you seen crazy man with big round ship?' over and over, all along the sea coast. Many told me no, others tried to kill me, but Hercle is not so easy to kill, you know. Some of them even wanted to eat me, can you believe it?" He shook his head. "Many people very hungry, and not much food. It is sad. But I keep looking, asking. Eventually, someone who came by this way and visited other village over there knew about you."

"How did you get all the way here?"

"Hah! Ionic, before big kaboom, sent me over there," he pointed toward the large distant mountains "to make sure his pillars got finished. He make plans, we carve animals, set everything just so to line up with sun, moon, stars, all those things he wanted. We tell the story of this cursed comet. We build plenty of pillars on hills there, and over there, and everywhere. If one hit by comet, others will remain. We do a good job."

"Did you finish them?"

Hercle shook his head. "Not yet. The Great Flood didn't quite reach us, but we could see the water coming and almost lap at our feet, and the Earth shook terrible. We got hit with much rain, wind. The gods send their chariots across the sky, look like snakes on fire. There was some damage, but we fix it quickly. But it's much work. A couple of villages have cropped up nearby, several hundred living in mud and stone homes."

"How many people do you have working with you?" Ogenus asked.

Hercle laughed. "We have two, three dozen. Sometimes people come, sometimes they go. Cutting stone was easy at first. We used laser cutters. Then our power ran out and now we cut with steel and muscle. Takes longer. Not as good. A lot of polish needed. But we get the job done."

Hercle shouted some more when he saw the three young men he last saw as little more than children. He was introduced to their mates, and they talked, telling each other stories of their varied experiences. Hercle shook his head, wishing he had seen their round boat.

"So many called you crazy," he told Ogenus, "yet here you are, alive and well. Not so good for so many others."

"It wasn't easy," Inanna said, and everyone agreed. "But we're here, and so happy to see you. Your arrival gives us an excuse for another celebration."

"Celebrations are our only form of entertainment," said Iapetos.

Hummurabi had just taken a drink of water. He gasped, coughed, and sprayed water. "Not the only form," he croaked, wiping his chin. He glanced at Adante and saw her stifling a giggle.

Ogenus smiled again, then it died. He excused himself and Hercle from the others for a private conversation. He hesitated, then blurted, "Ionic didn't make it."

Hercle burst out in laughter, slapping Ogenus on the shoulder again and almost knocking him down. "Oh, but he did! The mighty ocean did not eat his flier. He and Eris are alive, both of them. Alive and well."

"He's alive?" Ogenus shouted, bursting into laughter. "He's *alive!* How? How do you know?"

"I have satellite phone like you, but yours is off. So he called me, said to find you and tell you he and Eris are fine. By some will of the gods, you landed here, far east of Kursatta" he spread his hands, "not too terribly far from my stone workshop. Five days walking. Downhill, easy. Not so easy going back. But this message is important. Ionic *lives!*"

*

Ionic gazed at the phone as he finished his last call with Ogenus. He turned the phone off by habit, saving a battery that would probably never see use again. He could tell that they were just moments from crashing into the sea. He stepped down from the passenger area into the cockpit where Eris was doing her best to keep their flier in the air. "I have bad news," he said. "We're out of fuel cells," Ionic said matter-of-factly. "We're going down."

Eris glanced at him. "I don't think so," she said. "Have you checked the emergency locker?"

"The what?"

"Over there. Push the yellow button. Full of emergency supplies. Should be a dozen fuel cells in there, too."

Ionic almost tripped getting to the locker. He pressed the indicated button and frantically pawed through a small compartment.

"Look down at the bottom," Eris said impatiently. The only thing keeping them in the air at this point were individual electrons, and few enough of those. "And hurry, if you please."

Ionic swept other supplies away, lifted a floor panel and pulled out fuel cells. He leapt to the power center and yanked the cover open. He removed two exhausted cells and replaced them with new ones. At once, Eris had renewed power and began slowly regaining altitude.

Ionic retrieved the remaining ten cells and refreshed the entire bank. He slammed the cover closed. "We have power!" He shouted. "Who knew commercial fliers had emergency cells?"

Eris laughed. "I did. It was part of my job. I was just about to refuel when you disappeared. I couldn't fly and retrieve new cells when power was this low. If you'd made me ditch...well, lifting this big thing off the water would have been a feat in itself. Then I would have killed you."

Ionic laughed in relief and sat in the co-pilot's seat. "I was talking to Ogenus." Then he sat forward suddenly, "and, by the gods, I hold him we were crashing into the sea. I need to call him back. He'll think we're dead." He rose and limped back to the passenger section where he had left his satellite phone. His attempts to raise Ogenus were unsuccessful. He switched channels and called for Hercle, and finally raised him.

When he returned, Eris was tapping the flier's computer screen. "We should have enough fuel to reach half-way up the western continent, somewhere near Mokaya Land. Might be some survivors there along the new coast line."

"I hope they fared better than the rest of the world, but I doubt it," Ionic muttered.

The next afternoon, they arrived at the location where Mokaya Land once existed. They found nothing. The entire coast line had changed. Far inland, they saw rising smoke from twin volcanoes.

"Keep an eye out," Ionic said. "There has to be some civilization down there somewhere, or at least semi-organized survivors."

212

They followed the coast, and in time saw a fishing boat. It was small and crude, but they were overjoyed to see three fishermen staring at them, who then started waving frantically. Since this part of the continent was thick tropical jungle, they brought the flier down on calm water and floated it up onto a small beach. People began emerging from the thick growth of trees, armed with spears and knives, staring at the large machine and shouting among themselves.

"Let's hope they're friendly," Eris said dryly.

"Indeed," Ionic said.

"They don't look too friendly."

"Then you need to smile."

When they exited their craft, they were surprised to find that most of those waiting for them were black-skinned, similar to the inhabitants of the large southeastern continent. They spoke a language from that area that Ionic understood. In his youth he had studied at a university there. When he shouted back in their own language, smiles appeared and weapons were lowered. They stepped into the beach and were immediately surrounded by a multitude of people asking a thousand questions.

He learned their leaders had heeded warnings and some set out in boats before the flood, with animals and supplies. Some of them ended up on the opposite side of the Great Sea, making landfall on the western continent, cut off from their homeland. Since then they had been busily setting up a village in their new home. Here, human survivors were few, and the indigenous nations had been destroyed even more thoroughly than had those in and near Oceana, which Ionic found hard to believe.

"We welcome you to our new nation," the leader, Omek, said. "Welcome bearded white man, and," he nodded to Eris, "his woman. We will sit at our evening fire and listen to your story, and learn about your working flier." He glanced at the machine half floating in the water and resting on the beach. "We'll tie her down so the tide doesn't steal her from you."

"I thank you for that, Chief Omek. Thank you for your hospitality."

The Chief nodded. "We have survived fire from the sky. We have survived wind and rain and the ocean at war with itself. We have arrived here, on this new land, and we are making it our own."

Omek and his people were stout and well-built, with wide, friendly faces. As Ionic expected, these immigrants to a new land were accomplished mathematicians and engineers. They knew of his plans for building large stone structures aligned to celestial points, and had designed their own large versions which they planned to work on as soon as events allowed.

Omek nodded. "We liked your ideas, but until recently we haven't been in a position to actually do anything. Recently we've begun working on some large stone statues. We also plan to develop calendars to know the cycles of days and years, far into the past and far into our future. Any changes, we will know."

Eris had gone with the village women. She observed as they prepared meals and wove animal hair into colorful cloth. She found a small group busy grinding lenses and testing them for accuracy. Later, as they prepared to eat their evening meal, Eris pulled Ionic aside. "They have telescopes!" she told him.

"Telescopes? You're sure?"

"I saw a group of women grinding lenses. They told me the men are working on an observatory. That can help, can't it?"

"Oh yes, it certainly can help. We can search for the comet, perhaps determine its next appearance. Maybe even find out if it's going to hit us again."

During their meal, Ionic related his observations of the feathered dinosaur when Mokaya Land was still a functioning nation. Omek and his people were excited at this news. Some of them wondered if it might be possible to recover the specimen. "Things have been shifted and churned so much, there is no remnant of the Mokaya Land cities," Ionic said. "They've been swallowed by the sea. I'm afraid our feathered serpent is lost forever."

"Not forever," Omek said. "We will remember it. We will make it live again in art and sculpture." Omek raised his arm. "Your feathered serpent will be remembered through the ages." He looked Ionic in the eye and nodded forcefully. "It will become the sign of this comet. We will make it so."

"I'm happy to know that."

The lives of Omek and his people were not entirely idyllic. Several tribes living deeper into the jungle were war-like and possibly cannibalistic. "We avoid them when we can, fight them when necessary. They are good fighters, but we are better."

"Hmm," mused Ionic. "Perhaps it might help if we were to use our flier to impress upon them that you have powerful friends. We might cruise at low altitude over their larger villages, then land nearby and have some of your warriors emerge."

Omek smiled. "An idea worth considering. Let me think upon it."

Ionic and Eris spent the next several weeks assisting Omek and his people to develop a functioning village. "You can add these chemicals to crushed granite rock to make a strong cement," he said to a group of workers. "You can use forms to shape building stones as you please. Much more efficient and less lifting."

The Chief Architect nodded. "I see that. But why do some have notches protruding from the sides?"

"Once you have the cement stone placed, you'll need to shift it back and forth, grind it down to fit the stones below, and the ones beside it. They should fit tightly. With various angles and sizes, your walls and buildings will be virtually earthquake-proof. If our comet reappears, or there are earthquakes, your work should survive anything, except a direct fragment impact, should we be so unfortunate."

They discussed the size and shape of the walls and various buildings, including an observatory. Ionic convinced the engineers that this should be a priority as it would allow him to determine what might come at them in the future.

They also dragged the flier along the sand to higher and dryer ground. Ionic didn't know how many more times it would fly. But he wanted it to be capable of flight in the event Omek decided to confront their enemy tribes from the air. His dream was to return across the great sea to where Hercle and Ogenus had found their new homes. In order to do that, they would need to find, or be able to recharge, the necessary fuel cells. The likelihood of that was slim.

So Ionic and Eris settled in for a long stay, knowing that they were unlikely to ever see Ogenus and his family again. They, Ogenus and Hercle, all had satellite phones. However, once the power cells were exhausted, those devices would soon be as useless as the flier.

A few of the surviving indigenous people drifted into the village. They were welcomed and accepted since there was much more work to be done than there were people to do it. Some of them were individuals from the nearby warlike tribes who had been banished. Others came from further away. These were short, stocky, brown-skinned people who spoke a language different from either Omek's people or the residents of the former Mokaya Land.

They quickly picked up the language of Omek's people, who called themselves The Me'catl, but they also used words from their own language. Ionic noted that sometimes they would point to him and use a word, "Kukulkan" which, when he asked, translated to "feathered serpent" as they had heard stories told to them by the Me'catl people, and their plans to immortalize the dinosaur as related to them by Ionic. Since he had white skin and a beard, he was looked upon by members of these primitive peoples as a god, who came from the east in a flying machine. They began to worship him when he wasn't looking, which annoyed him.

Ionic tried to suppress such irreverence, but the practice persisted. Thankfully, the Me'catl weren't as prone to superstitious tendencies since they, like he and Eris, had come from a highly developed scientific and technological culture.

Everyone worked hard, more refugees joined the village, and Ionic saw his observatory grow cement stone by stone. There would be no electricity. His plan was to use the telescope in the dark interior at night to search for his comet based upon past observations. The dome of this primitive observatory could be rotated, but with considerable difficulty as it was done by many hands, stone on stone, lubricated with plant oil.

He tried to maintain a patient demeanor, but found patience a limited resource. He wanted to go home.

*

Iapetos chipped away at one small stone with another, slightly harder rock. After a few more strikes, he examined his handiwork, then tossed it away in disgust. It landed on a pile of similar rejects. An hour later, he held up a later attempt and screamed in frustration. Hammarabi and Shemash abandoned their tasks and came over to see what was happening.

"It's pathetic!" Iapetos said, almost screaming.

"What are you doing, big brother?" Shemash asked.

Iapetos glared at his sibling. "I'm trying to make an axe head. But I just don't get it. Sabra had seen it done at an exhibit in her native country. She said it was easy, told me how to do it."

Hammurabi picked a stone from the pile. "This is not an axe head."

"You think not! Look at that pile. Ten thousand years from now, if somebody digs that up, they'll think I was no better than a monkey."

"All you lack is the tail," said Shemash, which set the two brothers howling with laughter.

"Like you could do better?"

"Don't know. Haven't tried. Why do you need a stone axe anyhow? We have a real axe."

"It won't last forever, my stupid little brother. Steel rusts and wears out. We'll need to replace it someday, and all we have are these stupid rocks."

"Maybe," said Hammurabi slowly, holding an example of his brother's efforts in each hand and examining them closely, "what you need is a harder rock."

"I figured that out, too," Iapetos said. "Haven't been able to find one."

"Well, then, you just keep on making these 'monkey rocks' for some ten-thousand year distant digger to find. He'll be impressed."

All three young men laughed at that.

Ogenus came out of his home, wearing a frown. "What's so funny, guys? And why isn't anybody working."

"Iapetos is working very hard, Father," Shemash said, grinning. "He's making you a new axe head."

"What's wrong with the old one?"

Iapetos tossed his rock down in anger and strode off.

"Show Sabra your axe," Hammurabi called after him. "She'll be impressed!"

His reply, while silent, was emphatic and resulted in more laughter.

Sabra announced her pregnancy within the next month, after a private audience with Inanna. Hammurabi was crestfallen. He'd wanted to be next to make a happy announcement, and he and Adante were trying very hard. He felt as if he were running last in a race.

Well, there was nothing for them to do, but to keep "working."

*

Omek walked with Ionic past some of the rock sculptures the Me'catl artisans were working on. The going was slow since Ionic walked with a cane and had trouble with his balance over the uneven ground.

"We smelt iron in small quantities," Omak said, "and the quality is fair. If we had laser cutters, the work would be done much faster."

"You're absolutely right," Ionic said. "If we only had more power cells or some way to recharge our old ones."

"Speaking of that, there was another raid by the mountain people last evening," Omek said. "Two of my warriors were killed and some others injured."

"And the raiders?"

Omek shrugged. "A few got away. The rest did not surrender. I hate killing, but sometimes it is necessary. Something interesting, though. One of the dead raiders had a fuel cell in his pouch." He looked at Ionic. "A fully-charged fuel cell."

Ionic stopped and stared at the Me'catl king. "And where do you suppose he got that?"

Omek barely smiled, "I would certainly like to know that as well. Had to be somewhere up in the mountains, near where they live."

"Hmm. If there are more, hidden somewhere within the territory of that tribe..."

"My thinking as well," Omek grunted.

"Perhaps," Ionic mused, he stopped and turned. "Perhaps it's time we paid a visit to these violent people and see if we can turn away their wrath and at the same time find out exactly what they've got."

"I have brave warriors, but I don't have an army, Ionic. How many of my people would die if we tried to attack those mountain people? Up there, the advantage is theirs."

Ionic smiled. "What if we used the cell you got last night, used it to supplement the remaining few in our flier, and came at them from the air? They don't strike me as the remnants of an advanced civilization. So they're probably hunter-gatherers who've always lived in these mountains."

Omek stopped and turned toward Ionic. "Brilliant, you are! They've probably never seen one like you, pink skin and a beard. You would appear to them as a god, coming down from the heavens. They'll worship you!"

"That's been happening all too often as it is," Ionic said sourly. "But I think it's worth a try. If we're wrong...well, I won't make much of a meal for them, will I?"

Omek broke into a loud, guttural laugh that echoed through the trees.

Ionic met with Eris and planned how to best use their flier to intimidate the mountain tribe. "The fuel cell Omek's people captured, plus what we have left already in the flier, will give us more than enough flying time to get up the mountain and, if we live, back down. But not a whole lot more. We need to conserve what fuel we already have, but I think the gamble is worth it. Perhaps we can stop these raids and, if we are sufficiently persuasive, secure a supply of fuel cells."

"Let's do it, Ionic. I'm tired of weaving cloth. Maybe we can find enough fuel to get us back across the sea."

Ionic's eyes lit up. "Now there's an idea. It would be good to see Ogenus and Inanna and their family once more."

"Indeed," said Eris. "Hopefully they're doing well."

It took them a month to plan. Eris proposed the idea of keeping herself in the shadows, armed with a beam weapon, just in case Ionic wasn't quite as convincing as he needed to be. They would pull off their Grand Deception at night, making their appearance even more mysterious and hiding some of the effects that might be obvious during daytime. "It will also hide my shaking knees," Ionic said. "A self-respecting god shouldn't tremble in fear."

"No, please don't tremble," Eris said. "You tremble, you're tomorrow's stew."

*

Out of the dark night, a giant serpent flew into territories of the Waryah mountain people, a people feared by all those nearby for their tendency to engage in blood sacrifices and ritual cannibalism.

As the serpent roared overhead, most of the war-like tribe members cowered in fear. The serpent turned and stared at the group, illuminating them with two powerful glowing eyes.

The Chief held his ground, hiding his fear. He glanced nervously at the Shaman, who stood defiantly, his ceremonial staff held at the ready. Be they gods or demons, this was his job. The growling serpent hovered momentarily as if assessing any possible threat. Then the craft descended and settled gently in a clearing near the primitive village. The roar of its anger faded away, and it closed its horrible eyes. Silence returned. Some of the more curious and bravest members of the Waryah slowly gathered around their Chief, but none dared step as close as the Shaman, who now began a soft chant used to ward off evil demons.

A mouth opened on the side of the serpent, causing the gathered tribe to step back almost as one. Out of the mouth a brilliant light. The Shaman raised his staff and shouted in defiance. A god emerged from the serpent and slowly descended to the ground.

The Shaman ceased his chanting with a surprised look on his face. This god was a man, such as himself, but his skin was white, and his face covered in a beard. This god carried a stick with him, but it was obviously not a weapon as he used it to help him walk. If this was a god, it walked like a man, and a weak man at that. There was nothing here to fear after all.

Nevertheless, the Shaman's staff dipped, and the rest of the tribe whispered among themselves.

The god, or man, walked slowly but boldly up to the Shaman, grasped the holy staff and jerked it from his hand. The god then tossed the symbol of power behind him, into the darkness. The message was clear; he was a god and carried no weapon. He needed no weapon.

Ionic then spoke a few words in the language of the Waryah, words taught him by refugees and a few captives that resided in the Me'Catl village. He had practiced his lines until his teachers could understand easily. What he said was, he hoped, "I am from the sky. You," he swept his hand to indicate the tribe, "are not people. You are no better than animals. Do you have any people here?"

The Shaman thrust out his chin. "I am."

"You are dust," Ionic said, pushing him aside with his cane. "Are there any people here?"

Angered and humiliated, the Shaman pulled his long knife. He raised the blade to slice at Ionic, but before that could happen, the Shaman's eyes opened wide, he clutched his chest and dropped the knife. Blood oozed between his fingers and he fell over, dead. Voices rose in astonishment.

In the shadows beyond the flier's hatch, Eris lowered her beam weapon. She did not like killing, but she and Ionic hoped that the death of one would prevent the death of many, including, possibly, themselves. To the Chief and the tribe members, it appeared that their Shaman had challenged Ionic, threatened him with a weapon, then simply fell over dead. A god that powerful was one not to be trifled with. The warriors looked at each other and broke out in shocked exclamations. They backed away, eyes wide in fear.

Ionic then approached the Chief. He faced the Waryah leader without fear, silently.

Finally, and slowly, the Chief tossed his knife away and knelt before Ionic, lowering his head in submission. The other tribes' members whispered among themselves. How could this be?

"It seems you are people after all," Ionic said loudly. "Because of this we have brought you gifts." Eris then opened the rear cargo hatch and wheeled out a flatbed filled with food. She pushed the gifts into the midst of the group, resulting in a growing and excited response.

"We accept your gift, O mighty god." the Chief said. "What do you wish from us in return?"

Ionic held up an empty fuel cell. "We wish these, as a tribute," he replied. "And we also require that you cease your attacks on the peoples near the sea. We will show you how to grow your own food, and how to capture and care for animals. These animals will make more of themselves if handled properly. Soon you will eat and have no more hunger."

"All of these things you will give to us?" The Chief shook his head in disbelief.

"We who own the sky will do this."

"We have those strange boxes. Many of them. We will bring them to you. We will no longer leave the mountains toward the sea. This I swear."

Ionic nodded and said quietly in his own language, "good enough then."

Over the next two days, tribal warriors brought load after load of charged fuel cells along with an equal number of empty, useless ones. They were, the Chief said, hidden deep in a cave complex a short distance from their tribal village. Other unknown treasures were stored there as well. Ionic asked the Chief to show the cave to Eris since he wasn't able to walk long distances.

Eris returned that afternoon very excited. "Must have been a military supply depot," she said. "I showed the Chief how to tell charged from dead fuel cells. I also showed him the supplies of rations and water containers. There are caches of weapons there as well, along with some military vehicles, much of it damaged. I told him that section was filled with power they could not understand, and it was taboo and to keep all his people away from that area."

"Good. We've almost got a full cargo bay load of fuel. You ferry those down to Omek's people and let him know what we've accomplished. Leave me here with the beam weapon, although I doubt I'll need it. I'll start these people learning agriculture and land cultivation. When you get back, we'll teach them domestication of livestock. In a month or two, we will have taught these people what we can. These mountains are not the best for agriculture, but terraces might work. Once we're finished, we can rejoin Omek's group and start thinking about going home."

Language barriers caused a delay of several additional weeks, but they at last got the concepts across, and members of the tribe had begun preparing suitable land for growing crops. The Waryah had many slaves to help with the work.

Eventually, Ionic and Eris were ready to leave. Ionic addressed the Chief and his people. "We are leaving now," he said to the gathering. "Do not forget what we have taught you.

Someday," he added, "we will return. We will come to judge you on how well you have used the knowledge we have given you. We expect you to send gifts to the people near the great sea. They will be happy with these small boxes filled with the power of the gods. You will take them as many as you can carry. When he wishes it, you will guide the chief of the sea people to your cave and allow him to take what he wishes. We will certainly return to judge you on your good relations with neighboring tribes. Choose a Shaman who is kind and strong as well as wise. That will please us."

Ionic and Eris entered the flier and the hatch swung closed. The great bird began to roar, then slowly lifted into the sky. It circled once, then headed out toward the great sea, disappearing into the morning. They did not go far, landing on the beach at the edge of Omek's village half-an-hour later.

Eris was excited to have a flier with a full complement of fuel. "How soon can we depart for Oceana? Or what's left of it?"

"I need to make some further observations of the night sky," Ionic said, "I don't know how long it will take me as most nights are filled with fog or these obnoxious clouds. It might take me a couple more months to make sure I have enough observations. We should be able to lift off just as soon as I've gathered my data."

Omek was overjoyed at the abundance of charged fuel cells delivered by the Waryah people. Powering laser cutters and other equipment found in the mountain cave would make completing their stone constructions much easier.

Ionic's "couple of months" turned into four. But when he indicated it was time to take flight, the elderly scientist looked worried and in a big hurry.

"What's wrong, Ionic?" Eris said.

He sighed, glanced at the woman, then looked away. "Whenever I look through a damned telescope, I come away with bad news."

"What now?"

"The worst, I fear." Ionic shook his head. He looked at Eris. "This time I'm really afraid."

Saying goodbye to Omek and his people was difficult. Whereas the mountain tribe had been lacking in technology, and were essentially ignorant, violent, and superstitious, Omek's people were civilized and fully cognizant of their vast knowledge. They had used that knowledge here to build a new civilization. Instead of metal and concrete, they now built in stone. They were masters of their art.

Ionic, of course, had encouraged them to build cities and include his plans for incorporating giant aligned structures. He told Omek to keep watch for the mountain people, who were expected to bring an additional supply of fuel cells as gifts to the sea peoples.

Omek assured their elderly friend that they would, indeed follow his wishes. Ionic was especially anxious after he had made his astronomical observations, although he didn't provide any additional details.

"Be vigilant," Ionic urged. "If you see a light approaching in the sky, move your people to higher ground, completely away from the sea."

"Are you predicting more comet strikes?" Omek asked.

Ionic placed a hand on the large man's shoulder. "I make no predictions, my friend Omek. But if it happens, do not delay. Move quickly. Take necessities only, and move fast. That cave near the Waryah territory might be ideal."

The Me'catl King assured Ionic that they would heed his warnings.

The entire village gathered at the beach, singing a farewell song and watching Ionic's large craft rise into the sky, heading east from a land that had once been the home of great nations to another land that had once been the home of great nations.

They flew toward lands that now held only a few surviving humans hanging onto a precarious existence. And he had bad news. Bad, bad news.

*

Once a week, Ogenus turned on his satellite phone and checked for messages. One day, a month after the birth of his second grandchild, he turned the phone on and was rewarded with a green light flashing receipt of a message.

"Ogenus," the message began, "Ionic here. If Hercle was able to find you, you know that Eris and I survived via an emergency supply of fuel cells that I did not even know existed on commercial fliers. Even better, when we landed on the western continent, we found a large cache of cells. We've loaded up the flier and are heading back across the Great Sea toward you. If you have moved from your original location, four days from receipt of this message start leaving your phone on. We can pick up your signal and home in on it. I'm afraid I do not arrive with good tidings, only with more bad news and difficult challenges. Forgive me, my friend. We shall see you very soon."

Ogenus turned off the phone and searched the sky. It was far too early to expect Ionic and Eris to appear, but he looked anyway. He would be happy to see them, despite Ionic's threat of more bad news. As requested, in four days he would begin leaving the phone on so that Ionic and Eris could find them.

"What is it?" Inanna asked, stepping from their small home.

"Ionic and Eris have found enough fuel to make it back here. From the date of his message, they should be arriving within a week or so. How amazing is that?"

"That's good. I'll be happy to see them and I know you have missed Ionic."

Ogenus smiled. "He's been a good friend over the years. I think I mentioned this before, but when my parents were killed, Ionic took me under his wing and kept me from making stupid decisions. I was badly depressed for several months, but his friendship helped me to recover."

"More than friendship," Inanna said, "love as well. Just as you loved me when I was abandoned and needed help."

Ogenus looked into his mate's eyes. He simply nodded and they hugged. No words were needed.

Several days later, Ogenus began leaving the phone on. He worried that the battery would die before Ionic could use its signal. It wasn't until five days later that Shemash spotted a flier in the distance. He was standing at the ocean's edge, trying his hand at surf fishing when a glint caught his eye. He watched it, finally realized what it was, then ran back to the encampment shouting.

Ogenus popped out of his residence at a run.

"A flier is coming!" Shemash said, pointing back toward the water. "It's coming."

Together, Ogenus and his youngest son ran back to the water's edge. They searched the skies, but couldn't spot the flier. "It was just there," Shemash said, "I *saw* it! I did see it!"

"I believe you, son. It's probably hidden in those clouds."

A few minutes later, as Inanna and Hammurabi joined them, the flier became visible again. It grew in size rapidly, circled their encampment, then swooped in for a landing about fifty yards away, settling onto the flat land a few hundred feet up from the water's edge.

By the time the hatch opened, four humans swarmed over the two who descended the flier's ramp. Ogenus was surprised to find tears staining his cheeks as he grasped Ionic by the shoulders and pulled him into a hug. "I feared you were dead," he whispered. He was surprised at how thin and frail his old friend looked.

"Believe me, my friend, it was close," Ionic said, smiling. "But Eris here knew more about the flier than I ever will. She saved us with a well-timed and a well-aimed point."

"And you're late," Ogenus accused.

Ionic nodded. "We took a little side trip to the northeast to pick up Hercle."

"He's here too? He left us many months ago to continue work on his stone pillars."

"He is, indeed, here," Ionic looked over his shoulder and frowned.

They heard some loud, crunching noises from inside the flier. Hercle appeared in the hatch, holding the back of a passenger seat. "When I leaned back to undo my belt," he said, "it just snapped off." He tossed the seat back into the flier. "It's pretty flimsy."

Ogenus burst into laughter, then welcomed the large man once again to their home.

A lavish feast was concocted to welcome the newcomers. Eris and Ionic were introduced to the three boys' mates, two of them carrying babies and the third very pregnant. "It is difficult to imagine you three grown with mates and children," Ionic said. He looked at the three young women, "I knew these boys when they were toddlers spilling milk and wetting their nappies." The women burst into laughter followed by pointing fingers.

Ogenus noticed that Ionic ate very little, and his elderly friend was more than unusually quiet while animated conversations went on all around him. He wondered if Ionic had pushed himself too hard. He was not a young man anymore. Perhaps Ionic was concerned about the bad news he had hinted at but was yet to divulge.

As evening came on, the talk quieted, and everyone basked in a warm glow from the fire and the warmth of good friends. When full dark had fallen, and the babies put down for the night, Ogenus felt a tap on his shoulder. He looked up to see Ionic and Hercle standing near him. "We need to talk," Ionic said quietly.

*

Ogenus rose and followed his two friends into the night. Light burst from the flier as the hatch opened. The three entered the large craft, and Hercle made sure the hatch was closed and secured. "I have two pieces of news, one that's interesting, the other...well, not good."

"Give us good news first," Hercle said. "Always better to hear good news before bad, eh?"

Ionic nodded. "That it is, my dear friend Hercle. When I consulted with the astronomers of Me'catl, I learned they had records of this comet and perhaps other comets going back for a very long time. Comets have, of course, appeared in our skies since before the times of humans on Earth. Me'catl astronomers traced comet sightings back through legends, prehistoric art, and accounts of our primitive ancestors. After that, they used geological layers to determine dates when comet fragments might have struck the Earth." He paused and took a deep breath.

"There exists an ancient list of the kings of earth. It's in some of the more esoteric history books, we touch on it in university classes, but we don't know the origin of this mysterious list. It's very old. Each of these kings apparently lived for many thousands of years before a new king was crowned, which is not logical nor practical. Human lifespans have never been nearly that long. I now suspect that this list does not refer to actual living people, nor some mysterious gods. I believe, and some Me'catl astronomers are inclined to concur, that these 'kings' were actually appearances of a comet or comets in our skies, and likely, at least in some cases, the very comet that has been tormenting us. The first king on the list ruled over 230,000 years ago. That king's rule lasted for 28,800 years before a successor was named, and the new king ruled for 36,000 years, and so on. This is, of course, absurd. No human king could live that long. We believe that each time a comet reappeared in close proximity to Earth, a new 'king' was announced. There were eight kings with extraordinarily long reigns. That would mean a comet interacted with Earth only eight times during that span of centuries. Sometimes fragments hit and caused destruction. Other times its passage was more benign, but certainly visible to those keeping watch. This may also explain why the ancients were so obsessed with observing movements of the planets and stars."

"Amazing," said Ogenus. "So you're saying comets are possibly the gods in our ancient history. That's going to upset a lot of people."

"There's more. You've seen the ancient petroglyphs, carvings, and cave paintings done by prehistoric peoples? Many of them are focused on and seem fascinated by snakes or flying serpents. We believe those are representations of the comet as it appeared over the Earth, a large head with a tail stretched across the sky."

"Snakes mean comets!" Hercle said. "We used the same symbol on your pillars. We asked, how can we send this message of comets and fireballs in stone carvings? Then we said, 'Aha!' they look like serpents in the sky. So we used the same symbol as these very old people?"

"In many instances, we believe that yes, snakes and serpents and even dragons portray the appearance of a comet. Depictions of what has been referred to as sun disks may have, in some cases, actually been references to comet sightings as well."

"So we've been hounded by comets for far longer than we suspected," Ogenus said.

"My friend, there are trillions of comets in our solar system. It's a wonder there were so many thousands of years between sightings. In fact, it's such a wonder, I believe we are missing something still. After the long reigns of these eight kings," Ionic continued, "the reigns of subsequent kings were substantially shorter, on the order of a thousand years or so. This could mean the appearance of a single comet, or a series of comets with different orbits, probably the result of increasing close approaches to Earth. And, according to the geologic record, these appearances became not only much more frequent, but more often deadly."

"Until recently," Ogenus said. "When these angry kings began showing up in our skies even more frequently."

"Just so. These 'kings' were sometimes referred to as gods who came down to the Earth from the heavens, comet fragment strikes near primitive settlements perhaps. Sometimes they rode fiery chariots that made loud noises."

"I've seen too many of those these past few decades," Ogenus said sourly. "So these early kings of Earth weren't actually human kings at all."

Ionic nodded. "They were 'kings' in the sense that they were crowned in absentia by terrified humans who had felt the wrath of the gods. They were given names, and in time, artists gave them the form of gods and later, depicted them as humans. Whenever you see a god in concert with a snake or, possibly a sun disk, think comet. Later on, as villages became nations formed from primitive tribes, human kings and rulers were instituted, and the lifespans of these human kings reflected typical life spans. But even in these instances, many human kings were referred to as gods, hearkening back to the ages when kings were comets, and they sometimes visited deadly wrath on their subjects."

"That's fascinating," Ogenus said, "but this isn't what has gotten you in such a glum mood. Time to spill the real reason we're hiding in here. You know, every time you call me into a private conference, the world ends. I'm beginning to get a little tired of it." He tried to smile, but it was not measurably successful.

"I'm afraid, my friend, that I will not disappoint you. Not this time. Especially not this time."

*

Ionic related the use of a new observatory built by the Me'catl people. "They are very good at what they do," Ionic said. "Like you, these survivors took to boats, and I understand their journey was much more perilous than yours, Ogenus. They set sail westward across the Great Ocean. They lost half their people, most of their supplies and livestock, and those who survived made landfall months later, half-starved, on an entirely different continent. Yet when Eris and I arrived, they had a functioning civilization going. They'd already begun construction of buildings, built pens for their remaining animals, and begun to clear and cultivate the land. Certainly they had troubles with the remnant indigenous peoples, but those were minor. Me'catl warriors are fierce and they tend to be rather large and menacing. At any rate, along with their other talents, they ground lenses for telescopes and built me a primitive but functioning observatory. Light pollution was not an issue, but overcast skies were frequent. We would have been here much sooner had I been able to get decent observations. When I did get good seeing, Ogenus, what I saw terrified me. What's coming at us this time is either a huge chunk of the comet or a giant asteroid."

Ogenus shook his head. "So still another rock is headed for Earth?"

Ionic nodded. "Only this is not a small comet fragment, it's a really big chunk of some god's anger. And, to the best of my ability to determine, it's coming in straight at us. The Me'catl astronomers working with me concurred."

"And I assume that's a bad thing."

"It's as bad as it can get, my friend. Look, most of the comet fragment strikes we've faced so far have come in at oblique angles. A lot of the mass was burned up in the atmosphere. Not so with this 'king.' This one will punch through the atmosphere like nothing you can imagine, straight down. It will hit hard." Ionic stopped, unable to continue. It took a moment before he regained his composure. "This time, this rock will most likely destroy every living thing on Earth larger than an insect, and most of those as well. Ogenus, Hercle, if that thing hits like I think it will, we're all doomed, every single living human."

"So what can we do?"

Ionic shook his head. "If it had come at us first, before we lost everything, we might have been able to deflect it with nuclear-tipped rockets, but even that's doubtful. Except..."

"What?"

"If we only had some form of ground-based beam cannon. There was some research done along those lines in the far east, weapons that might have been able to inflict at least some minor damage on the rock. Jiahu scientists hypothesized that a nuclear-powered array of extremely large lasers coupled with a particle beam weapon might have been able to reduce an incoming asteroid to pieces before it entered our lower atmosphere. Not likely, but possible."

"But we can't build such weapons now, can we?"

"No, Ogenus. We couldn't have built them before the first comet fall. Such technology was beyond our capabilities. The scientists and engineers in Jiahu were apparently engaged in preliminary planning stages when everything started falling apart."

"Maybe," Ogenus said, "this rock will hit on the other side of the Earth."

"That," Ionic said softly, "is the rest of my bad news. Our calculations show that the rock will impact directly somewhere on the great southern continent across our local sea here. Exactly how close to us is just a guess. A thousand miles, maybe. Or a few hundred."

Ogenus said some words he hardly ever used.

"The one good thing," Ionic said, "we won't linger as the Earth is pushed out of its orbit and our atmosphere ignites. We'll be dead by the time we see the rock. Those on the opposite side of the planet will have a few hours before a massive firestorm reaches them."

"How soon is this thing going to hit?" Ogenus asked, not actually interested in hearing the answer.

"We have maybe a month. It's coming in fast. This time there won't be a warning tail in the sky, no serpent to announce the crowning of a new king. Just a rock, silent, invisible, falling. We'll see it, feel it, hear it just in time to die from it."

"Could we move into mountains? Maybe one of those underground cities?" Hercle asked, turning and pointing.

"Wouldn't help," Ionic said, touching the large man's shoulder. "Even if you're underground, you still need to breathe." Ionic looked at the other two. "First the gods destroy the earth with water, then they send a rock to destroy it with fire."

With that, the three men were silent. There was nothing left to say.

*

Ogenus wandered back to his home and family. He called them together and related Ionic's news. They were frightened and angry, but there were no outbursts. They had long ago been resigned to the Camel following them through the desert of life, eagerly wanting to kneel before them and bring their existence to a close.

"Weeks," Iapetos said softly, holding his baby son close. "It's not fair, Father. Why us?"

"That's a question for the gods, my son, not me."

"Bother to the gods," Hammurabi said forcefully. "We kneel to them, we hold our children up to them, we give them thanks for our good fortune, and how do they repay our dedication? Like *this?*"

Ogenus shrugged. "I don't have answers for you, my son. I wish I did, but I used up all my answers long ago."

"Perhaps if we build an altar to them," Adante suggested, a hand on her swollen stomach.

"How big an altar would it take to interest them in removing this rock from our world?" Shemash asked bitterly.

No one tried to answer that question.

"Let's sleep now," Inanna said. "Tomorrow..."

"Tomorrow we shall celebrate," said Nala with a lightness she didn't feel. "We'll make merry and laugh and eat and celebrate the end of life on Earth." She smiled, but tears lined her cheeks. "We'll end this in uplift and joy." She looked at her mate. "We'll play with our daughter and tell her she's a good girl." She fell into Shemash's arms and sobbed.

"Hold onto that thought for just a moment," said Eris, stepping into the family group. "Perhaps..."

"What now?" growled Ogenus.

"Ionic sent me. He has just heard from a colleague via satellite phone, an acquaintance in Jiahu. Seems the first comet fall didn't do them as much damage as it did us, and the flood largely bypassed two of their main cities."

"What does that mean for us?" Inanna asked.

Before Eris could reply, Ionic limped into the group. "They still maintain some parts of their technology," he said, "despite their brief participation in the nuclear war."

"Enough technology to stop that rock headed our way?"

Ionic shook his head. "Not from ground level," he said. "But they have a rocket, and it was not damaged in any of the upheavals."

"And they propose to use it to save the Earth?" Ogenus asked. "How?"

Ionic stroked his beard. "They have something else that might be of use."

"Which is?"

"They dug into a damaged military base and found an intact nuclear warhead. They can use the rocket to launch that warhead at the asteroid, and perhaps, if we are very lucky, burst it into pieces."

"And how will that help," Iapetos asked. "Then we'll just have a thousand little pieces falling on us instead of a big one."

"Ah, yes. But the smallest pieces will burn up in Earth's atmosphere."

"Leaving a slightly smaller big rock to kill us instead of a larger big rock?" Ogenus asked.

Ionic smiled slightly. "Jiahu scientists, technicians and military crew are on their way here even as we speak. They're bringing an array of lasers and a particle beam cannon. It seems their military had reached a breakthrough just before the first comet fall. They've been working since then. These weapons have barely been tested, and they might not work at all. They are merely prototypes, and not full-powered military weapons. But maybe, just maybe, after the warhead does its best, we can further carve up that large rock with the beam, then burn pieces with the lasers."

"Have you told them we have no source of power?"

Ionic grinned. "They're bringing with them a portable nuclear reactor."

Nala looked up from Shemash's arms. "Is there any reason to have hope?"

"I always have hope, my dear," Ionic said softly. He glanced at Eris, and she helped him back to the shelter where he slept.

*

A week later, four very large fliers appeared in the sky. The Jiahu Dragon Ships settled near the small family community, and everyone ran out to see this amazing sight. The dragons were larger even than passenger and cargo fliers that had once belonged to Oceana. They were heavily armed military vessels and looked frightening.

With Eris' help, Ionic limped out to meet the Jiahu scientists and military leaders. They spoke for quite some time, then Ionic turned, and he and Eris slowly re-joined the anxious group.

"Do they think they can actually do this?" Adante asked.

"They're committed to trying," Ionic said. "While their language is unlike any we've experienced, one of their scientists studied for a time at Kursatta University, and he is fairly fluent in our language. They want someone to accompany them to the southern continent and assist with operation of the array, if the rocket succeeds. They've brought all the scientific instruments they might require for sighting and tracking the asteroid."

"Accompany them? Why? Don't they have their own technicians?" Hammurabi asked.

"The only one available with the necessary skills is the launch control officer who's going to launch and guide the rocket. He can't do that and be here in time to do this. It takes

238

someone with a fine touch and experience with guidance control systems."

"And who have you selected to accompany them?" Inanna asked, glancing quickly at Ogenus.

Ionic took a long time to reply. "I think you know who, my dear."

"But you can't. I won't let you do this!"

"This equipment is basically untested. We need someone who has technical training. Name one other person here that fits that requirement."

"Hercle! You can take him!"

Ionic shook his head sadly. "He is a master at what he does, but he is not a technician."

"Eris then," Inanna said, not looking at the other woman. "She can..."

Ogenus glanced at his mate, then stepped close and hugged her tightly. "She can't. She's an administrator. There is no one else. It's settled then," he said softly into her hair. "I'm needed. I must go."

"You're needed here, Oannes. You must stay."

Ogenus shook his head.

"You'll be right under that thing when it hits."

"Only if we don't destroy it."

"If you can't destroy it, I want you here, with me, with your sons and grandchildren."

"That would be my fondest dream, my soft and gentle love. But my duty is giving you," he looked up at his extended family, gathered close, "giving you all one more chance at life."

"It won't be life without you," Inanna whispered.

"Yes, it will," Ogenus replied. "You'll go on. You will lead our family and you'll survive. Your name will go down in history. You will bear many names, as one will not be enough to contain your love. Legends will tell of your life, my love.

239

You're the strongest and smartest person I've ever known. And you know, in your heart, there is no other choice."

They held each other for a long time, silently, hanging on. Hanging on.

"Your name, too, will live forever" Inanna whispered into his ear. "You will be a man of renown, a Giant, down through history."

Shouting from the Dragon Ship caused Ogenus to step back and glance at Ionic. The old man nodded. "We have very little time. There is much work to be done before..."

Ogenus stepped away from his mate, then turned back to her. "I have to go. I really have to go." Then, one last embrace for his one love. He discovered that a last kiss is forever, and inhumanely brief.

Each of his family came to him for a hug and a cry, and a kiss for his grandchildren. Shemash was last in line. His voice shook, "Father, what's going to happen to us?"

Ogenus grasped the boy by the back of his head and pulled him in close, gazing into his eyes. "What's going to happen to you, my son? Nothing. *Nothing.*"

He said farewell to his oldest friend. They said goodbye with their eyes. Ionic and Ogenus simply looked at each other. Their choices had defined them. This final choice would preserve a world, or doom it.

Eris stepped up to him and took his hand. "You saved me once, when all hope was lost. I'm counting on you to do it again."

"I'll do my best."

Ogenus turned and walked away. Much as he wanted to, much as he needed to, he didn't look back. Leaving tore at his heart, and fear gripped it. He approached the liaison and nodded. Together they entered the lead Dragon Ship and a few minutes later it lifted off into the sky. The four Dragons formed up and headed toward oblivion or salvation.

Ogenus watched from a window as the ground slipped by. He saw Ionic limp over to his family and join them, with Eris helping. He got one last brief glimpse of Inanna and his sons, then they were gone, out of sight.

The Jiahu crew and technicians did not speak with him, although several glanced at him from time-to-time. They passed over the sea from which Oceanus had gotten its name. After an hour, they passed over the edge of the great southern continent. As land replaced water, it was clear that the climate of his huge area was slowly changing, and not necessarily for the better. What had once been a lush jungle was quickly becoming a Savannah, with fewer trees. Lakes were smaller than they had been, and there were fewer rivers. At least one bomb had detonated several hundred miles south of their intended landing place, during the brief war that had taken place between comet falls. They passed over a herd of elk, and watched them run in fear from the ships above them. Ionic had told him this entire area might one day be a desert. He couldn't imagine it.

Two hours later, the Dragon Ships settled down in a large clearing flanked by dead and dying trees.

Ionic's Jiahu colleague, Kwan, called him over. "This is where we will set up our equipment. According to the calculations by my colleagues back home, they will launch their rocket in exactly seven days and four hours from now. We have to be set up and ready to fire our beams and lasers shortly thereafter. That thing is moving so fast that the time between rocket strike and impact on our heads is in the order of minutes."

"That sounds impossible."

"Doing the impossible," said Kwan with a slight humorless smile, "is merely a matter of careful preparation and planning. We have done the planning, now we must prepare."

"How close are we to the point of impact?" Ogenus asked.

Kwan looked surprised. "Ogenus," he said, stomping his foot, "*this* is the point of impact."

"Oh. Of course."

Hundreds of technicians and soldiers exited the Dragon Ships and began unloading equipment at a furious pace. The nuclear reactor would remain in the hold of one ship. It was large enough to provide power to a medium-sized city. The electricity it generated was sufficient for the particle beams as well as the array of lasers.

"The lasers themselves are unable to penetrate the mass headed toward us," Kwan explained. "What remains after the rocket detonation must be cut into smaller pieces with the particle beam cannon. The lasers will then vaporize many of the smallest pieces."

"You can't hope to eliminate them all," said Ogenus.

"Of course not. Our goal is to obliterate enough of the incoming object so that it doesn't cause irreparable damage to Earth."

"But what remains will cause damage to this area, right?"

Kwan was slow to answer. "The smaller fragments will, of course, burn up in the atmosphere. There is a high probability that larger pieces are going to impact here." He shrugged. "We are here for the benefit of all mankind, friend of Ionic, not ourselves. Whatever happens to us is of little consequence, just so long as we succeed."

*

Crews worked frantically to assemble the equipment and get it all connected, run in with the controls, and tested ahead of a fast-approaching deadline. Errors and glitches needed to be fixed. After it had been almost completed, Ogenus wandered over to the narrow steel frame which housed the lasers and particle beam array control center. He opened the door and looked at controls that were both unfamiliar and familiar. He wondered if he still had the delicate touch needed. He was, after all, much older than the confident young man who docked cargo ships.

Kwan joined him.

"What is it, exactly, you are expecting me to do?" Ogenus asked.

"Ionic told me you used to be a navigator on large ships."

"That's correct."

"While we have people who know how to operate this weapon in general, the purpose for which we intend to use it now requires a very light, delicate touch. The distance from here to the asteroid is extreme. The slightest adjustment here will result in a very large movement at the target above Earth's atmosphere. Even a tiny movement might cause a complete miss. You will have no margin nor time for errors. There is no leeway of even a tiny amount." They climbed onto the control cabin, trying to stay out of the way of workers. "These controllers," Kwan said, indicating two hand-sized knobs, "control left and right, up and down for aiming. One foot pedal controls firing the beam and the other the intensity. You will be wearing this," he held up a thick face mask with a large cable leading from it. "It will give you a high-magnification telescopic view of the object in three dimensions. In the center is a red circle. Use the controllers to center your circle on the object, and the foot pedals to fire the weapon. During the few minutes you will have to break up the object, you need to keep that red circle centered. That is crucial. Any deviation, and you won't have time to correct."

"What about the lasers?"

"They will fire automatically, computer-controlled, using radar, once the smaller fragments reach a lower altitude. You don't need to worry about them. You only need concern your-self with the primary target."

"Why not use radar and computers to control the entire array, including the particle beam."

"I wish we could," Kwan said, "but radar doesn't have the range and isn't precise enough at the high altitude needed. Human touch is required."

Ogenus blew out a deep breath. "You're giving me a lot of credit," he said softly.

"We're giving you the future of the world," Kwan said dryly.

*

Hercle gently knocked on the door of Inanna's home. When she answered, her eyes were red and swollen. "Yes? Hercle, this is not a good time."

"Sorry, Lady. Ionic believes we should move back from the sea. He thinks we should move over those hills. Give us a little protection."

"You mean if things don't work out?"

Hercle smiled briefly, a sad smile. "Even if all happens as we hope, the effects here could be substantial, Ionic says."

Inanna took a deep breath. "We are over a thousand miles away. How big…? Let me talk to Ionic. Take me to him, please."

Hercle hesitated, then nodded. "Come with me."

The big man led Inanna to a small hut her sons had built for storage but had not yet been used.

As she started to enter, Hercle grasped her arm. "He is not well, Lady. His years...the stress..."

The big man was trying to tell her something, to prepare her. Inanna opened the door. Inside was dark and musty, with an odd sour odor.

"Who?" A feeble voice asked.

"It's me, Inanna. Is that you Ionic?"

"Come in, my dear. I'm afraid my years have finally caught up with me." His voice was weak and broken, and higher-pitched than normal. A cold chill enveloped Inanna.

Ionic said, "I'm so sorry that I can't receive you in an upright position. However, I'm happy you're here, and your timing is expedient. Selfish of me, of course. I hesitate to place more burden on you, but I dislike the necessity of dying alone."

As her eyes adjusted to the gloom, she saw her old friend lying on a pallet. He looked so small. She tried to smile. "Who told you you were dying?"

Ionic coughed, cleared his throat. "It's the Camel, my dear. He's been following me, lately. He's out there right now, kneeling in front of the door. Strange you didn't see him." He coughed again, a wheezing, wet cough followed by a groan of deep pain.

"You can't" she sobbed. "I've already lost..."

"You've already lost way too much, I know. I know." Again the cough, followed by a long moment of ragged breathing. "If there was anything I could do, I would. But...listen to me now, you need to move your family, every-one, away from the open sea. Follow Hercle. You don't want to lose more than you've already lost, dear Inanna. Please, do it. Go now."

She knelt beside the pallet and took one of Ionic's hands. The skin was cold, but damp. "We can take you with us, Ionic. Please let us take you."

"No. I'm sorry, I can't go this time. But thank you," he said softly. Then there was silence, a long, empty silence. She could no longer hear his ragged breathing. Inanna sat with him for a while, hoping to hear Ionic's sweet voice again, maybe just one more time.

Finally, Inanna stepped out of the small hut. She looked at Hercle and gave him the barest shake of her head. Tears ran down Hercle's face, and he quickly wiped them away. "We must go now," he said gruffly. "We need to quickly pack supplies and get everybody moving. Come now."

Before they could begin, Eris strode to the small hut. "I'm here to see Ionic. I have something important to tell him."

Inanna wiped her eyes. "You're too late."

The older woman brought a fist to her mouth. She glanced at the door, then back to Inanna, then over at Hercle. "I never got to tell him. I was planning to, more than once. But now..."

Inanna placed a hand on her arm.

"He meant so much to me," Eris said.

"I'm sure he knew."

Eris shook her head. "That's not the same as hearing it."

"He knew," Inanna repeated. She gently led the other woman away. It was time to start packing, getting ready to hide from the wrath of the gods one more time.

*

Ogenus spent hours practicing in the un-powered control booth, getting a feel for its joysticks and the pedals. He adjusted, then tried on the headset, but it showed only a black screen at the moment, so he saw nothing but the red aiming circle. He would continue to see nothing more until full power was applied. Yet still he practiced, working to develop a most delicate touch. The controllers were precise and calibrated for use as a weapon, but its function now required a much more feather-like touch. He did not know if he could master it in time, but his long-dormant navigational skills slowly returned. He kept at it, ignoring the chaos around him as workers continued their feverish race to construct the tools he would need in a terrible few hours.

He stepped out of the machine and found Kwan. "How soon?"

"The rocket will launch in an hour. Impact, if all goes well, two hours after that. We hope to have twenty-five minutes for you to fire the weapon before what's left enters the atmosphere. Once that happens," Kwan spread his fingers and shrugged.

Ogenus strode purposefully back to the control cabin. He wasn't quite sure how his hosts would take it, but he pulled out a knife and scratched his name on one of the beams.

"Your purpose?" Kwan asked.

"For luck," Ogenus said.

"It is not necessary to believe in luck," Kwan said, "only in adequate preparation." He was silent for a moment, then smiled. "In this case, however, I will make an exception." He borrowed Ogenus' knife and scratched his name on another section of the metal housing.

Final preparations had been completed. The reactor successfully initiated and was generating the megawatts of electrical power needed to activate the array. All lasers had been test-fired successfully. Ogenus gently depressed the pedal that fired the concentration of ionized mercury nuclei, and he heard and felt the particle beam hissing into the atmosphere. His headset was live now, but showed no target as yet.

"Test fire successful," Kwan said. Then he paused and listened to his earpiece. "Launch initiated!" he shouted in English, then in his own language. "Launch successful!" Everyone cheered and some looked into the sky, but there was nothing to see and it didn't last long. They still had two hours to wait.

*

Inanna and Hercle led their people north. The low, rolling hills were not sufficient, Hercle said. "We need to keep going."

Hours passed, and the hills grew higher and the going more difficult. Everyone was hungry, dirty, and tired. Babies cried in frustration. "Keep going," Hercle said again. They eventually reached a rather sharp drop into a valley.

"Here," Hercle said. He slid down a steep drop-off onto a relatively flat ledge, then helped lower the others down. "We'll stay here. This should be safe, if anywhere is safe."

"That doesn't sound exactly promising," Hammurabi said.

Hercle shrugged.

Inanna made sure everyone was counted for and as comfortable as possible.

Hercle knelt next to the woman. "In a couple of hours, we will know," he said quietly.

Inanna glanced back up the rocky hill. "I'm going back up there," she said, "where I can see."

"You shouldn't," Hercle said. "If there is anything to see, it will probably kill you. But if you insist, I'm going with you."

Inanna told everyone to stay put, then accompanied Hercle back up to where they could see over. They were far enough inland that the sea wasn't visible, but their location allowed them a distant view. They lie down on their bellies and waited. A few minutes later, Eris joined them. "I always liked to play with fire," she said with a smile, quickly gone. They waited, and waited some more. The day was warm, but a soft breeze brought some cool, marine air over them.

High overhead, and a bit to the south, came a brilliant flash that dazzled their eyes. All three turned away and slid back down to the ledge. They waited for more, but there was no more.

"I think that was rocket, hitting the stone. Good!" Hercle said, "They didn't miss."

"Now?" Eris asked.

"Now," Hercle answered, his usually gruff voice as soft as a distant breeze, "now we shall see if we receive good value for the price we have paid."

*

Ogenus settled himself in the control cabin. He fastened the seat and shoulder belts, flipped the power switch, and settled the headset over his eyes. This time he could see stars. A tiny radio receiver in his ear came to life. "Rocket impact was successful," Kwan said softly. "Prepare to activate beam array."

Other technicians initiated the computer-controlled laser weapons, waiting to vaporize chunks of the asteroid as they were cut from it by Ogenus.

Ogenus stared into his headset. It and the beam array were tied into a radio telescope system that should zoom the object into his viewing area. It was Ogenus' job to fine-tune the aim, get the particle beam hitting the exact center of their target.

So far, he saw nothing. Then his view shifted and he could see the asteroid barely glowing, and a few fragments accompanying it. "I've got it," he said into his throat mike. "Looks pretty intact. I don't see many fragments. Hopefully, they are outside my field of view. Preparing to fire." He adjusted his controllers so that the red circle in his headset was centered on target. He depressed the firing pedal slightly, then all the way down. "Firing." He heard the crackling roar of the beam array.

Ogenus could see the beam strike as it began boring into the rock headed their way. The red circle began drifting to the left. "Adjust" he heard Kwan's soft voice.

"Adjusting." Ogenus worked the controls and brought the circle back to center. It took constant vigilance and tiny, gentle adjustments to keep the target centered. He had less than half-an-hour to do as much damage as he could. Sweat poured down his face but the headset kept most of the moisture out of his eyes. The asteroid began glowing brighter.

He kept firing the beam and could see the center of the object begin to flare, but it didn't look as if there was much damage. "Keep firing," he told himself. "Inanna is counting on you." He could hear the sizzling sounds of the laser array firing as fragments entered its range.

A sudden burst of light dazzled him. He blinked, then waited a second for his vision to clear. The red circle had drifted again. He brought it back to center and saw a large hole in the middle of the asteroid. He continued firing, but began to slowly shift the beam up and down, left and right, trying to cut the rock into pieces. It grew larger in his view, and the telescope adjusted. Then it adjusted again, and again. The asteroid was coming in fast!

Once the rock hit the upper atmosphere, it began to burn brightly. Ogenus knew he had only seconds left to finish his job, or fail completely. And he couldn't fail! He. Could. Not. Fail.

*

Inanna, Eris, and Hercle kept their eyes on the distant horizon, gazing to the south. They observed a flicker very high in the sky. Then the entire horizon lit up brighter than the nuclear detonation. The three humans covered their eyes and slid down below the hill's edge. It took several moments for the green and orange dazzle to clear.

Inanna climbed back up and glanced over the edge. The southern horizon was aglow. Another green flash was followed by two more. They waited to see if a wave of final destruction would roll over them, destroying everything. They waited, searching, watching. The sky became filled with lines of fire, as fragments of the asteroid reached the lower atmosphere. Most burned up, but hundreds of pieces too large to vaporize, impacted, some very close by, raising dust and dirt and trembling the very ground. An odor of sulfur and smoke permeated the air, causing Inanna to cough.

Despite the hundreds of roaring, burning objects blasting down from the sky, total destruction didn't come. Several fragments, however, did impact the valley in which they had taken refuge, but Inanna made sure none had struck close enough to harm her family.

Burning fragments roared overhead, but a wall of incandescent atmosphere didn't wash over them. They watched, and waited. And it didn't come.

Almost an hour later, their ears were assailed by an ear-piercing *crack!* Followed by an equally loud low-pitched rumbling that lasted a long time and echoed off the hills and distant mountains. There were two more cracks loud enough to hurt their ears. This was followed minutes later by a sudden gale-force wind that threatened to fling them off the hill. Then the sky was at once filled with more fireballs, big and small. Most of them burned up before reaching the ground, but a few impacted nearby, causing even more shaking of the ground. The fireballs and the wind didn't last long, but toward the south, a flickering glow continued for two more hours, slowly dimming.

"By the gods," Hercle said reverently. "We're still here. They've done it!"

"How can you be sure?" Inanna asked.

"If they had failed, we would be dead now. That blast was the rock exploding in the atmosphere, not by hitting the ground. We need to go tell the others! We will live!"

"You go, Hercle. You and Eris. I want to wait here for a while."

Hercle stood and looked at Inanna. "You will be okay?"

"I'll be fine," she said dully. She looked at the other two. "You go now."

The big man shuffled off, followed by Eris. He stopped and looked back, then turned, grasped Eris' elbow, and began to hurry them down toward the others. Inanna could hear his shouting echoing from the hills and she smiled. Then she began to cry, deep sobs that could not be shared with anyone. She cried for Oannes, and for Ionic. She cried for her parents and little brother, and all those lost in the cataclysms. She fell to her knees and cried into the ground, wanting to become the dirt and stone, to merge with it.

Everything in life, it seemed to her, was fleeting, temporary. And that which one loved the most departed soonest. That wasn't true, she knew. But it seemed that way. "You will live on, my love," she whispered to the south, "Legends will speak of you down through all of time. I will see to that with all my remaining days." Having said that, she did not know how to find the strength to go on for another single moment. Then, in the distance, she heard a baby cry.

She stood, watched the glow for another minute, then she turned and made her way back to the family that remained. They would live on. They would live on.

*

Two weeks later, the small band of refugees reached a hill about two hundred miles to the northeast. This was the location where Hercle had been building Ionic's pillars arranged in circles, each one weighing as much as 10 tons. They were T-shaped and Hercle said they represented humans surviving. The site also featured the work of artists who carved animals and other symbols onto the pillars, some of which

Hercle didn't quite understand. "These are messages to another time," he said. "Ionic wanted men thousands of years from now to know about us. We plan to build ten pillar complexes like this all around here, each on a hill so that all people will know about it."

"And what will they learn from all your work, Hercle?" Inanna asked, sadly.

"They will know who we were, what we did. Ionic gave me plans. This, he said, will be a giant hall of records, too big to ignore. And," Hercle said quietly, "they will learn one more thing. Earth no longer takes its kings from the sky. Some may still worship them, but someday comets will no longer crash into Earth, no longer be considered gods. For a while at least. So we build, to tell them. So Ogenus will be remembered through the ages no matter what."

Inanna placed a hand on Hercle's arm. "Thank you," she said.

"And thank Ionic."

"Yes. Always we thank Ionic."

*

Two months later, Sabra, her infant daughter in one arm, looked at Iapetos' handiwork. "An axe head, you say?"

"Yes, it's an axe head, my sweet but infuriating love."

"Looks like it was made by a monkey," she said, smiling.

Iapetos tried to reply. His lips worked, but no words came out. Sabra handed the stone back. Iapetos examined it under her watchful eye. Then he glared at her, and tossed it to the ground near the base of a pillar, and strode away.

"You have other talents, my love," Sabra called after. Iapetos ignored her words, and her laughter.

*

Across the great sea, Omek gathered his people. They were immigrants to this land, he said, and they had created a wonderful civilization. But many had the desire to move on, to eventually make their way back to the homeland on the great southern continent. They also had a desire to see more of the world. They were mathematicians, astronomers, scientists, and artists. They had brought with them their calendars, and improved upon them. They had observed the stars and comets, and knew that Earth had narrowly avoided destruction. Their stone monuments confirmed that Earth's orbit had not been altered.

They remembered Ionic and his tale of the feathered serpent. They incorporated images based on this into their art, and related the story to some of the less aggressive peoples they encountered. Ionic had promised, someday, to return. When he did, he would find what Omek's people had left for him, giant carved stone heads of themselves.

As the legends were passed down from generation to generation among many tribes, the plumed serpent became Kukulkan in some places, Quetzalcoatl in others, and Gukumatz in still others.

The world awaited Omek and his people. They left behind remnants of their civilization, gifted to the indigenous peoples. Omek and most of his people moved west, through the jungle, fighting warrior tribes, animals, and insects. When they encountered friendly tribes, they rested a while and related their tales. They taught, and listened, and often learned. When they reached the west coast, they constructed boats similar to the ones that had brought them through the flood and to this new land.

At this point, the nation faced a quandary. Some wanted to sail southwest and others wanted to go northeast, and a few wished to remain where they were. Omek split his people into three parties. He and about a third of his people sailed southwest and after 3,000 miles of facing the worst an angry ocean could throw at them, arrived at a small island. Omek and half his people elected to settle there. The remainder moved on, looking for larger lands upon which to explore.

Omek and his people lived a hard life on the small island. Subsequent generations were taller and thinner, and they lost much of their scientific knowledge. There they began the task of carving a thousand statues of Ionic, called Moai, with their friend's thin lips and stoic expression, in the event he should return someday. They placed the statues around the edges of their island and left them waiting. When Ionic returned, he would recognize himself and know that he'd found Omek's descendants.

Those who moved on discovered a continent-sized island and many hundreds of other islands. They merged with the indigenous peoples and settled these lands, carrying with them remnants of their former civilizations.

Those who headed northwest came upon a chain of volcanic islands, and settled there. None of them, it seemed, ever made it back to their original home.

*

Hercle finished Ionic's pillar project and eventually made his way back to the Crecopia. He had many adventures along the way, and more after his arrival. Of those adventures, many became the basis of legends. While he missed the golden cities of his youth, he did not mind the more primitive living conditions. Eris accompanied Hercle. While they did not become mates, Eris shared in many of Hercle's adventures, and they remained close for the rest of their lives.

*

Inanna became the matriarch of a large, growing family. She grew old and happy, surrounded by her sons and their children and even more children through several generations. She lived long enough to see a mighty civilization arise from the ashes of chaos. She told those many generations of children about her life with Oannes, the wise and kind Giant, the fish god, ruler of the sea and bringer of knowledge.

This new civilization never reached the heights of the Giants and their technological marvels, but they lived comfortably. Generations, many thousands of years later, still remembered Inanna, and what they remembered most was the depths of her love.

Epilogue I
c. 2003

A well-equipped Land Rover motored through the endless desert of Libya. The four occupants were looking for glass. About 300 miles southeast of Cairo, Egypt, they found what they were looking for; a giant field containing chunks and layers of greenish glass spread out over many square miles. Each of the scientists had seen a similar field of glass back in the United States. That glass was created when sand became instantly super-heated and fused during the process of a nuclear explosion.

This field of glass, however, was not the site of a nuclear explosion. At least not a recent one. This glass was far older. Some said it was ten thousand years old. Others dated it as far back as 26 million years. No one knew for sure, but one thing they did know was that there shouldn't have been nuclear explosions thousands or millions of years ago.

The only alternative explanation was an atmospheric detonation of an asteroid or comet fragment, but the mechanics of such an event remained a mystery. "It would have come straight down," said one, "and bam!"

"No crater," said another. "Would've made a huge crater, not glass."

"Must have exploded in the atmosphere, somehow." The third shook his head.

The scientists collected samples of the glass. They took radiation measurements, and found one small location where readings were slightly higher than background. Not high enough, of course, to even raise eyebrows.

The field of glass was large, dozens of miles north to south and about two-thirds of that east to west. Whatever had caused it had been massive.

"Hey, look at this!" one of the scientists called.

The other three found him pulling at a piece of metal that was partially sticking out of the ground. It was pitted, corroded, bent, and rusted. The four pulled at it until it either came loose, or broke off a larger piece still buried in the sand.

"Looks like a girder," one said, noting the two rows of holes along the length.

"Burnt to hell and back," said another. "Half melted."

"How long you think that thing's been in there?" another asked.

"I'd guess World War Two, probably part of an airplane or a tank or something similar that got blown up or crashed. In this desert stuff's buried and unburied by the sand and wind all the time."

They took a couple of pictures of it and were just about to toss it back when one noticed a few scratches along one side. They brushed it as clean as possible, and the scratches became somewhat clearer, although the metal had a tendency to flake. "Almost look like hieroglyphs."

"Nah, that don't look like any hieroglyphs I've ever seen. Probably just random scratches."

"Or maybe somebody's initials," said another. They all laughed.

They looked at it for a moment longer, then tossed it back to the desert. They took their samples of glass and drove away.

Epilogue II
c: 2018

Josh, now a full-fledged archaeologist, finished his site survey. He'd walked the entire hill and what he saw excited him, and he hated it. Vandals had dug up some of the pillars, and damaged them, but he had no trouble recognizing them. They were very familiar to him. And he hated that even more. He had been working at the original site in Turkey for the past twenty-two years. That site, 20 miles southeast of where he now stood, began excavation back in 1995 and was now considered to be the very first megalithic stone temple ever made by humans. It was proclaimed unique since it had been built at the very end of the last ice age by hunter-gatherers who had no business building temples.

But now…the hill on which he stood was almost certainly just as artificial. He fully expected that below the dirt they would find a series of ten-ton T-shaped pillars in a circular formation, ala Stonehenge. He fully expected that ground-penetrating radar would show the entire hill filled with similar circular formations. He fully expected this site would also date to the end of the last ice age. And, he fully expected to find that this site had been deliberately buried thousands of years after it was built. Just like the original site. He hated it, hated the very idea of it.

"What the hell is going on?" Josh asked his assistant, rhetorically. "How can there be a second site? This is just not possible!"

"I've got bad news for you, Boss."

"Keep it to yourself, Danny. I've already got a headache." He was silent for a moment, then shook his head. "Oh, hell, tell me!"

Danny couldn't restrain a smile. "There's another one Boss, a third site, filled with T-shaped pillars. Across the valley, about 50 miles east of us, over on that ridge," he said, pointing.

Josh did not reply, but looked like he wanted to kill his assistant.

"And there might be more of them, Boss, four or five hills, maybe more, scattered all over this area of Turkey, hundreds and hundreds of pillars in circles under artificial hills, all of them deliberately buried. What does this mean, Boss? These things shouldn't be here."

"I don't know what it means, Danny. Right now, I'm only sure of one thing."

"Yeah?"

"This changes everything."

Author's Notes

This is a work of fiction. The Prologue and Epilogues I and II are fictionalized accounts of actual events. The dates are estimates, but close.

This novel uses standard U.S. English vocabulary, slang, and measurements, as if scrolls had been found in a cave and then translated for a general audience. However, I included enough differences in terminology that would indicate to the reader that "we're not in Kansas anymore."

Names of characters in this story are archaic versions of well-known mythological entities. Inanna, for example, later became Ishtar and Aphrodite in later cultures, the goddess of love (and other things). Ogenus is a variation of Oceanus, the god of the ocean. Inanna's fond variation of his name, Oannes, is the name of an Apkallu, a Sumerian god, a fish-man, a wise man. Ionic is a made-up name from various ancient references to a numeric system, an alphabetic system, and other scientific disciplines. Eris is the Greek goddess of strife and discord. In this novel, strife and discord are not overt and obvious, but more subdued and inferred. Hercle is, of course, an early form of the god Hercules. The three sons of Ogenus and Inanna are variations of Noah's sons (and, in a couple of instances, their wives).

"Noah's" ark in this novel was built by Ogenus and his sons. It is round, as some scholars now believe this is how the ark in the Epic of Gilgamesh was constructed. A group recently tested this hypothesis by building a round, but much scaled-down version of the Gilgamesh ark, including a cabin at the top and space for animals below. This test vehicle did float, and was stable. Interestingly, everyone who saw it sail by exclaimed, "Look, it's Noah's Ark!" Indeed, from any ground or water-level view, it resembled an artist's version of a child's fanciful Ark, with a highly up-swept bow and stern.

As with times and locations, I have played fast and loose with some, tying them into real and imagined historic events. The *Younger Dryas* is an actual event that took place about 12 thousand years ago, during which Earth's temperature fluctuated wildly from ice age to temperate and back again. There is some evidence of possible comet impacts as the cause for this fluctuation. I have compacted the time frame between these atmospheric events from hundreds (perhaps even thousands) of years to a few decades in order to maintain the same cast of characters. Since none of us was there, and since evidence is sparse, I might even be right!

I also explored the concept that the prevalence of snakes and serpents in ancient prehistoric artwork, writing, and sculpture could possibly be interpreted as referring to comets. In Central and South America, many ancient cultures worshiped the Feathered Serpent (and, interestingly, today's depictions of dinosaurs indicate many were feathered). In Asia and England, we find ancient tales of dragons. Reference the serpent in the Epic of Gilgamesh and the Bible, and other snakes in various holy books. And there are more: Apophis, the great serpent in Ancient Egyptian lore, the enemy of the sun god; ancient serpent cults in India; in Australia, the Rainbow Serpent created the landscape; in ancient Greece, serpents ruled the world, and there the word for dragon originated; Pytho, the enemy of Apollo, a serpent. Hurakán is the Mayan god of wind, storm, and fire and caused the Great Flood. He is described as having one human leg and one leg shaped like a serpent. Typhon was a Greek God upon whose shoulders were one hundred snake heads that flashed fire and made unspeakable sounds, and was alternatively described as humanoid from the waist up and snake coils for legs. In North America, the Serpent Mound is the largest of its kind in the world, and is located over a meteorite impact site.

Those real and mythical creatures had one thing in common: a snake or serpent. Such creatures often sport a large head and a long tail. Just like a comet stretching across Earth's sky. What if, tens of thousands of years ago, and perhaps longer, comets were much more prevalent than they are now? And what if those ubiquitous "chariots" of the gods, the descent of the gods to Earth, were periodic flaming and roaring comet fragments through Earth's atmosphere? And the punishment, wars, and conflicts with the "gods" were the instances when comet fragments impacted the land or water near human habitations? "What if" is the bedrock of fiction.

The Crecopia is, of course, now called the Greek Acropolis. Kursatta existed at the southern edge of what is now the island of Crete, famous for its ancient ruins. During the ice age, sea levels were much lower, so the area today known as the Aegean Sea, was primarily dry land.

Hercle dredged the two-mile gap between the southern edge of Italy and Sicily. With lower sea levels, that would have been the only navigable way out of a much smaller Mediter-ranean Sea, and only then at high tide, until Hercle fixed it. So, fictionally, the Pillars of Hercules were located at the narrow, two-mile space between Italy and Sicily rather than its current location further west. The great southern continent we today call Africa. The great western continent? The Americas.

This novel was built on a foundation of actual, suspected, and imagined events, and peopled with characters that are a complete fabrication of the imagination. When I first began contemplating this novel, Ogenus was to have been the main character. During the writing of it, Inanna came in and took over, making the novel more about her, which I welcomed as she is the more interesting and charismatic person.

You may have wondered at the lack of physical confron-tations herein (i.e. blood and guts), as well as overt descriptions of sex. There are no depictions of giant battles or messy deaths or steamy bedroom scenes. I decided to focus, instead, on the people impacted by the larger events, and kept most of the blood and guts, as well as intimate encounters, mainly off stage.

A modern civilization, suddenly and violently flung back into the stone age would not fare well. Co-existing primitive hunter-gatherer tribes would continue on much as before, their lifestyles pretty much unchanged. In time, from these tribes, new civilizations might arise, eventually re-inventing writing, science, and government. What if, however, survivors of a hypothetical modern technological civilization mixed with these primitive tribes? What might each have learned and taught? What legends and myths might be handed down from such encounters?

You hold in your hands my answer to that question. It is certainly not the only possible answer. Nor, perhaps, not even the most likely. Fiction is like that.

Made in the USA
Monee, IL
13 February 2020